# "Why Jersey City?"

Laura Jarrett asked after we'd settled into a bar near Washington Square Park. I was working for her ex-husband.

"A matter of balance," I suggested. "New York has nine hundred private investigators, most of them tied into security. It's big business here, with all the edges rounded off. But for me it's still an art, full of mystery and surprise. I like to take chances."

"Why murder?"

"It's the ultimate crime with the ultimate risk. And it's clear-cut. Only winners and losers. Either I get them or they get away."

"Do many get away?" she asked.

"Too many."

Her eyes were diamonds fired by a million years of tension, her mouth a cut in the cleft of the earth. I'd seen that look before. Murder turned her on, the thought of a murder or the talk of murder. Hopefully even the investigator of murder . . . I began to feed my own fantasies.

"You must like Bogart," Laura laughed.

"Bogart who?"

# JERSEY TOMATOES

## J.W. RIDER

PUBLISHED BY POCKET BOOKS NEW YORK

This novel is a work of fiction. Names, characters, places and
incidents are either the product of the author's imagination or
are used fictitiously. Any resemblance to actual events or locales
or persons, living or dead, is entirely coincidental.

POCKET BOOKS, a division of Simon & Schuster, Inc.
1230 Avenue of the Americas, New York, N.Y. 10020

Copyright © 1986 by J. W. Rider
Cover artwork copyright © 1987 Enric Torres

Published by arrangement with Arbor House Publishing Company
Library of Congress Catalog Card Number: 85-20046

All rights reserved, including the right to reproduce
this book or portions thereof in any form whatsoever.
For information address Arbor House Publishing Company,
235 East 45th Street, New York, N.Y. 10017

ISBN: 0-671-64018-6

First Pocket Books printing June 1987

10 9 8 7 6 5 4 3 2 1

POCKET and colophon are registered trademarks
of Simon & Schuster, Inc.

Printed in the U.S.A.

For Jay Bell

Who got shot down somewhere
short of his dreams.
He was the best man I ever
knew.

He was some kind of a man.
What does it matter what
you say about people?

—Marlene Dietrich,
   in *Touch of Evil*

# JERSEY
# TOMATOES

# one

WHEN THEY SANK THE Holland Tunnel eighty feet into the Hudson River back in 1926, everybody saw a golden age for New York and Jersey City on opposite ends. One paper even called them the new twin cities, like Minneapolis–St. Paul, I suppose, or maybe even Sodom and Gomorrah. Either way it didn't work out like that. What happened was New York got all the gold and left Jersey City only the age. It just got older.

Which bothered some people, a lot of people, like Cooper Jarrett. To him urban decay was a mortal sin and empty space a crime. He was a local real-estate developer, a self-made man who'd made millions. Now he was trying to make himself immortal. I stood next to him facing the New York skyline and wondered if a bunch of buildings would guarantee immortality. Jarrett had no doubts.

"Someday soon we'll look just like that."

"Is that good?" The thought of living through a steel monument left me cold, but so did New York.

Jarrett scowled my way. "It's money, Mr. Malone."

"That's good."

"Big business means money, and money is life."

I wasn't going to argue with him.

"Cities are a lot like people, you know." He sounded disappointed. "Both need new blood all the time."

"Which is why you called me," I prompted.

"Which is why you came," he snapped.

We met on Caven Point beach, twenty minutes by car from midtown Manhattan. A square mile of weeds and scrubby beach in the shadow of the Big Apple.

"All right," I admitted, "so I've heard about you."

"What have you heard about me?"

"That you've got a lot of blood."

"You mean money."

"I mean blood money."

He tried to smile. Smiling didn't come easy to Jarrett. He'd started with rented rooms, then whole blocks. A shark.

"Anything else?" he asked.

"Just that you've been known to empty your buildings too fast."

"It's called improving the neighborhood."

"Changing it, anyway."

Around us was a picture postcard, the kind you sign *Wish you were here* and send to enemies. Refineries and factories whistled alongside crumbling piers and abandoned bulkheads. Beached ferries groaned in agony. A Jersey landscape, ugly and in ruins. But the view of New York was good, even great. And if you were greedy enough—or sadistic enough—to see the same for this side . . .

"So if you know that much, you can guess the rest." He didn't seem happy I knew anything.

"I'd say you're a man with a problem."

"I'm a man with a mission."

"The new Harbor Terminal?"

"The dream of a lifetime."

"That's your problem," I told him. "Dreams are only what we see in mirrors. They can shatter."

Jarrett took in a great gulp of salty air. "So you have a way with words." Exhaled. "What else do you have?"

"A busy schedule."

Sharks don't really smile, it's an optical illusion. But Jarrett came close. A thin twist of the lips.

"Not too busy. I had you checked."

"Maybe they lied," I said. "I could be competition."

"People don't lie to me."

"I'm lying to you."

The lips turned cruel, beating the eyes by a blink.

"I told you I'd meet you here, but I didn't really show up. You don't have a problem and I don't have the time. I'm on another job."

It took him a second to adjust. "They warned me you were too independent."

"You should've listened."

I looked over at the Statue of Liberty's ass, almost close enough to kiss. The only one I ever would, too, money or no money. But people in the market for private investigators always got strange around me, uneasy. It was what I did for a living, they didn't know how to handle me. When they saw they couldn't, they had to make decisions. I just hurried them along.

"We shouldn't meet like this," I said. "People might think I work for you."

Jarrett made up his mind. "How long you been in the business?"

"Twelve years plus my whole life."

I watched a couple of nudists walking near the waterline.

"What's it take to get a license in Jersey?"

"A clean record and five years' experience," I told him. "That's all?"

"Did I mention the five-thousand-dollar surety bond?"

"Where'd you get your experience?"

It was too far to tell age but one of them seemed very young, his walk mostly.

"Miami," I said after a moment. "Before that the FBI."

"You're from Florida?"

"I'm from here."

"Why'd you go there?"

"I heard they had snow."

"Snow? There's no snow in Florida."

"So I heard wrong."

She kept coming back like a song, her face. Two years made no difference. I was back in Florida watching her fall, the knife flashing red against the bronzed body.

"And the FBI?"

I squinted at Jarrett, a blob of white under the dark sky.

"Four years." Hell, it wasn't his fault.

"What made you leave?"

"I got too old to stay."

"You must be Catholic," he said.

"Mormon."

The sun strayed out of the clouds again.

"Sounds Catholic to me."

"Does it matter?"

"Not to me it don't."

"Then I was born one," I said. "Jersey City's ninety percent Catholic."

"So's the FBI."

"They're changing too."

Jarrett nodded, like he approved of the FBI changing. Which made me think he was either a Communist or a crook, my paranoia courtesy of the Bureau and the seminary all the way back to St. Peter's College. But I had to admit he didn't look like a Communist. No horns, not even a tail.

"They told me you take only murder cases."

"Only homicides, that's right." The two nudists were looking our way now, the older man a head taller. "And threats of homicide."

"Why only killings?"

"Keeps me awake."

Jarrett nodded again, but not like he knew anything about nightmares. Or even daydreams.

"The age of specialization, I suppose." He let out a huge sigh, a broad man with soft hands. Only the eyes gave him away, the kind you see in pictures of predators. The rest of him was Jersey City solid, a blend of Barney's and Burma Shave and Thom McAn. The vest didn't reach the shoes. Not even the pants.

"A murder's committed every twenty-three minutes," I said, and checked my watch. "We're about due for one."

"How do you solve any with your attitude?"

"I wear 'em down."

Jarrett was hooked and he knew it. I turned toward Ellis Island. The buildings were baroque, another time, and so was the dream. Twenty million people had their first close look at America and saw Jersey City. Some, like my parents, crossed the few feet of water and stayed. German-Irish were like that, stubborn, rooted, religious. To them New Jersey sounded like the biblical land of milk and honey—and meat. The New Jersey, the promised land.

"What do you know about local politics?"

To others it must've seemed like the end of the world. Wasn't New York the gateway to America? Ellis Island was just the back door. When I turned away from the bleak buildings, the nudists were gone.

"Politics? It's all just rock 'n' roll to me."

"It's money to everyone else."

"Really."

"And I don't mean nickels and dimes," Jarrett said. "Big bucks." His eyes began to sweat. "There's a revolution going on here, a building boom."

"I think I read about it somewhere."

"Downtown's already like a bitch in heat. New housing projects, condos. Everything. Look at Hamilton Park, you wouldn't recognize it."

"I'd recognize it."

"Started with a brownstone revival, now it's spread all over town." The spread seemed to excite him. "And private developers are taking over."

"Developers like you."

"We're turning the city into New York. Giving it a smart new image."

"I liked the old image."

"Who cares what you like? The point is nobody can stop what's happening. And what's happening now is business development, getting banks and corporations to come over from New York. That's the next stage. That's where the big money will be."

"What's all this have to do with politics?"

Jarrett's brows raised. "We're talking hundreds of millions between the city's redevelopment agencies and the private market. You can't build on that scale without getting involved in politics." The voice lowered. "Politics says who gets what."

"And you got Harbor Terminal."

"It didn't come cheap."

"That's politics."

"Smart guy, right?" Jarrett frowned, held it while I watched the wheels in his head turn. Or maybe just the wheels he wanted me to watch. The man didn't get here from there by being dumb. "Not everybody was happy," he said finally.

"Can't please 'em all."

"Made a lot of enemies."

"Like who?"

The frown turned into a scowl. "People with power, who else?"

I didn't say anything.

"There have been calls, anonymous. Different people calling the office." His eyes went wide. "They weren't kidding."

"You talk to the police?"

"What do they care about calls?"

My second thought was what's he doing on a secluded beach if his life's in danger. He was a sitting duck standing here. Then I thought better. Professional killers don't make calls. Maybe it was just some of the poor who got pushed out of his houses.

"You need a bodyguard," I told him. "I don't do that kind of work."

Jarrett snorted. "I can take care of myself."

"Then what do you want?"

"What I want is for you to take care of the callers. Find them and lose them."

"Lose them?"

"Yes. You know, maybe they suddenly disappear. Lose them."

"What you want," I said evenly, "is a couple of goons." Another TV nut, the second this week. I started to pull away in disgust.

"All right, for chrissake. So scare them off."

"Why not buy them off?"

That made Jarrett wince. Money was important to him, maybe it was everything. I decided to find out.

"When you had me checked, they tell you my fee?"

"No."

"Three thousand advance against three hundred a day," I told him. "For that you get a written daily report and a final summary when the case is closed."

The wince came back as the color left. But I gave him credit, at least he didn't cry.

"Kind of exclusive, aren't you?"

"Depends how you look at it. I only work seven days a week and twelve months a year. Taking out the dry spells, I average about half that time on pay. Eight thousand a month times six months is about fifty thousand a year. For maybe getting shot cleaning up other people's lives. That sound like too much?"

"What'll you do with all that money?"

"I'm going to buy a castle and live like any other P.I."

"Smart guy, right?"

I owed him that one.

"Three hundred a day." He squeezed the words out until they sounded like three thousand. "All right, what can I lose?"

"Three hundred a day." I made it sound like thirty cents.

"But no lunch hour!"

I let him have that one, too. "You'll get the contract in the morning," I said.

"There's something else."

There always is, I groaned as my eyes turned into pinheads. That's the kiss of death in this business, we call it the Widow. Three little words that have killed a lot of good men.

"What else?"

Jarrett ran a tongue over his lips. It wasn't forked so I figured he had at least two. He was beginning to look more like a Communist every minute.

"I got this partner who's received some of the calls—most of them, in fact. I'm out of the office a lot."

"So?"

"So she's shaky."

"She?"

"It's my ex-wife."

I looked down at my shoes, kicked at the sand with a wing tip. The last time I'd heard the Widow, it cost me three weeks in a hospital. And I was starting to get that same feel.

Jarrett wet his lips again. "We divorced about a year ago. But she owns half the company, so we stayed partners. She's good window dressing, knows a lot of people." He was on the dark side of forty but still had all his hair and maybe even all his teeth. I wondered who he was biting now. "But I do all the deals."

"She local?"

"Connecticut."

"What about you?"

"The West Side," Jarrett said defensively. "Are you trying to point out our differences?"

"Just trying to find out what they are."

"Whatever they are don't concern you, Malone. I'm paying you to stop the calls. She's out of it."

"She's taking them, isn't she?"

"Only because I'm not there much." This time he bit his lip. "Jesus, you don't think they really mean to—"

"We'll see." It's a funny thing about ex-husbands: They're usually solicitous for the woman in a way they never were while married. Maybe it's just relief.

"Jesus," Jarrett repeated, and went back to swiping the lips with his tongue.

The beach was almost deserted. April was still too cold for crowds, which never came anyway. Only knots of men, fishermen of all sorts.

"Let's go," I said.

"You coming to the office?"

"I have another appointment."

"So cancel it."

"I'd rather cancel you."

He didn't like that.

I looked him over. He was a head short and forty pounds light. I could crush him with my size twelve shoes.

I used my smile instead. "Smart guy, right?"

Walking away, I kept thinking it's a shame about Caven Point. Hardly anyone knows it exists. Can you believe that? The nearest beach to Manhattan and nobody knows it exists. Which didn't really matter since it wouldn't exist much longer.

"Nice beach," I said to my client on the way out.

"What beach? Soon this'll all be mine."

# two

I COLLECTED CHARISMA KELLY and her entourage from in front of her ashram on Kennedy Boulevard. That's what they called it, an ashram; I don't know why. An ashram was supposed to be a religious retreat. It struck me as strange for their line of work but I let it pass. Which wasn't strange at all. In my line of work I had to let a lot of things pass.

Only her chief hack made it through the first five minutes; the hangers-on fell off somewhere between the sidewalk and our destination. It was my car and my time. They all smiled sweetly, on their best behavior, and hoped I'd have a nice day. What they meant was I should burn in hell.

Charisma Kelly sat in the back seat, a commanding presence. In the rearview mirror I saw an angel where many others saw the devil. She wasn't a day over thirty or an ounce overweight, a younger Jacqueline Bisset. Her face said she had nothing to hide and her eyes hid the rest. I wondered why the devil an angel needed help.

Her assistant's name was Kassam, an Arab. He started hating me when I told him I loved *Lawrence of Arabia*. Apparently his people had worked for the Turks. "Somebody had to," I said, trying to make him feel better.

"May you live forever," he mumbled. But his look was a slicing scimitar.

Looking elsewhere, I thought I caught a glint in Charisma Kelly's eye. Or maybe it was just a mote in the mirror.

"We could have talked just as easily in my office," she finally said. "When I summoned you, I didn't anticipate a kidnapping. How much further? I should warn you I don't like cars or country."

We were about ten blocks from Journal Square on our way to Pershing Field. Some country! I followed the bend of the boulevard, trapped in a slow traffic dance. In another hour it would turn into a parking lot. But the goal was worth the journey. The track was a perfect oval and the stands were always empty. I liked to run around the field in the early morning; there was a Brueghel feel to it. Charisma Kelly and the Arab probably didn't believe in Brueghel either.

"You didn't answer my question," she said as I turned off the boulevard.

"Sorry. I was saving my mouth to kiss off kidnappers."

"You'd do better licking stamps with it. How much further?"

"Few more minutes. It's hard to tell in this open country."

She tilted her head to the Arab. "Where did you get him?"

"Someone in the prosecutor's office. They said he knew his way around."

"Around what, a comedy hour?" Her voice dipped into a sigh. "Maybe we should talk to someone in the defender's office."

"There's always Legal Aid," I said.

"Just keep driving."

She made some scratching sounds in the back, like she was scraping the shine off the imitation leather. When she got to the imitation floor mats, I was going to put my foot down.

"When did you get this car, anyway?"

"Not anyway," I answered. "Most particularly. When it was new."

"Must be at least three years old."

"They made 'em last in those days."

I found a space by an entrance and led them across the track to the stands. A few runners were faking it, others did honest resting. Afternoons were for amateurs.

I picked a third-row seat. The stone was hard, but so was

life. We sat facing the sun low in the west, a fading ball in a darkening world.

"Why did we come here?"

"I heard the mob was going to whip your ashram, thought you might like me if I saved your lives."

"That's not funny."

"Sorry," I lied.

She looked pointedly in three directions, noticeably avoiding my quadrant. I decided she didn't like to repeat questions, so I tried the truth.

"It's usually a good idea to meet prospective clients away from familiar surroundings, throw them off-balance a bit. Less lies that way, or at least fewer evasions."

Her face was triangular, a sign of passion, which could be a good sign or a bad sign. Or even no sign at all.

"I don't lie," she said. "Not about important things."

"Swear to God?"

I could see her face flush. In the light a bit of the bloom was off the rose, but she still looked like an angel and even walked like an angel. Only she didn't talk like an angel, probably because she didn't believe in angels or anything else. Which was why the locals saw her as a devil in disguise.

"Miss Kelly is an atheist," Kassam said needlessly. As if everyone in the world didn't know, at least the world according to Catholic Jersey City. "Christians Anonymous?"

"Does that bother you?" she asked.

"Not at all. Some of my best friends eat lions. Are you looking for converts?"

"I just wanted to make sure you understood the background."

"I haven't heard any yet."

"And to see how you felt about us."

"Us?"

"My work, then."

"That's your work. My work is murder. Is there a connection?"

"Some people think that's my work as well."

She managed to sound pleased and offended at the same time. Christians Anonymous was patterned after Alcoholics Anonymous and offered help to religious addicts trying to kick the habit. The group had chapters in several states and was spreading largely through the efforts of Miss Kelly, who was considered charismatic. I gave her the benefit of the doubt.

"Since we're in the background phase," I said, "I suppose you should know I spent two years in a seminary."

"Which one?"

"The Jesuits."

"Not the worst."

"Not the best."

"But you got out," Kassam said.

"I didn't get out, I was let go. There's a difference."

"Why were you let go?" Charisma Kelly asked.

"I had a very bad temper years ago, maybe I still do. When I get real mad, I shake a lot. I got mad too much in the seminary."

"So they wanted you out."

"I was diagnosed as epileptic. A section of the church's canon law excludes epileptics from the priesthood."

Her eyes suddenly became animated. "You know, of course, that in centuries past epilepsy signified possession by the devil as a result of ancestors committing unnatural acts with animals."

"I've heard tell."

"And much of Catholic canon law," she said quietly, "is very old."

"They railroaded you," shouted the Arab.

"Let's just say they had probable cause. There'd been a car accident earlier that could've brought it on."

"But the injustice made you turn detective."

"Hardly." I grinned in memory. "By then I was simply more interested in bodies than souls."

"So the joke was on them," Charisma Kelly said.

"On me." The memory turned sour. "Took me six months to learn I wasn't an epileptic after all."

In the sky the scavengers circled the city while on the ground they spoke in seductive tones.

"The world," she said, "is much more chancy than the religionists would have us believe. Things people get into by accident have enormous impact on them, and this happens over and over."

"The dice just keep on rolling," I agreed.

She brushed strands of hair away from her face. Dark hair in sunlight, much like Karen's. "Why tell me all this?"

It was hard to say. In going from the Jesuits to the FBI, I'd just traded one seminary for another. Now I was someone else in another life and I didn't relish reminders. Maybe it was just that. Maybe. "I might not be what you need," I said hesitantly, "or you what I want."

"Prejudice?"

"Practical. I'm doing all right."

"In that car?"

"So I'm down to the bare luxuries."

Her first smile, half-smile. "And it doesn't bother you that I'm a demon exorcising priests? That doesn't shock you?"

"The way things are going, it wouldn't surprise me to see parents who've eaten their kids come out of the closet demanding recognition and respect."

She studied my face, the eyes peeling away my skin. "You have good bones," she decided.

"Good for what?"

"Especially the jawline. A sign of strength."

"Or stubbornness," I suggested.

"He might just work out," she said to Kassam, and turned back to me. "If you're not afraid of designing women, that is."

"As long as they don't try to design me."

"Is there a chance?"

"Not a chance in hell, if you'll excuse the expression."

"The expression's fine. I believe in hell. Only it's other people and it's right here."

We sat in Pershing Field and watched little kids throw pebbles at each other. Soon they would grow into rocks.

"If you're still interested," she said after a moment, "I should mention that I have a cause to which I devote all my energy. I am a workaholic. My work is all that matters to me, nothing else. I believe in what I'm doing. In my own way, I'm as duty-bound as any religionist." She took a deep breath. "Outside of that, I am thirty-five years old and—"

"That's funny. You don't look an ounce overweight."

"I beg your pardon?"

I shook my head, seeing fallen angels all over the place.

"—and my real name is Constance."

I'd been a workaholic too, after Karen's murder. But my cause never worked out and neither did Miami—that died with her. "Why Jersey City?" I asked.

"Because it's almost New York, the communications center, but it's in New Jersey, the most densely populated state in America. My movement has broad mass appeal for the right kind of masses." She wrinkled her nose. "Besides, New York isn't even part of America."

Listening to her I could think of another difference between New York and Jersey City. In Jersey City nobody is a nobody.

"So what do you think, Malone?" It was the Arab, who'd wished I live forever. A curse if I ever heard one.

"You talked to the people in prosecution so I assume you know my specialty and my fee. What's the job?"

"Three weeks ago Miss Kelly's mother died of a gunshot wound."

"The papers called it suicide, if I remember."

"Not suicide!"

The Arab pressed his lips together in a frown. "Miss Kelly obviously does not believe it was suicide."

"Families seldom do."

Kassam nodded. "Her mother was shot once in the right temple with a .357 Magnum. The police say there were powder burns inside the wound, indicating the weapon had been placed tightly against her head. Apparently tests showed she'd recently handled a gun."

"Suicide so far," I told him.

"Except for the fact that so far the gun's still missing."

I studied the assistant in his three-piece suit, fastidious even for an Arab. He would be the kind who wore pajamas with pockets. And remembered everything he'd ever seen or heard. "Anything else?" I asked.

"The medical examiner's report found the powder burns to be more consistent with suicide than homicide. Also, the bullet had taken a suicide track through the skull."

"So the conclusion is that the woman shot herself and someone else took the gun before police arrived."

"Exactly."

"It's happened before. Is that the official finding?"

"It's official."

I turned to Charisma Kelly, dry-eyed and defiant. "I know how hard it must be to accept the fact that a loved one would commit suicide—"

"I didn't love my mother and she didn't commit suicide."

"What then?"

"My mother was murdered."

"Murdered, you say."

"It would have been impossible for her to take her own life. Utterly impossible."

"A woman who believed in nothing at the end of her life?" I snapped. "Unloved by her own daughter. What did she have to live for?"

"You don't understand."

"What don't I understand?" My voice bristled, pressing her. "Why couldn't she commit suicide?"

"Because my mother was a devout Roman Catholic," Charisma Kelly hissed, "and was totally opposed to suicide on religious grounds."

# three

CONSTANCE KELLY WAS BORN in Philadelphia, Pennsylvania, of loving parents who had her by the grace of God and then could have no more. When she was six, according to her account, the family moved to Jersey City, where her father worked for Colgate. Four years later he died of cancer. Constance never forgave him for leaving her, or her mother for remarrying. Her new stepfather sexually assaulted her for two years before abandoning his family. By age sixteen she was already questioning the efficacy of her mother's religious beliefs; nothing had ever gone right for them. After high school Constance left home.

Over the next decade she drifted around the country, caught up in some of the protest movements of the 1960s and early Seventies, all the while nurturing her distrust of religion until it became an obsession and then a crusade. By now she'd been herself abandoned, saw her own child die of disease. In Philadelphia at age thirty, Charisma Kelly started Christians Anonymous. Two years later she moved back to Jersey City.

"Your mother remarried again, you said."

"Seven years ago. For companionship mostly, I would think."

"You like him?"

She shrugged. "The best of a bad lot, I suppose. Very quiet. He never mistreated her that I know of."

"Where's he work?"

"For the city, one of the agencies."

"Any significant money?"

"They owned a nice house in a good section, if that's what you mean. And a summer place at the shore. Possibly some savings, not much. They weren't rich. Most of what they had came from a negligence case my mother won five years ago."

"Who gets it?"

"My stepfather, of course."

"Your mother's married name was Stiles?"

"Yes."

"All right," I said, "let's get back to the missing gun."

"Doesn't that mean murder?"

"Not always."

She didn't understand. How could someone shoot herself if there's no gun?

"Usually the gun is found within a few feet of the body," I explained. "It's held anywhere up to about eighteen inches, but the recoil could push it out maybe another foot or two."

"Still not very far," Kassam said.

"Four, five feet tops. At least for a handgun." I made a mental note to check on the Arab. "You said it was a .357 Mag. That's just an overloaded and lengthened .38 Special. Any chance it was a .38? Lots more of those around."

He shook his head. "From what I was told, the bullet was definitely a .357 Mag factory cast."

"So. Maybe five feet for a handgun," I repeated for her benefit while I wondered how he knew the bullet was a factory load. "Now a shotgun obviously has a bigger bang and more recoil so the distance from the body could be greater."

A demented teenager ran by, radio blaring. The Rangers had lost again.

"Then there's the full-fire weapons," I said in sudden defeat. "The assault rifles and submachine guns, even the machine guns that shoot rifle slugs." Six in a row! "Not to mention the exotics." How was that possible? In my despair I was working up to bazookas and howitzers.

"Wasn't it a revolver weapon?"

The war games snapped. I blinked back to Charisma

Kelly and decided she knew nothing about guns. Either that or she was the greatest actress since Doris Day.

"I mean that is what's missing, isn't it?"

Directness was also a sign of strength, my second decision about her. "You're right," I said. And started wondering about my own jawline.

She was worrying a knee with the heel of her hand. Her fingers were long and slim and so were her legs. "Then how did it disappear?"

"There are ways," I said. "Could be some mechanical magic that whisked the gun out a window or up the chimney after firing."

Her perfect lips were parted, with the tip of her tongue showing between her perfect teeth. A perfect commercial for McDonald's. "The police went over the room a hundred times," she said. "Even outside. Nothing was there."

"Could also be a remote-control device from another room, fired through a tap in the wall."

"They searched the whole house."

I watched a pigeon with one leg draw closer. The will to survive was everywhere.

"Any bits of metal found near the body?"

Kassam said he hadn't been told of any.

"Nothing that could've come from an explosion?"

"No."

"Too bad."

"Why?"

"Some of the new plastic stuff could make anything disappear," I said. "What about water?"

Kassam snapped his fingers. "An ice gun that melt-ed."

"There are no ice guns," I told him. "Only ice bullets, but that's not what's missing."

Charisma said, "A flood."

"Flood the room and rig the door to open when the gun fires. It's then flushed out."

"I told you they searched the whole house."

"If a storm drain were removed, the gun might follow the water down the drain."

She shook her head. "I found my mother's body. There was no flood."

A flock of pigeons flapped their wings, landing in a graceful glide.

I tried again. "People fatally shot through the head have been known to go three hundred feet before dying. That's plenty of time and distance to hide a gun."

"Except the police say it happened in the bedroom where I found her."

"A hundred fifty feet one way," I said slowly, "to get rid of the gun. Then a hundred fifty feet back the other way. Did they search the whole block?"

Charisma Kelly didn't like the thoughts I was forcing on her, but I wasn't going to let that stop me. I'd met other women who saw guns as part of a man's world of incomprehensible caliber codes and bullet types. Unless, of course, she knew all about guns and was the greatest actress since Veronica Lake.

"If you find that hard to believe," I added, "there are cases of people shooting themselves six times in the head or chest. Or shooting someone else three or four times before themselves, then reloading and finishing the job." The one-legged pigeon watched hungrily as the others fought over a few crumbs. "You don't always die right away."

She slumped in her seat, a moment's retreat to get her wind back. The weeks had taken their toll. And the guilt, always that. I knew the feeling. I'd been through it all myself.

"They didn't find the gun," she insisted. "Damn it, it can't be suicide."

"They didn't find the gun," I said gently, "because someone took it before they got there."

"Do you believe that?"

"What I believe is irrelevant. It's what the police believe."

"The police believe I took it."

The season was almost over and the Rangers were 26–39 in the won-lost column. The best they'd probably do was fifth, and there were only six teams in the division. It was a bad year all around.

"Did you?"

"No."

And getting worse.

"Why would they think you took the gun?" I asked.

She said, "So it wouldn't be considered a suicide."

"Any motive?"

"An insurance policy my mother kept with me as beneficiary. It was her way of making certain I got something."

"How much?"

"A hundred thousand, I think."

"You think?"

"So I'm sure."

"And it doesn't pay off for suicide," I said.

"No, it doesn't pay off for suicide."

I stood up to lose the shooting pains in my legs. "You knew that when you found the body."

Her eyebrows raised. "Exactly what does that mean?"

"Exactly what I said. Insurance policies have a suicide clause and you must've known that when you discovered the body. It's common knowledge."

"I don't think I like the implication," Charisma Kelly said sharply. "In fact, I resent it. Knowing something that is common knowledge doesn't mean I took the gun."

If their eyes were small and close together, you had trouble on your hands. Hers were wide and far apart, which only proved there's a sucker born every minute. And I was up.

I sat down. "But you could see how the police would think so. They always look for the obvious motive."

"You are not the police," she said. "You are here to listen to me and learn what it is I need. The police have not done their job, they have taken the easy answer. They have accepted a murder as suicide, and that is simply not good enough for me. I do not believe in the hereafter, with or without gods. This life is all I have or ever will have and so I require justice, here and now. You are going to be hired to get me what I need. You are going to get me justice."

"Am I?"

"Yes. I have listened to you and learned all I need to know about you. Or care to know. You are direct, and seem to possess a certain code of what used to be called manly conduct. I for one think it a shame our age has lost sight of that. You also seem clever enough, or perhaps just stubborn enough, to get whatever you're after. If you are not intimidated by the prospect of seeking a gun everyone assumes is in my possession, Ali here will handle the terms."

"I won't stop there, you know. I won't stop with just the gun."

"That is precisely why you are being hired. I want the man who murdered my mother. I want him punished."

It's funny how you can know someone for a whole hour and not really know them at all.

"And the other reason?" I asked Charisma.

"What other reason?"

I sat very close to her, our eyes locked in combat.

"Your mother was a devout Catholic. Unlike you and me perhaps, devout Catholics do believe in life after death and the Last Judgment. At which time their bodies will rise again to be judged before the throne of God." I clipped the words off. "Until then, their bodies are buried in consecrated ground to await the resurrection and the life."

"I don't see what this—"

"Buried in consecrated ground," I said, "unless they died by their own hand."

It was all coming back to me, even the exact wordage. Things I never wanted to think about again.

"Now you see?"

The voice—when it came—seemed to swell in my ear and soon I heard, or thought I heard, the little girl who sat between her parents in church and sang God's praise. Or maybe it was the little boy.

"You are quite right, Malone, if that makes you happy. My mother was a frightened, helpless woman who prayed for death all her life. Death and her damned god." Her eyes blazed out of control. "I want the official verdict changed to murder. I want my mother buried in a Catholic cemetery."

They say women's eyes tend to be more moist than men's. Or perhaps it was just the glint of the sun as she turned away.

"Please?"

# four

COOPER JARRETT HAD HIS office in one of the bank buildings overlooking Journal Square, which itself overlooked anything. But it was cheap and easy to get to and so it became the heart of the city. Legend had it that on this site in 1979, nothing happened.

The office door said Sons and the inside said money, which meant all the furniture matched. I stood in the lap of luxury while the receptionist offered encouragement, radiant in a Kanzai sweater. I asked for Laura Jarrett and she asked for more. Somehow I had the feeling I couldn't afford her.

We traded thoughts for a moment, mine full of Mozart and magic. Behind her a hallway stretched to a distant window full of poison ivy. Halfway down, a door opened and a vision floated toward us, robed in a Lagerfeld that lost nothing in translation. I watched her approach and saw Cleopatra entering Rome. And I was Caesar who was epileptic. I was prepared for anything but what I said. "Did you know that father and son form the most dangerous animal relationship on earth?"

She smiled and swept me under her thumb. "Then we must be satisfied with second best."

It was all a mix-up in my central switchboard. Over breakfast I'd read of the boy who stabbed his father forty times, another Lizzie Borden or else a blow for male equality. He was on my mind when she stole it. About all I could do was swear I wasn't Caesar or ask if she read the papers.

"Only in bed," she said, luring me on.

We loped past the receptionist, whom she pointedly ignored. "Her name is Virginia," she sniffed, "though I don't know why."

I put it down to friendly female rivalry.

"In here."

Her office was warm and inviting, much like the woman herself. Spontaneity was a great gift and only women had it, some women. Laura Jarrett had it. She could cut your heart out and make you feel alive.

"The outer door said Sons," I started.

"One son, not mine." She sounded relieved. "It's morning so he's probably sleeping."

"What's he do in the afternoon?"

"He gets up."

"Sons?" I was curious.

"My loving ex," she said sweetly, "has an ego problem. He thinks women are only for fucking." She motioned me to a chair. "No brains, no business. Just body. You know the type." Her eyes raked my face. "You may be the type yourself. It's hard to tell anymore."

"Sons mean at least two."

"You're looking at her. I'm the other one." Her sigh spanned the desk. "He didn't want Partners or Associates on the door—too equal. And as for a woman? God forbid! 'It's a man's world,'" she imitated Jarrett, "'and a woman's place is on her knees.' He's very oral, my ex. 'Who cares what you like? Smart guy, right?'"

Her imitation was good, especially the rhythm. Made me wonder if we all sound that foolish to them.

"You don't really look the type," she admitted. "Are you?"

"Do I call you Miss Jarrett?" I asked.

"You call me Laura."

"When I spoke to Mr. Jarrett on the phone, he said he'd be out for the day."

"He never lies."

I said, "Must be hard."

"Easy. Whenever he's caught he calls it old age, like he just forgot."

"How old is he?"

"Forty-five."

She had at least twenty years on him. Two or three anyway. I couldn't tell anymore, they were all beginning to look like lollipops to me.

"I married young," she said, seeing the sticks in my head. "Better that way, get it over with. Like measles or chicken pox."

I didn't say a word.

"You married?"

I told her no. "With me two's a crowd."

"You must hate dancing."

On top of that I'd run a check on the dead mother. She was fifty-nine, but her last husband was only forty-seven. Charisma Kelly said they were married seven years. Which meant that when he was forty he married a woman who was fifty-two.

"Do you know a Henry Stiles?" I asked Laura. "With the city's redevelopment agency?"

She'd never heard of him.

"I just thought with your husband a developer—"

"Ex-husband," she meowed. "A whole year last month." And stretched like a cat. "After a dry spell, a whole year to catch up."

"On what?"

"What else?"

They'd been wed four years, Jarrett had said. But in that time she'd played the hostess and walked away with half. Hardly a cat, I thought, more like a fox. Or maybe even the one that has the best of both, the wolf.

"Would you like a cigarette?" she asked.

"I'd rather have ice cream."

Except she couldn't walk away, it was a family business. Cooper Jarrett and Sons. How do you split sons who look like daughters? What about daughters who look like that?

She reminded me of Gene Tierney, the same Chinese eyes and alabaster skin and hair of India ink. It was *Laura* all over again, my first love, and I was on a train that was passing through.

"Did Mr. Jarrett tell you why I'm here?"

"The phone calls, I imagine."

"He says you're shaky. Are you shaky?"

"Should I be?"

"It would be natural."

"Then I'm just being foolishly brave, I suppose."

Soundly chastised, I sat at her feet and thought of reasons to stay. The phones, for one.

"How about the others?" I said. "Anyone else get a call?"

"Charlie Weems got a few." She pursed her lips. "And Cooper, of course."

"Can I get into his office after I finish here?"

"What are you going to do?"

"Fix your phone."

"My phone?"

"So it records everything."

Her smile lit the room. "You're going to trace the calls."

"I'm afraid that's not—"

"I saw it in a movie," she trilled. "They traced this call in New York? All they had to do was keep the person on the line as long as they could."

I shook my head. "Sounds like a lot of fun, but it doesn't work that way in real life. Tracing a call in a big city is almost impossible."

"Then why—"

"Voiceprint identification," I said. "Maybe later we can match the voice to someone."

"Like fingerprints?"

"Same idea."

"But how?"

"Speech," I told her, "is a randomly learned process, so each voice is unique. What we try to do is match a recording to a suspect when we have one." I spread my hands. "Simple."

"Simple." She laughed.

"Not foolproof," I cautioned, "but good enough. They ran a test a few years back on Rich Little? He can imitate anyone, so he did John Wayne. You ever hear him do Wayne?"

She made a face.

"Sounds exactly like him. But when they ran the voice

spectrograph, it wasn't John Wayne at all. It was Rich Little."

The phone rang. Laura quickly pointed to the extension by the couch and we lifted the receivers at the same time. It was a business call.

"When was the last one?" I asked afterward.

"Friday."

"And before that?"

"Almost every day for more than a week."

"Always the same?"

She nodded. "They'll kill us if we don't pull out of the Harbor Terminal project."

"Who's us?"

"I assume they mean Cooper and me."

"Can you still pull out?"

"Hardly." She hesitated. "I mean, it's going up."

"But can you?"

"By wrecking the company, sure." She thought that over. "I suppose so. But he never would."

"Jarrett?"

"This is the biggest deal of his life. He'd die first."

I let that sink in.

"You own half the company, don't you?"

"The wrong half. He controls it."

"But not you."

"Not anymore." She fiddled at the desk, some papers. "You think these threats mean anything?"

"They don't sound harmless, if that's what you're after. There's more than one person involved, they're directed at more than one person, and they've been going on for more than a week. Could be trouble." I looked at her, a piece of my past. "Why don't you get out while you can?"

"Get out?"

"Sell your share of the business. You obviously know what you're doing in real estate. Start your own company."

"Did Cooper tell you to say that?"

"Is that what you think?"

"I think he'd give a lot to get my half. He could've paid you to come here and scare me."

"Am I scaring you?"

"You're damn right."

"That's good. You should be scared. Mad, too. Some-body's playing games that could end in tragedy."

"Suppose it's nothing, a prank?"

"Suppose it isn't?"

She thought that over. "You apparently get paid for doing this kind of work," she said slowly. "If there's no threat, there's no pay. My getting out doesn't change anything. So why are you doing this?"

"Doing what?"

"Telling me all this, like you cared what happens to me."

She was *Laura* again, home suddenly and confused to find a cop in her apartment gazing at her portrait over the mantel. But for me she was Miami and the mother of my unborn child, cut down in the middle of life and dying on a darkened street, her eyes oozing love.

Why am I doing this? I said to myself.

"Someone needed help once," I heard myself say, "and no one was there."

In the room fingers of light spread slowly across the floor. It was so quiet you could hear a gunshot.

"Who was she?" Laura Jarrett asked after a while.

"Just someone I used to know."

Morning light was so honest.

"It's a funny thing," I said. "That's the first time I ever told anyone the story of my life." Trying to build bridges. "How about you?"

"Not much to tell." Her fingers traced the edge of the desk. "I grew up in Greenwich with money and then I grew out of Greenwich and the money disappeared. When I married Cooper my parents disowned me. I never saw them again."

"After your divorce?"

"By then they were dead. An accident."

"Holding up all right?"

"It was a few years ago. I'm fine now."

"Why the divorce?"

She shrugged. "Things happen."

Much of my life was random information, a sponge soaking up debris. "Anything specific?"

"Nothing worth talking about."

Somebody knocked and I half expected to see Jarrett walk in—would be just like him to check on the help. In a way I felt sorry for him, losing someone like her. But the truth was he never had her at all.

*"Entrez!"*

She was just too much class for him.

"Sorry. Didn't know you were busy."

He had shocks of white hair around a dissipated face. Alcohol was my guess, a steady diet. The kind that functioned well at work but took its toll over the years.

Laura introduced him as Charles Weems, financial VP and the third principal in the company. He'd received two of the calls.

Weems nodded in my direction. "Just wanted to know if Coop'll be in later."

"All day in New York," Laura said, and turned my way. "Chase is renting space for some of their back-office operations."

"I really must talk to him. What about tomorrow?"

"Flying to Georgia for the state Tourist Commission. They're ready to sign." Another client, she indicated. "Why not call him tonight at home?"

"Yes, I should do that." He appeared distracted. "Tonight, you say. Right."

"Anything you could tell me about those calls, Mr. Weems?" I explained what Jarrett had hired me for. Weems listened carefully, which surprised me. Then asked what I'd found so far.

"Just starting," I told him. "I'm going to tap the phones now. Mr. Jarrett's, Laura's here, and I'll do yours if that's okay with you."

He put up a little fuss, like most people, and I tried to calm him by pointing out the possible gravity of the threats. Only it didn't calm him at all. I watched him grow more disturbed by the minute.

"I'm really not up to violence," he said. "I—I didn't think something like this would happen."

"Let me worry about that. Is there anything you can tell me?"

"About what?"

"About anything."

The phone rang again but I didn't move. Laura picked it up.

"Not here," Weems said uncertainly.

"Where?"

"Tonight, my house." He pulled out a pad and pen, wrote down his address. I folded the paper in my pocket. "About the calls?"

"I'm not sure."

I saw I wouldn't get anything out of him in the office.

Laura replaced the receiver. "It wasn't them."

"I didn't think so." According to Jarrett, most calls came in the afternoon.

Weems left, saying he'd be gone for the day, and I said I'd see him at nine.

"Something's bothering him," I told Laura.

"Could be the liquor. Charles is very capable, but . . ."

"Smells like fear to me. How long's he been with you?"

"About three years. Before that he was with the county political machine. There was a shortage, one of his people, but he took the blame. It was a bad blow."

"But Jarrett wanted him anyway."

"He came in with money at the right time." Her voice registered disapproval.

"Anything else?"

"I understand he has many friends of both sexes."

"Are you saying something?"

She laughed. "Just that he might have a secret life outside the office."

"Doesn't everyone?" I said.

# five

I SPENT THE LUNCH hour in the park with friends. Jarrett's phones were tapped, his people warned. I'd even asked my informants to keep their ears open for booking jobs, Jersey talk for extortion. You book a business for so much; if the owner doesn't pay, you whack the guy, kill him, or blow his business, ruin it. Sometimes you take it over. I figured if it wasn't a killing, it could be that. Which wasn't my game but I'd decided to stay in till homicide was ruled out. Laura Jarrett might have had something to do with my decision.

"Two cases! Getting kinda greedy, ain't ya?"

"They get billed every other day," I said. "Comes out the same."

Manny snorted. "Never be no millionaire that way."

"Don't wanna be a millionaire."

"Must be one of them throwups."

"You mean fuckups."

"He means throwbacks," Luther said. Luther had been listening to Manny for twenty years. "A dinosaur."

"Them dicks went out with Bogart," Manny said. "Now they all wear cream-color suits and sleep between bunnies. Don't you watch TV?"

To Manny we were all dicks. I was long and large, so I was a big dick. Local detectives were hick dicks. When we said investigators, he heard alligators. But Manny knew more about Jersey City politics than anybody since Frank Hague.

"Not like the Hague days, eh, Manny?" Kidding him about old times was usually a good way to get political information.

"Now *there* was a mayor," Manny beamed. "When he said 'I am the law,' the whole town shat."

"He means shit," said Luther.

"Goddam right," Manny growled. "One day he said to me, 'Manny, there are only two kinds of money. My money and your money.' So right away you knew he knows what he's talking about."

Luther scoffed. "Probably had his hand in your pocket when he said it."

"Frank Hague never had his hand in nobody's pocket," Manny snarled in derision. "He had plenty of pockets of his own."

"Only two kinds of people worked for Frank Hague," Luther said gravely, "the living and the dead."

Local politics was a love-hate relationship that had kept them fast friends for two decades. Luther longed to look forward and Manny held him back.

"So what've you got now?"

"At least this mayor's moving us into the twentieth century."

"Better he moves to Rome, then all we'd have to kiss is his ring."

We sat in Lincoln Park, the best in the city. Only two highways ran through it. From almost anywhere on a good day you could see smoke.

"Who's it this time?" Manny wanted to know.

"Just came by to say hello."

"So goodbye."

"Charles Weems," I sighed. "Worked for the county?"

"Charlie Weems." It wasn't said with affection. "What you want with him? He ain't news no more."

"When was he?"

"Three, four years ago. He was a bagman for the party, a heavy."

"What party?"

Manny looked at me with disgust. "The Democrats, what else? This is Hudson County we're talking about, right? So one of his boyfriends got mad one day and ran off with the loot, maybe a hundred grand. Maybe more—nobody ever knew for sure."

"One of his boyfriends?"

"He was a fruitcake. Gave some of them jobs in the money end where he was and one just took off. Guess he got jealous."

"Did it make the papers?"

"In Jersey City?" Manny cackled. "Who you kidding? It made nothing but trouble, so the whole thing was hushed down."

"Up," said Luther.

"Fuck off."

"Hold on." I grimaced in thought. "Didn't the party bosses see what was happening, what he was?"

"They didn't care what he was. He was a fruitcake. We're talking the new Democrats, right? Hague woulda killed him. They just let him go 'cause the money was gone."

"Any chance he was in on it?"

"Weems? No way. Besides, he's a lush."

A functioning lush, I reminded myself, who'd come to Jarrett's with money. Where'd he get it? A split? Maybe now the boyfriend was broke and looking for a new bankroll. Blackmail? He could shake them over the phone, then threaten to talk about Weems. Make people lose confidence in the company's projects.

"So why ain't you robbing the rich?"

I trailed a diesel's plume into the sky. Things were looking up. "All I want is a pig's foot," I sang to Manny, "and a bottle of beer."

"While you ride around in your Cadillac—"

"Dodge."

"And sit in your house on the hill."

"So I got in on the ground floor."

"Not for nothing, but there are a few floors above you worth about eighty grand apiece. Right?"

"Things are never what they seem," I quoted in defense.

"Machiavelli!" He turned to Luther. "Now *there* was a politician for you, just like Frank Hague."

"But that's not what Machiavelli meant," said the retired teacher. "What he meant—"

"He's at it again," Manny said, rolling his eyes.

I took the shortcut to the medical examiner's office. Split-second traffic lights, cowboys in crowded lanes, death-wish pedestrians, blurred faces and spawning scars honed my instincts. My job was to find the answers to questions, but first I had to find the questions. Like how did the callers get the three phone numbers? Jarrett's office had private lines and only the receptionist was listed. Think about it, whispered the callers in my ear. Who helped us?

"Inside the wound," the pathologist said enthusiastically, "rather than on the surface skin. Small particles of un-burned gunpowder and molten metal driven into the lower epidermal layers by the explosive gases. Fascinating." He rubbed his hands together. "The gun had to be absolutely jammed against her head."

"A .357 Mag."

"Absolutely."

"No bullet distortion?"

"Plenty. But not enough so they couldn't tell the caliber."

"What about the body? Any terminal illness that would make her do it?"

"Nothing yet."

"No killer pains?"

"Shouldn't have been, she was only fifty-nine. For a female that's hardly mid–middle age biologically." He leered. "Why, I could tell you stories—"

"I don't want to hear them."

Dorsey was young and zealous, a nice combination in pathology. It meant he talked and I listened. When his mind wasn't on lipstick.

"What else you got for suicide?" I asked.

"Just the usual things. A female seldom does it in the nude; this one was fully clothed. They almost never do it in the face. Female vanity, you know. And most gun suicides are one shot in the right temple, like this one." He paused. "What've you got against?"

"Most gun suicides are with a .22," I said, "the vast majority. A .357 Mag is too big, especially for a female. And they don't pick a gun anyway. They're prone to poisons and pills. Plus there was nothing really wrong with her, you say, and her life seemed in order, at least what I checked."

"Sometimes things go wrong that can't be checked."

"Like what?"

"In the head, I mean. People sometimes lose their way. Women who are childless, for example. It could prey on their minds in later life, might even make them drift into melancholy until it's too late." He shrugged. "Maybe that happened here."

I hated practical jokes and pathologists who played them. "What are you saying?"

"Just that it could've happened that way."

"Childless?"

"Yes."

"But she wasn't—"

He saw my eyes and mistook confusion for doubt. "I did the autopsy. No kidding."

"One of us," I said in a strangled voice.

"You mean you didn't know?"

I stood there stunned. Mrs. Henry Stiles was a woman who believed in God and had a daughter who believed in nothing. Her name was Charisma Kelly and she lived at—

"Mrs. Stiles had no children," he said. "It's all in the report."

"No children?"

"Here. See for yourself."

On the way to headquarters, I saw a city spun with cobwebs and seven miles of spiders storming the streets. They were all in my head. I didn't like to be used by anybody, nobody. Clients lied all the time, okay, but not like this. Like what? She wanted the insurance money so she needed a murder instead of suicide. Nothing new there. Then why was I so mad? Because she was an impostor? An atheist? A woman?

The spiders began to disappear. Okay, I told myself. Men can't help lying and women can't help telling the truth, that's the way God intended. So she broke the natural law and lied to me. Not the first time it happened, or the last. I had to face the fact. She was beautiful and I was hurt. What a basis for business. Some P.I. By the time I got there, I'd laughed the rest of the webs away.

"Who are you?" the guard wanted to know.

"Just another asshole," I told him truthfully.

Upstairs Bernie ran me through the police reports. "Everything points to suicide," he said.

"Everything but the gun."

"That's incidental in this case."

Sometimes Bernie liked his little joke, too.

"No kidding, Malone."

"How can a murder weapon be incidental?"

"Not murder. Suicide."

"Whatever," I said, exasperated.

"It's incidental because we know who took it."

"She says she didn't."

"She lied to you."

I didn't say anything.

"You know women," Bernie groaned. "They lie all the time. I think it's in their blood." He shuffled the papers. "The bullet, the body, all indicate the mother shot herself. When the daughter walked in, she thought of the money so she took the gun. What else could she do?"

"It doesn't bother you that the dead woman had no children?"

"So she's adopted. Same thing. She gets the *gelt* if it's murder. *Capish?*"

Bernie's father was German, his mother Italian. He turned out first-generation Jersey City. And a good detective who went by the book.

"What about the trace-metal test?" I asked.

"Nothing unusual. The lab sprayed the decedent's hands with a chemical agent under ultraviolet light, and the fluorescence showed up metallic particles of iron. Like from a gun."

"But not the shape of a gun."

"That hardly ever happens and you know it. Far as we're concerned, she held a gun."

"But there's no proof she fired it," I insisted.

"Meaning?"

"Maybe the killer pressed the gun in her hand afterward."

"Why would he do that?"

"I don't know. He could've wanted it to look like suicide but needed the gun, too." I smiled into Bernie's jeer.

"Maybe he read about you clowns and knew you'd fall for it."

At the door I had another thought. "Did you give out the information that the bullet was a factory load?"

"No, but a .357? They almost all are, around here anyway. Does it matter?"

"Not anymore."

Dinner was in a dive downtown near the piers. At least it was a dive during Prohibition when this part of the Hudson was still called North River and the boats would bring the booze in from Canada. Now it was a pricey health hangout that catered to Moslem vegetarian warriors trying to rid the world of witches.

Marilyn didn't agree.

"These are very nice people here, very nicely dressed."

I made a face. "Yuppies squirming up the ladder of excess."

"They're just finding their own means of expression."

"Some expression," I said. "In the Sixties they marched in the streets for the poor and now they run through them in ninety-dollar sneakers."

"Shoes are very important for good health."

Marilyn was a traditionalist. Clothes made the man, and the man made the woman. Which made sense if you liked clothes. I'd worn them all my life and never gave them another thought. It was our only big difference.

"I've decided to marry Peter."

Marilyn said something like that about once a month. But we always had a good time together. I think she liked me.

"Any comment?"

"A man's gotta do what a man's gotta do," I told her.

"Don't be a retromingent."

She was always saying things like that, too. Marilyn was a serial painter, someone who specializes in a single object. Her serial was the wolf. All her paintings were of wolves as human beings, doing human things. They were weird and funny and very original. And she made big bucks, which made it all right for her to be weird and funny and original. She was also a big reader, and sometimes a small pain in the ass. But I'd be a retromingent for her anytime.

"That means someone who pisses backward."

I grunted, feeling very macho wrestling with my curds and whey while she inhaled a spoonful of tofutti.

"Why do you love this place?" she asked between sniffs.

"Because you're not elsewhere."

"What happens when I marry Peter?"

"I'll probably go back to caviar and truffles, or maybe a bread sandwich."

Her face formed a question mark.

"Two hamburgers with a slice of bread in between."

"And never come in here again?"

Like all artists, I suppose, Marilyn was very romantic.

"This food wouldn't keep you alive anyway," she sniffed. And very practical.

While she went on about her day and yesterday, I took in some thoughts of my own. Stiles married Charisma Kelly's mother two years before her quarter-million settlement, so it couldn't have been for money. So why'd he marry her?

"Maybe I won't marry Peter," Marilyn said.

Charisma called it companionship, but it could be respectability. Hiding what? Or maybe the woman did kill herself and the other took the gun. She lied to me, didn't she?

"He's too wrapped up in his work."

I decided to drop the case. Who needed a bunch of bananas saying there was no God? Just more Communists.

"Are you listening?"

Artists were funny. All they ever thought about were their own problems.

"I always listen."

At least the liar had a family now, even if they were all crazy. All I had were my cases. They were my family, the people in the cases, even the dead. Even those who killed them. They were the black sheep of the family, and I was the Lone Ranger.

"It's a hard decision," Marilyn said. "About Peter."

"I know but I've decided to keep the case."

"What case?"

"Who's Peter?"

When Ray Price came over I was still toying with my soy

steak, an angry mass that resisted temptation. But I didn't care. I liked to share things with Marilyn.

"You're supposed to kill it first," Price said.

"If it doesn't kill me."

Ray Price had the name of a singer and the soul of a tout. He worked the crime beat for the local paper and was always ready to help. Or hinder. But I liked to read his stuff, the way he made New Jersey the head of the country and Jersey City the heart of New York.

"Do you know New Jersey is the cocaine capital of America?" Price sat down. "Stepan Chemical in Maywood is the only plant in the country that can legally process coca leaves into raw coke. Forty dollars an ounce."

"Do you know Marilyn?"

"Do you know New Jersey has the largest condom company in America? No joke. Young Drugs in Piscataway, fifty-three percent of all drugstore sales." He called the waiter over.

"Do you know me?"

"I knew you"—he ordered a liquid yogurt flambeau—"when your idea of a good time was to go to an Italian restaurant and listen to them eat."

"You have a good memory for your age," I told him.

"What age? It was only a few months ago." He turned to Marilyn. "You've done wonders for his disposition, I hear."

"He still mumbles in bed," she lied.

"In that case, his complexion seems to be improving too."

"Crime and sex," I said. "That's all the media know. Why don't you say a couple words about life itself?"

"Crime and sex."

"See what I mean?"

"Did you know New Jersey is the crime capital of America?" Price looked pleased. "The mob's even planning to open a 'free crime zone' at Newark Airport for international travelers. Trying to capture the terrorist market."

Reporters loved to romanticize the mob. They were good copy, a kind of terminal Disneyland. But Ray had contacts and liked to do favors. What I wanted was a line on the Arab.

"His name's Ali Kassam."

"An Arab working for Christians Anonymous?"

Unbelievers everywhere!

At nine o'clock I faced the house, the long front yard ending in a Cyclone fence festooned with gnarled shrubs. Behind it a ribbon of concrete ran back to the steps.

Weems had won his privacy. He'd escaped public wrath by political dealing, then wrapped himself in concealment. The house said nothing of its master, a slab of stone on a block of bricks. Under a bright moon I hurried up the walk.

To my left a tree threw grotesque shapes against the sky, feeding my paranoia. Ugly shoots stretched upward past the first-floor windows. I loved nature, everything green was poison ivy and everything red a rose.

Up the three steps I banged on the door, annoyed at myself for indulging in death symbols. Trees always held hideous shapes at night, shrubs grew prodigiously, and darkened houses loomed like medieval battlements. Night or day, the shit was all the same. Only the flies changed.

Then everything changed.

The first shot came with my hand on the knob, the second a blink later. By then I was racing for the rear, my mind on suicide. Two quick shots meant one gun. I bolted the small porch, smashed through the screen door. Sure it was dumb, but I was so certain it was Weems. The man, the psychology, the circumstances—it all fit.

Except it didn't fit at all. Nothing fit. I caught him still crouched over the body, his back to me. There was just enough moonlight to see forms, and I had seen first. The gun was already in my hand.

"No tricks," I barked. "The weapon on the floor, then you get up."

He kept his back to me, Lucifer rising. He was thin, even youthful, and my first thought was robbery that ended in homicide. And nothing to do with me, just a coincidence. Only there were no coincidences in my business, and nobody ever gets a free ride.

The noise was behind me, to my right. The instant I heard it I knew it was too late. Funny but what flashed through my mind was not my past but the future, the plans I hadn't made yet, the people I didn't meet. My body had 639 muscles that seemed to explode all at once. Falling into darkness, I caught a last look at Lucifer running, something about the way he moved.

I never saw the other devil at all.

# six

"ALL RIGHT," BERNIE SAID, "so you got a hard head."

"Everything's good for something."

"So what else you got?"

"There's a hole in the top if you're into that."

"Lucky it wasn't filled with lead."

Bernie sat backward on a chair at the foot of the bed and peered at me through the bars. The bed was old, about as old as Christ Hospital, and the painted iron rungs were peeling yellow.

"Must be the Irish in you." He grinned.

"The other half's German, like you."

"Even worse."

They'd found me on the floor near the body, dead to the world. Weems was just dead. A bullet in the back of the neck and another behind an ear made it a contract job.

"What's the doc say?"

"Same as you, a hard head and lots of luck." I leaned over the edge and spit into a metal pan. "Only it wasn't luck."

"What then?"

"They weren't getting paid to take me out. Just Weems."

Bernie nodded. "Professionals."

"All the way." I fingered the top of my skull, thick with bandage. "A sap in a paper sack so it's not enough to kill."

"So why Weems?"

I pulled my hand away. A dozen stitches were still enough to hurt. "When I find out I'll let you know."

Somebody grunted, but it wasn't me.

*"If* you find out."

I counted the bars, Bernie behind them. One of us, anyway. "What's that supposed to mean?" I growled. And counted to ten again while he got up and went to the window.

"I can remember this town when everybody lied about it." His eyes ran over the dirty glass. "We all told lies 'cause it was so bad."

"What's better now?"

"Now?" He turned away from the window, faced me. "Now it's all different. Everyone's talking about us. The Gold Coast of New York. We're even getting a Miracle Mile like Chicago and L.A." The voice registered disbelief. "You know what I mean, Malone?"

It was either hear him or strangle him, and I was too weak to walk. "Spell it out, Bernie."

He shrugged uncomfortably. "Just that the big shots downtown feel this thing should be kept a little quiet."

"How you gonna cover up murder?"

"Not cover up," he bristled. "What's the matter with you? They just don't want any bad publicity out of it. A lot of big deals are in the works."

"I'll bet."

"This Weems was with the county a long time before he took a dive."

"I know all that."

"Plus his life-style and friends. People might get the wrong idea."

"About what?"

"About the city," Bernie wheezed. "What else?"

"You mean about Hudson County politics, don't you? The county and the people who run it."

Bernie spread his hands. "Jeez, I'm just telling you what I was told."

"To tell me to lay off."

"To tell you to go easy."

"How easy?"

"A little cooperation, all right?"

"Is that a two-way street?" I asked.

"For starters, tell us what you know about Weems."

"By now you should know more than me."

"And whatever you find out."

I'd been in the hospital fifteen hours and Bernie was at least my tenth visitor, which meant at this rate I would soon run out of people I knew. Only Marilyn's early morning love-in made sense. Unfortunately it also made noise.

"Don't buy an iron bed," I warned Bernie. "They squeak."

"That's not what I wanna hear."

"Just trying to save your marriage. Isn't that what friends are for?"

The door opened and Ben Casey walked in. That was his real name, and he looked like Vince Edwards, too. Same scowl, like he'd turn a cold into cancer if you crossed him. A real medical charmer. He had a cigarette stuck behind his ear, the way they wore 'em in the old movies. It was smoked down about an inch.

I pushed myself up against the railing, trying to look alert. "When do I break out, doc?" My voice dripped health. "This morning you said this afternoon."

The doctor sized me up for a triple coronary bypass, then decided on a spinal injection of Airwick instead.

"In Hong Kong it's still yesterday," he mumbled. "You got plenty of time."

"If it was yesterday, I wouldn't be here tomorrow."

"Then think about today."

"How about this minute?"

Another scowl. "They're all alike," he said to Bernie. "Type A personalities. Always telling everyone else how to drive. No self-control." A hand pulled the cigarette off his ear while the other reached for a match. "Memory okay?"

"There was a young man from Siam—"

"How many fingers?"

"Twelve."

"And on this hand?"

"Three and a stalk of nicotine."

"Nicotine doesn't stalk," he said. "It attacks. You can go this afternoon."

"This *is* this afternoon."

"Then later this afternoon."

"When later this afternoon?"

"Six o'clock."

"That's this evening."

"In Moscow it's tomorrow morning," he said. "See how lucky you are?"

I turned to Bernie for support.

"Time is a relative," he announced with a wave of his hand.

"That's either a direct misquote," I fumed, "or the worst Italian accent since the Pollack pope."

"These cheap peepers," Bernie winked at Casey. "They all have a Christ complex."

"Type A personalities," the doctor repeated on the way out. The butt went back behind the ear. "Your tests showed nothing," he shot over his shoulder. "Keep it that way."

*"Jawohl!"*

"Do it!"

"I don't think he likes you," Bernie suggested when the door closed.

"That's just on the surface," I explained. "Deep down he hates me. To him all cops are paranoids and all paranoids are trouble."

"So's life."

"That's why he likes death. Says only death is no trouble." I reached for the metal pan again. "Shows how much he knows."

"So what about Weems?"

A neighbor saw me run toward the back when the shots were fired. Then two shadows came out and he called the cops. Trouble was he didn't get a good look. No description? He thought they might've been people. What about the spaceship?

"Let's trade," I told Bernie. "You tell me what you know and I'll listen."

Bernie showed teeth. "There was this rape case I remember a few years back. Before you come up here? According to the victim, the rapist wore sunglasses and a pillowcase over his head."

I lunged for the phone on the first ring. The last thing I

needed now was Bernie's rape cases, the sonofabitch loved them. Talking about them.

"Can you imagine? A pillowcase."

"Maybe he slept on the job." I listened to the voice, a soft sigh. "Still hurting," I told Laura Jarrett.

"Perhaps I can help," she hinted.

I wanted to think that over, turned back to Bernie. "Sunglasses, you said."

"The kind with the mirrors so all she could see's herself. The whole time he's on top of her she kept her eyes open, but all she saw was she needed a nose job."

"Malone?" Laura urged.

"I'm here."

"When she came in she had no description of the guy, nothing. What could we do?" Bernie shrugged helplessly. "She thought maybe the pillowcase came from Sears 'cause they were having a January white sale and I told her this was February. Took her a month to report it"—his eyes sparkled —"then it turned out the pillowcase was blue. Can you believe the nerve of some women? Holding back important information like that."

You had to be a little nuts, I suppose, to be a cop. Bernie didn't believe in rape. Using force was felonious assault and the rest was just revenge.

"There was another call before," Laura Jarrett said. "Maybe I'm not so brave after all."

"Brave enough," I assured her.

"Only thing she saw on the guy was his pecker, said she couldn't miss it." Bernie bubbled with enthusiasm. "Least a foot long."

"Wishful thinking."

"No, one of them silicone jobs where the stuff shifts along the shaft like wax. That's what gave me the idea."

"I know Cooper's paying you," Laura was saying, "but I'm the one who needs a soft shoulder. Are you available?"

"Usually," I demurred, and glanced over at Bernie. "What idea?"

"Best I ever had."

"Tonight?" she breathed.

"Seems the silicone leaves your pecker with half a hard-on. Imagine that?"

"So the guy's half cocked. What you do, run a ballistics check?"

"Better." Bernie smiled. "When the silicone moves around, it can do some pretty weird things." He fingered his earlobe. "She said it looked like an old Chianti bottle."

That did it, sex and wine. "What's your address?" I said into the phone.

"I'm in New York. Greenwich Village."

"Where?" I reached for the pad.

"West Tenth, right off Fifth Avenue."

I took down the number.

"Ever see anything like that?"

"Every morning," I growled at Bernie and returned to the receiver. "About eight."

"Hard to forget." He pulled at the lobe. "And easy to spot, especially in a lineup."

"Cooper called from Georgia this morning. He's worried about Weems."

"Too late now."

"We're next," Laura confided. "That's what Cooper says."

"Not necessarily."

"He's scared," she insisted.

"I'll talk to him."

"So am I."

"We paraded five of them in front of her," Bernie suddenly said.

"Five what?"

"Five peckers, what else? And everyone of 'em bare-assed."

"You made her day."

"Who?" screeched a feminine voice.

"Made the suspect's, too," he purred proudly. "Positive ID."

Even cops broke the rules. You shall not kill, except in the line of duty, but the line can be infinite if you know what you're doing. In Miami I was so desperate I cut the Ten Commandments down to five. Was Laura Jarrett meant to be my salvation? All I could see was Gene Tierney, who looked like Karen.

"Eight o'clock," I swore into the phone, and rang off. "Now what's all this got to do with Weems?"

Bernie shrugged, a gesture of innocence that fooled nobody. "All there is," he said. "We got the guy and the woman got a memory."

"I hope you mean seeing five in a row instead of what I think you mean."

He shrugged again. "Life is funny, you know?"

"You gonna go back to pulling your earlobe?"

"What I mean is, anyone who says no when he should say yes better mail his nuts to a new address."

Bernie was a twenty-year man, a city detective who had no love for the county cops. His big dream was to live in Alaska.

"Run that through me again in English."

"Charles Weems." The eyes rounded in good-fellowship. "You got sapped out before you had a chance to see his groin. Somebody castrated him." The voice hinted of close cooperation. "Sounds like a homosexual killing, don't it? Is that what you were working on?"

# seven

**I** USUALLY NEED ALL the help I can get. Private investigators have no police powers of arrest, no stop-and-search privileges. My gun, unlike James Bond's, was licensed only to carry, not kill. Without official credibility I had to rely for information largely on my native cunning, namely deceit, deception, and seduction. When that didn't work I turned to favors.

"One hand washes the other," I wooed the politician.

"Money follows money," I baited the businessman.

"A bird in the hand is worth two in the bush," I promised the worker.

*"A bird in the hand is dead."*

So were cynics in my business.

"Favors," I had reminded a City Hall informant, "are a form of friendship. People helping people, a Christian concept."

I'd helped him on an indecent assault, a gardener planting bulbs. Then a bulb bloomed.

"Henry Stiles," I'd said to City Hall, "what he did, what he didn't do at the redevelopment agency. The mistakes, the whispers. Everything."

Local agencies all had pipelines into the Vatican, verbal conduits that stretched like silken strands across every facet of municipal business. There was always someone who knew something, always a trade to be made.

"So what's the five-day forecast for New York?" City Hall had asked.

"Two days. What about Jersey?"

"Looks good."

"How good?"

"Money is gold or platinum. Unless it's stone, like a house. The only thing better than owning one is owning ten; if you're in politics, you own twenty. Poor people are lazy and the work of the devil, who wants them in Newark. The Natural Law is survival of the richest, which Darwin discovered in Bergen County. Bayonne is ethnic. Hoboken's worse. The only way to survive in Jersey City is by a miracle or in a natural way. The natural way is by a miracle. So what's with this Stiles?"

After Bernie left I stared at the wall until I conjured up Charisma Kelly. Her eyes were frozen vapor, the mouth a slash of ice. On her forehead was the letter *A* the Puritans used to brand an adulteress. Which also meant atheist, someone without faith, unfaithful.

Served her right, I snarled, and wiped her off the wall. A devious woman, and deep. I'd have to watch her carefully. Hadn't she fooled me already?

The nurse fooled no one, her face a basket of cheer. "Three more hours," she announced.

"Why must I wait?"

"To give the medicine time to work."

She said it so disarmingly I had to laugh. Like doctors, most nurses saw patients as children to whom truth was irrelevant. Much as I saw clients. Why weren't the other murders mentioned? You had enough on your mind.

She fussed over the patient in the next bed until he shooed her away.

"She likes you." I smiled across at him.

"Mae likes everybody," he grimaced. "No discrimination."

"Love's better than hate," I clucked.

"Mae's problem is she can't distinguish between them, so she feels each with equal passion."

"Sounds like a dangerous woman."

"The most dangerous."

I thought again of Charisma, a little more kindly this

time. Her hate was obvious, and so was her passion. But where was the love? Did she ever have any? Was any left?

"You're getting out today." He regarded me wistfully, the ultimate lottery winner.

"Just a scalp wound," I said. "Didn't look behind me when I should have. What about you?"

The frown came back. "I'll be here a while," he droned. "Been here before and be here again."

Metallic footsteps hurried down the hall, lending an urgency to the moment. Hospitals were hotbeds of stress.

"What are you in for?" I asked.

"My blood." The frown deepened. "It's a life sentence."

"Could be worse," I said, trying to cheer him up.

"Don't see how," he allowed. "What's worse than a life sentence?"

"A death sentence."

His eyes closed. "It's that, too," he revealed and turned to the wall.

I stared at the huddled form a long time, fighting dark thoughts of cosmic jokes. Brooding over Charisma Kelly who came out of nothing and had nothing to go back to. How far would she fight to keep what she had? Despair often leads to violence.

Or the politician who talked about garbage the day I got out of law school. "You think garbage is empty tins and chicken bones and candy wrappers. That's all you know, that's the world you live in. But it ain't that at all, nothing like that. I'll tell you what garbage is in the real world, what it's always been. Garbage is people."

He was only half right. There was also honor in people, some people, and unbelievable courage that stuns the heart. Much of it was the quiet courage of people who had to cope. And that meant most of us.

That's what I was thinking when the buxom blonde, not Mae, breezed in.

"Got another visitor," she gushed. "Must be something about you I can't see."

"You'd have to feel it to believe it," I reported truthfully.

She giggled, a nice girlish sound. "That's what the last one said."

"And?"

"I was still able to talk."

"Before or after?" I asked smartly.

"During," she gasped on the way out.

Me and my big mouth. Hospitals were hotbeds of sex, too. The next moment Dancer Fitzgerald waltzed in the doorway. I'd have known him anywhere, the same flashy smile and tilt of the head. The same insouciance.

"Gotta be ten, fifteen years," he drawled as his boxer's feet skipped across the room. "Christ, you don't look no different."

"Both of us," I said as we shook hands.

"Some of the boys were talking about you the other day, saying how good you was doing." The eyes fed the smile. "A private cop. Hey, like all them TV shows."

"That's TV. This is J.C."

"It's home, right? Hey, everybody comes back to Jersey City." He pulled the chair over to the bedside. "It's good to see you, no kidding."

"Good to see you, Fitz."

"Hey, no kidding. A private cop. Wow! Where's your gun? Under the pillow?" He lunged for it and I rolled my right arm under his and formed a gun with my fingers.

"Bang!"

"Fast," he growled in appreciation. "Wow! Just like the movies."

Dancer had fast hands himself, and even faster feet that took him to the Golden Gloves. Trouble was he had no punch. Which didn't bother the local crowd when he turned pro—they liked to see him run around the ring at the old Jersey City Garden. The sportswriters quickly dubbed him Dancer and the name stuck, but everyone who knew him called him Fitz.

"Hey, here you are."

"You too."

"So how's it going?"

"No complaints. You?"

"I make my weight," Dancer shrugged. "They got no beef."

"You fought some of the best," I lied.

"Some good boys."

"Ever see any of 'em?"

"Here and there, you know how it is." A flicker of past glory creased the eyes. "Hey, but you. I hear you got sapped."

I patted the top of my skull. "One of those things."

"You wasn't looking. Happens to me." His head bobbed up and down, a puppet. "Hurt?"

"Like one of your punches."

That made him laugh and we sat there smiling, me propped up in bed and him on the chair.

"Hey."

"Yeah."

Dancer was a homeboy for the county political machine, meaning he had a soft job in one of the wards but his real work was whatever came up. It used to be padding payrolls and stuffing ballot boxes and banging heads. But times had changed.

"Too bad about Charlie Weems," Dancer said.

"Too bad."

"He worked for the machine. Did you know that?"

"Heard some stories," I admitted. "Nothing definite."

"When he left"—Dancer lowered his voice—"a lot of money left with him."

"Wasn't it one of his people?"

"Same thing." He waved away the distinction. "Hey, a lot of money."

I waited for the count.

"Two hundred grand."

"I heard a hundred."

"There. You see?"

They were still looking for it, I told myself. Which probably meant more than a hundred, or maybe even two.

"All that money." Dancer sucked in air for emphasis.

"You don't know that Weems—"

"We know."

His visit said I was somehow involved, at least now. Or else why would I go after Weems?

"Someone who found it would get a piece," Dancer said.

"The money—"

"Don't belong to Weems. Everybody knows that."

"Then who?"

"The county machine. Who else?"

A war chest was my guess, maybe even unreported. Some kind of secret campaign fund.

"You went for the money," Dancer said. "Who sent you?"

"It had nothing to do with politics."

"In this town?"

"It happens."

"Not here it don't."

"Even here," I insisted. "The man was a homosexual."

"A fruitcake. So what?"

"So sometimes they get stepped on."

He thought that over.

"Sometimes," I said quickly, "they even fight back."

"Gimme a name."

"They didn't leave a name. Just kept calling him where he worked."

"What they want?"

"For him to change a business deal they didn't like."

"What business deal?"

"He didn't tell me. But everyone in the office knows about the calls. I even have a tape of one."

Keep it up, I was thinking. Trying to stretch the truth without telling him anything.

Dancer followed my lead. "And he hired you to find out who it was."

"That's what I was working on."

"He didn't mention no money?"

"Nothing."

"Nothing about what they done with it?"

I shook my head.

Dancer frowned. "It's weak, pal. Real weak."

"No weaker than your story," I snapped, trying to get his mind off me. "You come in here waving stolen money but when I say how, all you can say is Weems."

"What else? It's gone, ain't it?"

"Why Weems?"

"It was his girlfriend took it."

"And took off."

Dancer tilted his head in a defensive crouch. "Not for nothing, but Weems was responsible. He shoulda took care of the money."

"That's all you got?" I said scornfully. "What about the guy who grabbed it?"

"He didn't get far."

I kept hearing Bernie say Weems was castrated. That made it a revenge killing no matter how you looked at it.

"They found him in Detroit a couple months later. He was broke, not a nickel."

"Broke?"

Dancer caught my surprise. "Didn't Weems tell you? Hey, maybe you wasn't lying after all."

"But he must've cleared Weems when they questioned him."

"Didn't clear nobody," Dancer snorted. "The sap hung himself his first night in jail."

So much for the revenge motive, but where the hell did the money come in? I reached for the pan and Dancer stood up and poked a finger in my gut. He was smiling again, friendly. Even conspiratorial.

"First the girlfriend and now the fruitcake," Dancer's voice jabbed at my ear. "That leaves only the money alive somewhere. Think about it."

# eight

**F**REE AT LAST!

"But it's only five o'clock," Mae squealed in exasperation. "The doctor said six."

My socks went on first, all wool. I was high on escape. Who could stop me?

"When he said six," I pointed out calmly, "he was using eastern standard time. But my bed faces west so I'm running on central time, and we all know six o'clock eastern is five central."

Get me wool or get me home, the Irish girls used to say behind the sheds. Nothing like a little virgin wool to make you feel like a man.

"That's the most—most outrageous rationalization I ever heard in my life," Mae sputtered.

The German girls just said hurry up.

"The pants are next," I warned her.

"You wouldn't dare."

I dropped my pajama bottoms as she raced for the door. Mae was a Catholic convert and they're the toughest.

"Like others of the police persuasion," she sniffed, "you are a moral degenerate."

"Send in the big blonde if you've seen it all," I shouted after her.

"All the time," her voice bounced back from the hall. "My three-year-old son's about the same size."

Nurses were like cops, I reminded myself. They'd seen everything too.

Defeated, I finished dressing and laced up the shoes. Next came the watch from the bedside table. In the drawer I fished for the gold locket with Karen's picture, the last link to a dead wife. It went in my pocket on the way out.

"Leaving so soon?" said the buxom blonde at the nurses' station.

"The story of my life between Thursday and Friday," I noted on the run.

"Next time make it between Sunday and Monday," she giggled. "It's my night in."

Ten minutes later I was on my way to the office.

"You're lucky," the cabdriver told me.

"How's that?"

"A quarter-million people in this town and they all want a cab tonight." He ran a red light. "Must be a full moon."

"It's the second biggest city in the state," I explained.

"What's first? New York?"

"Newark."

"Never been there."

I took another look at him, thinking he might be from Mars. Who's never been to Newark?

"I'm from Georgia," he said, reading my mind. He made it sound like France.

"Never been there."

"Like I say, you're lucky."

"Here long?"

"Enough to know my way around." He surprised me by braking for a light. "Which way now?"

He had a lot of hair under a corduroy cap, the kind boat owners wear when they want you to know they own a boat. The braid was gold in case you missed the rest of him.

I waited for the light to change so he wouldn't start up and kill us both. "Straight ahead six blocks, then turn left for three more, then left again. Got that?"

"I used to hunt back home," he said, offended. "I can follow anything. Just I don't like to lead."

"Don't win much that way."

"Don't lose much neither."

He began to sound like someone I knew, namely myself. People were always surprising me. "What you hunt?"

"Whatever ran."

I glanced over at his hack license and scribbled his name in my head. Life was funny.

"Life sure is funny," I said so he'd think I was a nut and leave me alone. I had things on my mind.

In the detective business you either work with others or you go it alone. I guess I was too selfish to share, or maybe just too dumb. All I had was a secretary, which was all I needed. She was a fifty-five-year-old grandmother named Selma Now, a quiet woman of delicate ways who always greeted me warmly at the office door.

"Why the *hell* don't you hire some help around here?"

Her obvious relief told me I was right to return.

"Just *look* at this place. You go traipsing off to the hospital and leave a poor old woman with all this."

I glanced around the reception room. The furniture still squatted and the files still stood. The floor was swept, the walls plastered. I supposed my office would be the same disaster.

"All what?"

"All everything, that's what." She pointed to her desk. "All these—*documents.*"

I examined the documents carefully. A dozen call slips, the usual bills and advertisements, my Rangers tickets, and another possible pornographic picture from Jill the Slasher.

"Think of it," I said, holding them up. "In just one day."

"The damn phone didn't stop ringing the whole time."

"Must've been a run on wrong numbers."

"People barging in and out."

"You get the names?"

"It's a wonder anything's still here."

"Long as you're still here," I stroked.

"Only by the grace of God herself." She was running out of steam. "A poor old woman like me."

Selma owned two apartment houses and was looking to buy her third husband. Any sympathy I gave her would've gone to him.

"You use retired cops for special jobs and law students for

research," Selma cataloged, "and who knows how many informants."

"Many."

"Not to mention friends from the big agencies and occasional suspicious loners like yourself."

"Likewise."

"So why the hell can't you get some full-time help?"

I held her hand. "Selma sweetheart, if I took anybody on they'd take you off. I don't wanna lose you, sugar."

"You could lose a few junior partners, too." But the voice was starting to purr.

I straightened up, headed for my office. "Junior partners always scheme to become senior partners. Then where'd I be?"

"Less stress for you." She followed me in.

"I like stress. Keeps me awake."

"I thought murder did that."

"Stress and murder. It's an old Rodgers and Hammerstein tune." I wheeled her out of the office, singing a few bars. "Stress and mur-der, stress and mur-der, Go together like a Coke and bur-ger."

"You're sick."

"Who knows what sickness lurks in the hearts of men?"

"That's evil."

"What's evil?"

" 'Who knows what evil lurks in the hearts of men?' It's from 'The Shadow.' "

"Never saw him," I said from my desk.

"Before your time."

"Which reminds me, what time's my date with the prosecutor's squad?"

"Ten."

"And Cooper Jarrett?"

"Eleven."

A full morning. "All right, get me Charisma Kelly. The number's—"

"Christians Anonymous, I know." She hesitated in the doorway. "I don't like that woman."

"Because she doesn't believe in God?" I was curious.

"Sounds like she doesn't believe in *anything*. You don't have to be a religious nut to know that's scary."

"What about Laura Jarrett?"

"Her I like."

"Why?"

"She's got spunk."

I made a face. "Spunk's the male ejaculation. You mean grit."

"I mean spunk. John Wayne had grit."

"John Wayne had true grit. There's a difference."

"What's the difference?"

"Women wouldn't understand," I said airily. "What else you like about her?"

"She likes you."

See what I mean about Selma? Brains, especially when she agreed with me. Also character and nobility. The woman had true grit, and I was proud to be working for her. But I couldn't afford to let her know that.

"I'm gonna enter you in the Miss America Grandmother's Derby," I told her, "right after you get me Charisma Kelly."

"Why don't you drop the case? We don't need it."

"I gave my word."

"Look who you gave it to."

"What matters is I *gave* it." She wasn't the only one around here with character and nobility. "I gave my word."

"What happens if we don't get her check?"

"Then we drop the case, of course."

At 6:30 I parked in front of St. Lucy's near the Holland Tunnel and turned down the sun visor. The card read Hudson County Sheriff's Office, Honorary Member. Sometimes it saved me from a ticket and sometimes the local cops gave out two. In certain sections of the city, the other visor worked better. It was blank.

I quick-marched up the few steps and into the church, Jersey neo-Gothic. Confessionals flanked two rows of pews that stretched to the altar. In them a dozen worshipers waited for redemption or reward, while one waited for me.

The FBI regards informants as often psychopathic, people who are usually in conflict with society, grossly selfish, irresponsible, impulsive, and unable to feel guilt or learn from experience and punishment. Whatever else Marko was, he was never wrong. The best tool in town.

I sat down next to him and clasped my hands in my lap. Hands were useless in church if you didn't pray, and I hadn't prayed in two years.

"This place gives me the creeps," Marko said.

St. Lucy's was the perfect rendezvous, so far out of the way a strong wind would've blown us into Hoboken.

"It's like any other place," I whispered. "You talk and I'll listen."

"The talk is he's chipping some broad in his office."

"What's her name?"

"A receptionist."

Virginia! I knew I couldn't afford her.

"They go out of town when they go."

"Why out of town?"

Marko threw me a look. "Maybe she's so ugly he don't wanna be seen with her."

I was sitting there thinking impure thoughts. Jarrett was divorced, so why all the secrecy?

"What about his ex-wife?"

"Nothing."

"What's that mean?"

"That means nothing." He wrapped his paws around his knees; we were both too wide for the pews. "The locals would love to ball her, but they say nobody's touched home plate."

"She lives in New York."

"You just asked about Jersey."

Which meant she played across the river.

"Her ex had a tail on her for a while, but just over here."

"And?"

"Nothing."

"When was this?"

"Few months back."

"They were divorced a year ago."

"Life is shit. What can I tell you?"

"Who did the tail?"

"Benziger."

It didn't add up. Both kept their sex out of the city. What were they afraid of?

"That Weems guy?" Marko said.

"I already know about his lover. Killed himself in Detroit."

"Yeah, but he wasn't the only one."

"Only what?"

Marko shifted his weight, a beached whale. "They were into this S/M bondage thing, four or five of them. It's usually a master-slave relationship. The guy that croaked was Weems's slave."

"And the others?"

"Nobody knows nothing about them, just that there were at least two more. They used to meet at Weems's house for fun and games."

"How'd you learn all this?"

He blew into a red bandanna and it sounded like Joshua at Jericho. "Some guys like to watch fires," he said when the church settled down, "so they become a torch. I like to look at bodies so I'm a tool. That's what I do."

*Tool* was Jersey talk for the skin trade, someone who handled strictly sex. Especially the S/M kind. Marko probably knew more about Jersey City sex than anyone since Nellie Hart of the Boss Hague days.

"Think you could locate these guys?" I asked him.

"Not a chance. This kind of person, when they go they're gone."

He blew his nose again and a statue of Saint Joseph jumped back two feet. I was getting out before he parted the Red Sea.

"Only thing I can tell you is they like to keep pictures. Did you check Weems's house?"

# nine

NEW YORK WAS A woman waiting for a new love. She knew better than to cry over anything that wouldn't cry over her.

It took me twenty minutes to make the tunnel and two minutes to get across. I told the toll taker I wouldn't want his job for anything.

"Why's that?"

"Friday night traffic," I said over the music. "Must drive you nuts."

Didn't bother him at all. He looked fourteen and had a portable to prove it. When he grew up, he'd probably be a rock star. That's all they wanted to be now. Rock stars made millions and lived in mansions with drugs and drops. Drops were girls; you took 'em then dropped 'em. They all were under eighteen. There was no such thing as responsibility.

"Good luck," I shouted as the car inched forward. He was going to need it when *Fantasy Island* turned into the *Twilight Zone*.

Another ten minutes got me to a parking lot on the West Side piers. From there it was a fifteen-minute walk that took me thirty-five.

"I was just looking for a quick vacation," a voice in the mob moaned, "and she was the last resort."

The streets were alive with the sound of music, or something. People, too, dressed in every known style and shade—and many of them unknown. A weekend crowd in Greenwich Village, banal and tawdry, and stuffed with tourists from America wondering where the hell was all the glamour.

Someone should've told them all the glamour was gone a long time ago.

On Christopher Street two men glided by deep in conversation. ". . . tried to pick up a woman but couldn't, thank God."

I stood on the corner thinking maybe I was too old for this corner when she screamed, a piercing scream that caught nobody's attention.

"Did you scream?" I thought maybe it was me.

"At least ten times a day." She smiled. "Practice for when I meet my mugger."

"But no one noticed."

"But I wasn't mugged," she said, and stepped smartly off the curb as the light changed.

I love New York.

"So why do you live here?" I asked Laura Jarrett when I finally arrived at her six-room duplex.

"It's convenient," she confessed.

"To what?"

"The office, for one."

"And the other?"

She waved her hand. "The bright lights and excitement uptown."

I didn't tell her about Marko or the investigator Jarrett had put on her. It was none of my business.

"You like the bright lights?"

"Depends who's turning them on," she said with a throaty laugh. "What about you?"

"About the same," I lied.

"You said you were still hurting."

"Could be worse." I was thinking that living here also kept her out of Jarrett's grasp.

"Detectives are hard men," she sighed.

"Sometimes."

"Hope so."

So here we were, raping each other with our eyes. I watched her sip the wine, her sleek throat its silver chalice.

We sat in the living room beneath her moody portrait hanging over the mantelpiece. She was Tierney and I was Bogart the detective. Wait a minute—was it Bogart? No, it was Dana Andrews. No matter. It was always Bogart for me, Bogie and Laura. I reached into my pocket and fingered the locket with Karen's picture.

"When I left Greenwich I came to New York," Laura was saying softly, "to become a model."

My romantic reverie went up in words.

"That's when Cooper found me."

She was a statue in the still of the night, an earth angel. Or maybe it was just the city's glow through the skylight. Or even moonglow. Her eyes were ovals of intent, the lips a perfect pout. Smoke curled round her fingertips.

"You did some modeling," I prompted.

"Not enough," she snapped.

"It's a tough business."

"When we married I quit." She couldn't have been much in demand, I thought. At age twenty-one she would be too old for the fashionable kiddy porn and too chesty for the rest. But why resent it?

"Ever think of going back?"

"Too late." Her eyes flashed, just a flicker before the fires banked. "Besides, I'm a businesswoman now. Own half a company."

"Satisfied?" I asked.

"It pays well."

"Fulfilling?"

"Money denial is worse."

"What's better?"

"More money."

"Helps to know what you have to do for it."

"Not really." She smiled. "Cooper does it all."

"But now he's worried, you say."

"I said he's scared. So am I."

My eyes ran over the room, huge and expensively furnished, and there were five more like it. In the closets were couturier clothes, in the garage a Mercedes. She'd been bred on money, formed by it. Losing it would be like the kiss of death.

"Charles Weems was castrated," I said suddenly.

She hadn't heard. How horrible! Did it have anything to do with the calls?

"Could be a homosexual killing," I told her. "The castration points to that." I only wanted to ease her fear. Even a homosexual killing had to be tied somehow to the calls. The alternative was just too coincidental.

"The caller knew about Weems," Laura said, "about his being dead, I mean."

"It was on the morning news."

"He said now we'd better do what they wanted."

"But he didn't actually say they killed Weems."

I'd sent Bernie to Jarrett's office to pick up the tape, which was merely a repeat of their demand to get out of the Harbor Terminal deal. Could've been a group of preservationists or striped-bass lovers. Weems was mentioned, but only in passing and that bothered me. What good was killing someone to get others to act if you didn't claim the kill?

My idea of a homosexual murder seemed to depress Laura Jarrett, which surprised me. Maybe she saw through it. Women sometimes fool you, most of the time.

"Have you had dinner yet?"

"Not since last night."

"There's nothing here," she declared. "We may as well go out."

Out was the Fifth Avenue Hotel around the corner. At least it used to be a hotel, then a rental building, and now a co-op. I knew a drummer who lived there before he disappeared. Rumor had him bricked up in a wall when they renovated the apartments. Not murder, just literary license. He loved Edgar Allan Poe.

Laura had the sole amandine while I doted on chocolate ice cream because I wanted vanilla. It was a thing with me, a kind of self-discipline raising. Do without the little things you want so you build up resistance to the big things you won't get anyway.

"How's the chocolate?" asked the waiter.

"Got any strawberry?"

Outside again, we walked into Washington Square Park, surrounded on twelve sides by New York University.

"The Big Apple," Laura sighed under the arch.

"Excedrin City," I grumbled.

In the square people collided with reckless abandon, college kids pretending alienation and perverts mounting respectability. Mohawk cuts confronted Spandex curls. Glitz lashes and painted ears competed with lips that glowed in the dark. The Lana Satana look was everywhere.

Laura squeezed my arm. "They're just thinking Woody Allen."

"But they're talking Todd Browning."

Past the park the zoo upscaled to occasional gorillas beaten off with baboons. A few blocks down we found a bar on the corner of Walk and Don't Walk that served white wine without black nosegays. I almost felt deprived.

"You don't like New York," Laura observed after we'd settled in.

"Could be New York doesn't like me. It seems to suffer from reverse paranoia."

"Which is?"

"The constant belief that it's persecuting someone. When I'm around, that someone's usually me."

Her laugh was a musical ride. "And Jersey City?"

"Even worse. It doesn't believe it's good enough to be persecuted by anyone."

"Then why stay there?"

"A matter of balance," I suggested. "New York has nine hundred private investigators, most of them tied into security. It's big business here, with all the edges rounded off." I played with my glass, a perfect example. Rounded and empty. "For me it's still an art, full of mystery and surprise. I like to take chances."

"Surely there are more homicides here."

"Two thousand last year, but most were from petty crimes or drugs and the cops do better on those. They've got the manpower to beat down doors. With me it's the hunt for hidden motives, the *passion* of the crime, and the lies and evasions and distortions. Raw emotions. Murder's full of emotion."

"Why murder?"

"It's the ultimate crime with the ultimate risk. And it's clear-cut. Only winners and losers. Either I get them or they get away."

"Do many get away?" she asked.

"Too many."

Her eyes were diamonds fired by a million years of tension, her mouth a cut in the cleft of the earth. I'd seen that look before. Murder turned her on, the thought of murder or the talk of murder. Hopefully even the investigator of murder. But I'd seen that look before and it always came from a hungry animal, and the hungry animal was always a woman whose weapon was sex. I began to feed my own fantasies.

"You must like Bogart," Laura laughed.

"Bogart who?"

# ten

WE SKIRTED THE PARK on the way back, losing ourselves in the faceless college monoliths on the Square.

"Henry James lived around here," Laura reported.

"Obviously after anonymity," I announced. "That's why he called himself Henry James."

"What was his real name?"

"Jesse."

At its eastern edge the park boasted benches set in oblongs of brown and green reminiscent of conversation pits in suburban living rooms. Walks wound northward to the playground and on April afternoons the walks and pits were filled with human flotsam, a cacophony of color and emotion. Now there was only the darkness of night, and everything was shrill and desperate.

"I found a rabbit once when I was small." Laura pulled the folds of the chamois tighter around her waist. "It was sick and I wanted to keep it," she said. "But my father killed the rabbit."

We crossed Waverly Place to University.

"Later he brought the rabbit to my room and said now I could keep it. He made me so happy. I didn't know the rabbit was dead, you see. I scooped it up in my arms to kiss, my first love, and it was cold against my lips." Her head nodded in memory. "I screamed for a whole day and then I didn't talk for a month."

A siren sounded in the distance.

"When I did, I told my father I hated him."

We walked past the Mews, a narrow cobblestoned street of nineteenth-century gingerbread houses. I couldn't help thinking life was simpler then. There were no phones to make threatening calls, no cars to speed suspects away or information networks to learn anything about anybody. Charisma Kelly, for example. She'd never even been adopted by the dead woman she called mother.

Laura turned to me at the corner. "I don't know why I thought of that after all these years." She smiled, embarrassed. "Just forget it. Doesn't mean anything."

Up ahead was a flurry of movement, a mob pressing against someone leaving a hall. Trying to leave. I caught sight of her, a woman of independent schemes.

Speak of the devil!

"Damn!" I shouted, and swiveled to Laura. "Gotta go." I grabbed for her hand.

"What—"

"Trouble." We were a block from her house. "You go on." I hauled her around the corner, prodded her gently. "Won't take long."

"Shouldn't I wait?"

"I'll be there soon," I said on the run.

The next moment I spotted Charisma Kelly in the eye of the storm, a dozen angry bodies swirling around her. I put on my tightest smile and entered the ring. Its strongest link, at least the loudest, was a ton of fat with greasy hair and bad skin. When I got closer I saw the fat was mostly muscle and the grease sweat. The bad skin turned into a red face, full of anger and adrenaline. He could've passed for a Jersey torpedo but probably lived in Queens. Someone who mowed his yard and watched his TV, and what he saw was nothing but killers getting away with murder and devils doing away with God. America was falling down a rathole.

Charisma Kelly was explaining the law to him. "Get out of my way."

"Get out of town, you fucking Communist cunt."

Charisma shook her head impatiently. "I'll call a cop."

"You better call an ambulance."

"I'm a tow truck. Will that do?"

Her eyes melted into mine.

"I make things move."

Red Face looked me over while I sized up the rest of the ring. The women had pinched faces and bare heads—why is it activists never wear hats? They all wore makeup. The men were younger, more Manhattan, the glint of madness already in their eye. Probably down from some Westchester tax haven. Fanatics were never a problem in the short run; they had to wait for orders.

"Isn't it time you were getting back?" I said to Charisma.

"I thought I was," she replied coolly.

"Maybe I can help."

"That wouldn't be a good idea, pal." It was Red Face, his snarl worse than his spring. Like most people.

"You don't talk." I faced him down the barrels of both eyes. "If you had it, you'd have done it."

I could see he knew what I meant. Whatever he did now, he'd already lost.

"Come on," I said to Charisma, and turned my official smile on the crowd. They spread like Indian gas, all but Red Face who stood scowling, and a woman with hysteria working the corners of her mouth.

"She's *evil,*" the woman suddenly hissed. "Satan's whore."

"Oh yeah," I mumbled to myself. Here it comes, the real thing.

"She preaches *godless* fornication," the woman wailed, "and people *owning* their bodies and *owning* their minds, as if God didn't *give* them these things."

Her mouth gulped air and I pulled Charisma Kelly closer to me.

"She preaches *Satan's* word, and Satan's word is *death* for those who listen."

I inched us forward. "Your car," I whispered.

"At the corner." She pointed.

*"Hellfire* forever."

"Anyone with you?"

"The woman who invited me to speak. Over there."

A face at the edge of the crowd, of no interest to them. "She'll be all right."

"Judgment Day . . . is *coming.*"

I pulled her along. "What about Kassam?"

"Not here."

"It . . . *draweth nigh.*"

When I moved again so did Red Face and we landed in front of him.

"Around you or over you. Make up your mind."

He backed up.

"It is . . . *at hand.*"

We were almost to the curb. Another few feet and I'd hurry her over to the car and out of here. The things I did for clients! And I didn't even *like* her.

"I don't appreciate being hurried," Charisma Kelly complained at my shoulder.

And I sure didn't trust her.

"Fornicator!" someone shouted from the crowd, getting its wind back.

"Harlot!"

"Vampire!"

(New York is a show town, what can I tell you?)

I quickly pushed her ahead of me.

"And on that day when the *serpent* shedeth her skin, then shall ye know her by the *beast* at her *breast.*"

That was too much for Red Face, who probably saw us as King Kong and Fay Wray. I felt his paw on my arm, ready to swing me around, and I swung the opposite way and drove a hard left into his groin. A low blow there will stop a truck. As the air whooshed out, he dropped to his knees and I chopped an overhand right behind his ear. He was down before he hit the sidewalk.

Some guys never learn.

Even the hysteric hushed long enough for us to make the car. I shoved Charisma across the seat and grabbed the keys and fed the gas. "Nice friends you got," I snarled as we sped away.

"How did you find me?"

"I wasn't looking." We turned west on Ninth Street. "Just passing by."

"A coincidence."

"An accident. I won't let it happen again."

A red light held us on Fifth and I caught her eye. "I thought you didn't do New York."

"I don't."

"Just an angel of mercy this time."

"I was specifically requested by a group starting here." She smoothed her jacket. "And I don't like your sophomoric gibes at my faith."

"You have no faith."

"I have the faith that I'm right."

"That's called self-delusion."

"Your own is called faith," she snapped. "Everyone else's is self-delusion."

I pulled up near Laura Jarrett's house. "You can make it home now."

"Another client rescue?"

"Just relief."

"You must be very popular."

"Your average hardworking snoop," I told her.

"Maybe not so average." She slid behind the wheel as I got out. "You seem to get around."

"More than you know." I leaned into the window. "We have to talk. Not now. Sunday all right for you?"

"Isn't Sunday your day of rest?"

"Only those that have passed."

"Three o'clock at the ashram, then."

"In front of it. I'll pick you up."

She frowned. "Afraid of being influenced?"

"Contaminated would be more accurate." I started to turn.

"Malone?" Her face softened. "Thanks for your help."

"It isn't over yet."

"Could it be," she said as she slipped away, "that you have doubts about your own faith?"

I swore at her taillights. A shot in the dark can leave you just as dead.

To make matters worse, Laura was waiting in the lobby. Seated on a red satin settee. Across the narrow hallway a gold-framed mirror reflected her image and I began seeing Clifton Webb point the double-barreled shotgun. Me and my diseased imagination.

"I thought I'd wait here for you." She smiled at me.

It was just as well she did. Upstairs was a shambles. At her shriek I pushed her out of the way, keys and all, and kicked the door open. My hand went automatically for my gun and came up empty. I was a Jersey P.I. with no permit in New York.

"Downstairs," I barked. "Call the cops from the lobby. Go."

I waited till the elevator came for her—no use taking chances. Then I searched the apartment. They were gone, of course. I had to stay.

"How'd you know they were gone?" the cops wanted to hear.

"Nobody waited for us at the door."

I'd shown them my license, filled in as few details as possible. We went out for dinner and a walk, came back to this.

"She a client?"

"Her ex-husband, a developer in Jersey City."

"What's it about?"

"Just some threatening calls."

"To her?"

"She's partners with him."

"And you with her?"

"Strictly business," I lied.

"Sure, sure. Nothing to us." But he wrote it down anyway. "Think this was your caller?"

"Looks like it."

"Why the wreck? They after something?"

"Nothing that could be hidden."

"What then?"

I shrugged. "It's vague, exactly what they want."

"I'll bet." He put his pad away, went over to Laura. "We'll file a report, but it would help if you come up with a list of anything missing." He glanced at me. "Unless nothing's missing."

"How'd they get in?" his partner asked.

"I must have left the door open," Laura said. "I do that sometimes, just forget to lock it."

The cop looked blank. "You just forget."

The other went over to check the lock. "It's a dead bolt, all right."

"Anything else for now?" I rubbed my hands together in false enthusiasm.

"Guess not," said the younger cop.

"Funny thing," the older said on the way out. "Enough stuff tossed around for three gorillas, but the pattern is the same in every room. Like one guy did it all. What do you think?"

"Could be," I said.

"Let us know if you think of anything else," he fired from the hall as I closed the door.

I felt sorry for them. Half their job was playing games with rich people who trash their possessions when they tire of them so they can buy new possessions with the insurance money. Being a P.I. put me on the other side. They probably thought I did the trashing.

"I'm exhausted," Laura said when they'd gone. She slumped into a chair. "Who would do such a thing?"

"Who else has a key to the front door?"

"No one."

"Jarrett?"

"No."

"Any friends?"

"Nobody."

"There's always an extra key somewhere," I growled. "In a place like this—"

"Oh, the super, of course. But surely—"

"You know him?"

"Since I bought the apartment a year ago. But they told me he's been here forever. You don't think . . ."

"Probably not," I said after a moment. "My guess is nothing's gone or you would've noticed by now."

"Then why—"

"A warning, I suppose. Meant to frighten you, keep up the pressure. Who knows you live here?"

"The office, certainly. And friends in Jersey."

"Many?"

"I'm afraid so. And even more business people who have my number here."

"Which means they could easily get the address. Not much help there."

"I think I need a good night's rest," she said, rubbing her temples. "At least they left the bed intact."

"Sure," I said, "that's what you need."

She looked at me, her eyes watery. "Would you mind?"

"That's all right," I assured her, "you get some rest and you'll feel fine in the morning."

"Is there any chance they might come back?"

I shook my head. "They got what they were after."

She walked me to the door. "You were super, you know. I can't imagine what I'd have done if I found it like this on my own."

"All part of the service," I grinned. "You call, we come."

"I'll remember that," she said in a husky voice.

"Be sure to lock your door now," I reminded her.

She smiled, a nice smile full of promise. "I'll talk to you next week," she purred.

"You can count on it."

When the door closed I waited till I heard the snap of the dead bolt. It was the same sound I'd heard when we went out to dinner. Laura Jarrett had locked her front door.

On the way back to Jersey City, I kept thinking of her ex. Did he have a key after all? Or was Laura herself somehow involved? She'd waited downstairs for me. Why? And where did the receptionist fit in?

By the time I got home I'd decided that Laura Jarrett was behind everything. It was pure sour grapes. In all my steamy sex fantasies, I forgot that I couldn't afford her either.

Men are such shits sometimes.

# eleven

THE COUNTY SEAT IS on Newark Avenue near the old Hudson County Courthouse and holds the administration offices and criminal courts. It's a functional building designed for efficiency, unlike the old courthouse with its elegant murals and gold leaf. But all that was in a world where $3 million bought beauty instead of banality, in a time when they still watched Ziegfeld and heard Ravel.

I turned left at the elevator to the prosecutor's office. A county prosecutor commanded great power and respect, and though Hudson was the smallest of the state's twenty-one counties, it led in population density and criminal prosecution. Ninety percent of its people lived in urban areas, and it was the prosecutor's job to weed out the bad from the good. The local criminal-justice system flowed through his funnel.

I checked my watch. It was Saturday and I was on time.

"You're late," said the secretary. "They're downstairs."

I smiled and popped my head out the door. At least it was still Saturday.

They were in one of the sweat rooms, a holding pen for the courts. When I walked in, Harwood looked up and scowled. Gershon scowled without looking up. They were the pride of the prosecutor's homicide squad.

"You're early," the lieutenant said.

"Isn't this Friday?"

"Tuesday," Gershon grunted. He wasn't a lieutenant. "It must be Jersey City."

"Gentiles are like that," I mugged. "We never know what day it is."

"Except payday."

Gershon always kidded me about money, which meant we were friends. He thought I was greedy and I thought he was nuts.

"Who should know more about money?" I asked. "Look at Rothschild."

"Look at Hitler."

"You still get three hundred a day?" Harwood said.

"I'm thinking of making it four."

"See what I mean." Gershon shook his head sadly. "Christian greed."

"I hear you're in for a raise too."

"Yeah," said Harwood. "Four hundred a year." He made it sound like a cut in salary.

"If we get it."

"You'll get it," I told Gershon, "because God takes care of his own."

"Must be Religious Tolerance Day," he grumbled.

"Ain't that payday?"

Harwood lit a cigarette across the table. "Let's get to Gay Day."

Lieutenant Harwood was a pain in the ass, mostly because he didn't like me. There are some people who just rub you the wrong way. Harwood was like that with me. Except I did all the rubbing.

"We're very interested in Weems," said the voice at my side.

"If that's all right with you," the lieutenant rasped.

"What about the city?"

He looked at Gershon. "What's he mean?"

"Bernie's people."

"They're interested too."

"Great," I smiled. "That makes us all one big family."

"One big happy family."

"Not happy. I didn't say happy."

"What'sa matter?" Harwood was annoyed. "You don't want company?"

"Not if it gets in my way," I said.

"I can get you out of the way."

"And not if I have to report every hour."

"Who said?"

"You're making this case special, aren't you?"

"Not special. Just another homicide that—"

"Shut up, Harry." The lieutenant pushed back his chair, stood and stretched his legs like a sumo wrestler. "It's this way, Malone. We got a body we don't know what to do with. Weems worked for the county and knew a lot of important people. Other kinds, too. It could be just a sex kill, but we don't think so." He swiped his chin with a beefy hand. "There's a lot of angles here that could blow up in someone's face."

"Someone big?"

Harwood looked at his partner again. "What's he mean?"

"Just blowing air." Gershon turned to me. "He helped send the mayor to prison fifteen years ago, for chrissake. Who's left for him to cover? The governor?"

I had to admit Harwood was a good cop who worked under a load of pressure. If a cover came, it'd be from above and he'd probably try to fight it. On the other hand, how good could anyone be who didn't like me? A fatal flaw there somewhere.

"Right now the angles go everywhere," Harwood was saying, "so we got no real direction. If we end up with just a piece of the pie, somebody always gets hurt."

"Like maybe us."

"We have to nail down everything we got on the guy," Harwood said.

I agreed, meaning I needed to know what they knew. "What makes you think it wasn't a sex killing?"

"We had the Sex Crime Unit analyze it," Gershon said. "The guy's nuts were cut clean."

"While he was still alive?"

Gershon nodded. "Plus there's no evidence on the body of any sexual activity. No bruises or semen in the cavities."

"What about on his clothes?"

"Nothing."

"Too bad. Murder and sex often go hand in hand."

"Here too," the lieutenant said, "but not in the usual sense. We think it was a setup."

"For what?"

"We're hoping you could tell us. For instance, why'd you go to the house?"

"Weems invited me, said he had something to say."

"About what?"

"He never said."

"The phone calls?"

"I asked him that in the office. He wasn't sure."

"What's your guess?"

I shrugged. "Don't have any. But I agree it was a setup. These were no amateurs. Bernie told me they wrapped a telephone cord around the front doorknob so nobody'd enter."

"Which means they took their time."

"Any evidence of a search?" I asked.

Gershon made a noise. "Too good for that."

"Looking for what?" Harwood wanted to know.

"Letters," I suggested. "Maybe pictures. Weems was homosexual. Some of them like to look at photos."

"Not this time." He sat down again, lit another cigarette. "Okay, you're there to trace anonymous calls to Jarrett's office and Weems wants to tell you something but he's knocked off. Who knew you were going to meet him?"

I was ready for that one. "We met in Laura Jarrett's office, but she was on the phone when we talked." My hands spread apart. "I don't know. Maybe Jarrett himself. And anyone Weems might've told that afternoon. Could be dozens."

"Or nobody. How's Jarrett's ex fit in?"

"She got most of the calls. They threatened her too."

"Any proof?"

"You have a copy of the last one."

"Before that."

I hesitated. "Why would she lie?"

"You tell me."

"I'm telling you she's scared of the calls."

"You know women so well."

"I know it's hard to fake fear. Hers is real."

"You're sure."

"Damn sure."

I caught Gershon's glare and counted to ten behind my eyes.

"Why so protective?" Harwood asked quietly.

"Me? Protective?" I went into my shuck act. "Shucks, I thought this was the sewing scene from *Gone with the Wind*. Land*sakes,* I didn't know you gen'men all gon' crazy in the head from all dem long hours you works and all dat stress and strain and tote dat barge—"

"He's making me puke," Harwood groaned to his partner.

"—lift dat bale—"

"Shut up, Malone."

The lieutenant buried his face in his hands, rubbed his eyes. "There's a wise guy born every minute," he mumbled.

"Fourteen hundred every day," I said, "and forty-three thousand a month. You have to like the little rabbits."

He rubbed harder. If he asked Gershon one more time what I meant, I was gonna start rubbing my own until they both disappeared.

"The last wise guy I liked," Harwood recalled, "was a rapist I shot in the groin. Hurt more that way before he died."

"Maybe it was you shot Weems." I shifted to Gershon. "What about the slugs? Anything yet?"

"Monday."

"You'll let me know."

"Sure thing. We're all in this together."

"You mean I get to keep my license?"

"Of course."

"And my shiny automatic with the nineteen bullets?"

"Even your three hundred a day." Gershon smiled.

"Then we're partners."

"Absolutely."

"In that case," I snapped, "suppose you clowns tell me about the tape Weems made of his calls at home."

"How'd you know about that?" Harwood yelped.

"We're partners, right? Buddies?" I gave him my evil leer. "Why should I want you to feel guilt for holding out on me?"

I held the leer along with my breath. The rich get ice in the summer and the poor get it in the winter, so some people figure everyone gets an even break. But the only break is the one you make yourself. I made a lot of friends, only they were called informants and friendship had nothing to do with it.

The lieutenant speared Gershon with a look of disgust. "Tell him."

"Weems made a call the night he was killed," Gershon began.

"How you know it was that night?"

"The call was to Cooper Jarrett and Weems said he'd spoken to you that morning. He told Jarrett he had to see him, that they had to talk. Jarrett said when he got back from Georgia."

"You know anything about that?" Harwood pressed.

"Something to do with the Georgia Tourist Commission signing up for the Harbor Terminal." Back to Gershon. "What else?"

"Nothing else, like they didn't want to say more over the phone."

"Got any ideas, bright boy?"

I didn't. Except it had to be tied to the anonymous calls. Weems probably got the recorder at home when the office calls started coming in.

"No other tapes?" I asked them. "The calls began about a week earlier."

Harwood shook his head. "That's it."

"You searched the house."

"We know our job."

Which meant Weems erased the tape every day.

"No papers, no pictures, no tapes." I rubbed my hands on my pants, a nervous tic or maybe just oily skin. "You talk to Jarrett?"

"He was out of town yesterday."

Harwood coughed, the cigarettes his tic. "He's your client. We thought you'd want to ask him."

"He's a big shot, so why annoy him with an official investigation?"

"You must read a lot to get so smart."

"Only magazines."

"No books?" Gershon was surprised.

"No time. Magazines tell it all. Four minutes for an idea. Four sentences to a paragraph, four letters to a word. Don't you know all the important words have four letters? Love. Hate. Food. Wine. Home. Sex."

"Sex has only three letters."

"Any fool knows it should have four."

"Shit!"

"That too."

"How about fuck?" Harwood croaked. "Like in fuck off?"

I was pulling out a snappy one-liner but Gershon beat me to it.

"There's something else."

The Widow again. Last time I heard it was from Cooper Jarrett and I landed in the hospital sure as shit. Fuck, I told myself. And Piss, Damn, Hell, and Sexx.

"Like I say, Weems made only the one call, but he also received a call that night. After he talked to Jarrett."

"Who was it?"

"You ever hear of someone named Henry Stiles?"

# twelve

I MADE A FEW fast calls on the way out, my head in a spin. How was it possible? I kept asking myself. How could Henry Stiles know Charles Weems? They both worked the political fence, sure, but did they have to know each other that well? Did Stiles have to call Weems? Meaning, Why'd they do this to me?

My City Hall informant wasn't home. Not home? I gripped the mouthpiece. Where the hell was he? The voice asked if I was a friend? So far, I answered desperately. Was it something important? Only the fate of Western civilization. In that case, she said calmly, he was at his summer home in Sea Bright. In April? April to October, came the seasoned reply. I didn't ask if he wintered in Maine.

Getting the Jersey shore took tact, humor, and patience, so I got the operator instead.

"You can dial that number direct, sir."

"I can't. All my fingers fell off."

"How did you dial the operator?"

"I used my nose."

The ringing rattled me. So all right, Stiles knew Weems well enough to call him at home. Even enough to suggest they meet for drinks. They'd done it before, the voices were social. But there was also tension in them. Friends with a mutual problem?

"Sorry, no answer."

*Click.*

Operators were too sensitive.

I decided to try again. It was either that or go out and kick a cat.

"May I help you?"

"I can't dial because my nose is sore."

"Then stick a finger in it, buster."

*Bang!*

They were also too busy—probably got a lot of perverts on the weekend.

I talked to the phone for a minute to rebuild my ego. Charisma Kelly hired me to find whoever killed her mother who was married to Henry Stiles who knew Charles Weems who worked with Cooper Jarrett who hired me to find whoever made the killing calls. Coincidence? Why not? Any two cases could come together over someone who knew someone else. After all, Jersey City had only a quarter-million people. It was something I could understand and believe in. That and the Easter Bunny.

"You finished, Jack?"

"When I fall down I'm finished."

"Just don't fall on the phone."

Jokers everywhere. That was the trouble with the world. All of a sudden everybody wore a uniform. You couldn't tell the good guys from the bad anymore.

I tried Sea Bright again, let my fingers do the talking this time. At least I didn't crack in front of Harwood and Gershon. Did I know anyone named Henry Stiles? Sounded familiar but I'd have to check the files.

"Couldn't be the husband of the woman who committed suicide," Harwood had wanted to know.

"Maybe that's where I heard it."

"Like maybe from her daughter who hired you to prove she was murdered?"

Which only proved the police used informants too, which wasn't fair.

No answer from City Hall by-the-sea so I dialed the office. Selma worked Saturdays till noon, then switched over to the answering service. She didn't like the Saturday work, especially the phone.

"How come a poor old woman has to do *everything* around here?"

"How'd you know it was me?"

"I know your ring."

"Do you know Cooper Jarrett's?"

"Only by sight."

"I'm running late. If you hear his sight, tell him I'm on my way."

"Way where?"

"Can't say."

I rang off before she could call me paranoid. Which wasn't true at all. Just that I didn't want anyone to get a shot at me.

I glanced around and the uniform was gone, good thing for him. The nerve of some people, standing behind me like that.

My last call went to Marilyn, just to hear her voice. It was the Everly Brothers singing "Cathy's Clown."

"Me."

"Me too."

"You?"

"And you."

"Is this an obscene call?" she trilled.

"Hope so."

"I should tell you I'm all tied up."

I twirled my voice. "I like 'em all tied up."

She laughed in anticipation. "Six?"

"Sex? I can't wait."

"Don't forget to bring Hal."

A private joke. Hers was named Madge.

"See ya."

I walked out of the county seat thinking of Laura Jarrett, who filled my mind the way Marilyn filled my bed.

The cop was writing out the ticket when I got there. His uniform smiled.

"I already put money in the meter," I told him.

"What day was that?"

"Only been on the phone an hour." Rubbing it in.

"These meters only run an hour."

"Must've been fifty-nine minutes."

He wasn't impressed.

"Why aren't you out catching criminals?" I huffed. "That's what we pay you for."

"Caught one this morning."

"What you do, give him a ticket?"

He grinned until I saw his paper hand. "Guess."

"May you live forever," I prayed, but he took it nicely.

"And may you prosper until Allah—blessings upon him —catches up with you."

There we were, the only two in town who saw *Lawrence* more than once. What else could I do? I stepped in my camel and said, "Mush." Another four-letter word!

As I pulled away I saw him go back into the building, probably to call Kassam. He looked like an atheist for sure, one of those Arab religions.

Heading down Newark Avenue I was so mad at cops I began seeing the elevated subway in *The French Connection*, and soon I was Popeye Doyle in a commandeered car chasing the underworld killer. Except this was real life with rules, not some cheap fantasy, and only the killers were real. If I drove the way the cop did in the movie, I wouldn't make a mile before I'd be shot dead. Not to mention the fact that he never could've identified the suspect from the glimpse he got of the sniper on the roof. Or the fact that he didn't first help the wounded bystanders. Or that he couldn't know the suspect had shot two people on the subway and caused a wreck in which he'd lost his gun. But the cop killed the unarmed suspect anyway, in the back, and probably got a medal.

In real life he would've got fifty years on Devil's Island and a death threat from a retired police commissioner. Plus his pension would've been used to help pay off all the lawsuits.

Cop pictures were a pain in the ass and so were cops in my business. But we rarely did our own lab work or even legwork, so a strong link was important. In murder it was a must.

May you burn in heaven, I hollered out the window. At a red light I ripped the ticket into shreds and cast them to the wind.

By the time I got downtown, it was 11:15. I skirted Exchange Place and steered straight for Dudley Street and the Morris Canal Basin. Too late! Cooper Jarrett stood waiting in front of his Cadillac.

"It's after eleven," he snarled as I got out.

"I was just telling myself the same thing. How was Georgia?"

"Screw Georgia. How's my ex?"

"How's your receptionist?"

"How'd you know about her?"

"How'd you know about last night?"

That shut him up. Only one of us came here to ask questions and it wasn't him.

"So where the hell were you?"

"With the prosecutor's men," I answered. "Where were you?"

"What's that mean?"

"I called you at nine this morning. No answer."

Jarrett shrugged. "Must've been in the can."

"I called the can. You weren't there either."

"So I was out."

"Out of town?"

"What's the difference?"

"Virginia," I said softly. "That's the difference."

He walked over to the water without a word and I followed with a lot of them. "In Newark it could be any of the motels on the airport approach. Or maybe the strip in East Orange—that's always good for a quick one. Then there's parts of Bergen County—"

"What're you getting at, Malone?"

"You always take her out of town. Why?"

"What's that got to do with Weems?"

"I don't know until I find out. What's she got to do with you?"

He stared at the water. "Just something on the side."

"The side of what?"

"Of me," he growled. "She takes care of me."

"Why keep it secret?"

"I'm a private guy. What can I tell you?"

"The truth. If she's on the side, who's the main course?"

Jarrett's eyes went from water to me without a flicker. "There isn't any."

"Maybe you're back with your ex-wife."

"You're nuts."

"Or maybe you want to scare her with phone calls."

"Why'd I want that?"

"Why'd you want her tailed?"

His breath sucked in. "Benziger—"

"Don't blame him. I have my own sources."

"Smart guy, right?"

"Skip the compliments. Why was she tailed?"

I watched the eyes dart back and forth before finally forming the truth. "Laura owns half the company," he said against his will. "When she bought in, it wasn't worth all that much. Now it is." He was a businessman talking business. "I thought if I could get something on her I'd be able to buy her out cheap."

"Something like what?"

"Sex. What else?"

"Don't make me laugh. Anything goes today in sex."

"She goes both ways."

I stared at Jarrett a long time before I turned to the water. The Morris Canal was a leftover from another age when ships moved almost everything.

"You were married four years," I heard myself say.

He shrugged. "She gave me what I wanted."

"Until you wanted more."

Now the water was a film of sludge. You could drop a match and it'd burn.

"Laura was fifteen when her father got drunk one night and raped her." His voice ran over my nerves. "They had money so nobody said anything. I guess she was trying to get back at him."

"And you didn't care."

"So she takes a broad to bed once in a while. I got my own problems."

I closed my eyes and everything fit. Her talk about her father and not saying anything about the divorce. Brushing me off so quick, too. I didn't know whether to be sorry or mad. Then I thought of Charisma Kelly, who'd gone through much worse. Jesus, wasn't anybody normal anymore? But I already knew the answer.

"Happens a lot," Jarrett said defensively. "Some men just get the short end."

"Some women, too."

Something else suddenly fit: her not playing around in Jersey.

"Why'd you just have her tailed in town?" I asked Jarrett. "What about New York?"

"Figured if it wasn't here, it wasn't there."

"You gotta do better than that."

"A matter of priority." Jarrett shrugged. "She knows a lot of important men here. They like to fantasize. If they thought she was like that—"

"And New York?"

"Sin city, right? Nobody cares what goes on there. They wouldn't believe it anyway or they'd take it as a joke. Some of them go over to get things done, too, lemme tell you. But if it happened here, it wouldn't be no joke. She'd lose a lot."

"What about you?"

"She'd be squeezed out no matter what. I got the power; she's only got her act with the big boys. If that goes, she's gone." He nodded, another business deal in the making. "She'd sell out fast if she saw that coming." Squinted at me. "Laura's no dope, you know. Don't shortchange her."

I looked over to Hudson Street, the top of the Colgate clock looming above the sheds. The biggest clock in the world, it was fifty feet across and the minute hand weighed a ton. I felt it pressing on me.

"That doesn't explain Virginia," I told Jarrett. "You're divorced, so why sneak around?"

He scuffed his shoes on the dry soil, a dog trying to cover his tracks. "Got nothing to do with you."

"Convince me."

"The hell I will," he exploded. "You work for me."

"The hell I do. I'm cutting you loose."

I watched his eyes go from murder to broken bones to resignation. It was all in the iris.

"Virginia's a nice girl," the realist mumbled. "She gives me everything I need."

"And you do the same for her," I jeered, "but why should Laura care?"

His face formed a mask to hide the pain, even embarrassment. In Cooper Jarrett? Was I reading him right?

"It's not Laura we're talking about."

"Who then?"

"It's my son."

The mask slipped away and I stood there sizing him up. The emotions were real, I'd stake my life on it.

"Virginia used to be his until she came to work for me." The voice was soft, almost affectionate. "The kid didn't like it but he had to take it." Then the snarl came back. "What the hell, he works for me too."

I couldn't help what popped into my head, my first meeting with Laura Jarrett and what I'd said. Something about father and son being the most dangerous relationship on earth.

"How old's your son, Mr. Jarrett?"

"Twenty-four."

"Any more?"

He shook his head.

"You planning on more or is this just a Saturday-night special?"

"The girl's no tramp, Malone." I saw the beast come back, but protective this time. "After all, she was Miss Ohio a few years ago."

"So you take Ohio out of town to spare your son's feelings. Does he ever talk about it?"

"Never."

"But he sees her in the office."

"Very little. He's an engineer, works at the projects."

"But whenever he does," I persisted, "how's he treat her?"

"He says hello."

"That's it?"

"That's all. Nobody talks about what happened. It's over."

Brother, I thought, can you spare a crime? Sons and lovers would do it every time.

On the other hand, I had no sons or even daughters so

*101*

what did I know? The boy was probably pumping a new blonde and hoping his father made even more money before he died.

"Now what about Weems?" Jarrett asked sarcastically. "Or don't that interest you anymore?"

Standing at the edge of the canal I told him all I knew, almost all. One of the things I left out was Henry Stiles.

"So it was a sex killing."

"Or your phantom callers."

I played the tape for him, a copy.

"Same voice?" I asked.

"Hard to say. It's pitched so low, you know what I mean? But I think so."

"You got two of them, you said. The same?"

"Far as I could tell."

"Just like this."

He nodded.

"So where'd you get the idea there's more than one caller?"

"Laura said she heard different voices."

We were walking back to the cars. Jarrett's had wire wheels and a sliding sun roof. Mine was the other one.

"Am I in any danger?"

I listened to the electric seat go back, watched him adjust the collapsible steering wheel. Envy was always dangerous.

"Until we learn more about Weems, I wouldn't piss in the woods."

He didn't seem scared.

"By the way," I said as he pressed the auto-reverse deck, "did Weems ever call you that night? He mentioned he might."

"Guess he forgot."

"Too bad," I mumbled at the sliding tinted glass.

The time it took me to crawl into my tank, Jarrett's 747 was probably cruising somewhere over Fort Lee.

# thirteen

AMERICA'S THE GREATEST COUNTRY in the world. You can move up and down the social scale here, instead of being locked into genealogy like everywhere else. You can even step off the scale and disappear."

"So?"

"So out of all this revolutionary movement has come a whole new industry, with professional investigators on the cutting edge. But behind us are armies of people who track everything from dummy firms to lost heirs."

Frank Barnes was my sectional chief in the Denver FBI office. When I left, Frank shook my hand like he'd never see me again. He was right. A year later he was dead with a bullet in the back. But I never forgot the things Frank told me.

"America," he said, "is a nation of records."

Now I used law students for that kind of research, eager young piranha ready to eviscerate anything that fell their way. In training for the lawhood, they had all the morals of a falling rock. But they came cheap.

I pulled off Route 1 onto the gravel around the hot-dog stand. Felson was already inside munching away and when he saw me he ordered another. A foot-long frank. Who could refuse that?

"All beef," Felson said, licking his fingers.

I slid onto the seat. "How many of these you eat in a day?"

"Depends."

"On what?"

"On who's buying." He sucked a knuckle. "Sunday's the worst."

"What happens on Sunday?"

"They close."

Felson was tall and thin, claimed he hated to eat. What about the hot dogs? They were medicine, not food. Like ice cream for some people. A crutch? A drug. They made him feel better, not so lonely, more in control. The only hot-dog junkie I knew.

When the dog was ready, he brought it over and started cranking up his mouth. "You should try one," he garbled between bites.

"I thought I was."

"Get you high."

"Getting high just watching you."

The mouth was a third-year law student who commuted to Rutgers and lived on odd jobs and junk food. He fell in love with every girl he touched, which naturally made them run away. I figured he was just about all touched out. But Felson was good at what he did, and what he did best was background. There wasn't a reference he couldn't locate or a collection he couldn't crack.

"Remember the monograph on milk I found for you in the New York Academy of Medicine?"

"What about it?"

"You still owe me for that one."

"What about the UFO sightings from the Cycle Study Foundation? I paid you double."

"That's because I gave you two cycles."

"That's because you claimed the first came from the UFOs themselves."

"It did."

I watched his eyes leak mustard. "So what about Jarrett's company?"

"Interesting."

"Is that good interesting or bad interesting?"

"The monograph was hard to track," he mumbled.

I knew blackmail when it bit me. He had only half a foot to go. "Okay, I'll buy you another."

"They have takeout here."

I made a mental note to meet elsewhere next time.

"And they're closed tomorrow."

"All you can carry," I barked. "But in their smallest sack."

When he smiled I knew I'd lost again. The sonofabitch had clocked their bags.

That was the other thing Frank Barnes'd been trying to tell me. You can't beat research.

"Jarrett," I croaked in defeat.

"Nickel-and-dime stuff through the Seventies until he made some killings with small apartment houses. Then he went into block-busting, clusters here and there but still nothing heavy. In '78 he hit a big one downtown when they rezoned."

Felson bit off a quarter-inch and chewed it into chop meat.

"It turned his head from residential to commercial. Started buying up industrial sites."

"Where?"

"Wherever he could. You have to remember this was before the real boom began. The city had"—he checked his notes—"almost six hundred industrial plants and many of them were dying. Jarrett did his best but he was still small potatoes. We're talking maybe eight, ten million in holdings going into 1980."

"You call that small?"

"Compared to what happened later, sure. He was just doing what a dozen others did—they were all playing a hunch until the thing steamrolled. If the big boys in New York really knew what was going on, they could've come in and wiped these guys out overnight. But they saw Jersey as dead city and never even noticed the New Yorkers who'd been pushed out by rising rents beginning to come over here."

A string of sauerkraut fell on the notes but I was used to that. He'd once sold me some dipped in spaghetti sauce.

"In 1979 Jarrett bought out his partner—an old man moving to Florida—and reinvested the company, but it didn't help the problem. He was undercapitalized for the really big grabs. Then in '80 everything changed. He married into money and the fun began."

Also the frustration, because nothing that happened next made any sense.

"Her name"—back to the notes—"was Laura Cross, from Greenwich, Connecticut. The father was a corporation counsel, big bucks. They married in March and four months later her parents died in an accident and she got the money."

"How much?"

Felson looked up. "That wasn't part of my check on the company. You'd have to ask Connecticut."

I waved him on.

"Jarrett restructured the company and they split it. In effect, his wife bought in for two million dollars."

"But it was already worth ten million."

"That's in holdings, which means nothing. If you don't have positive cash flow to grow, you could end up losing everything. She brought in cash. With two million cash, you could buy twenty million in holdings."

"If his wife owns half, how come Jarrett's still the boss?"

"There are always things to do"—Felson smiled while I shuddered at the lawyer he would make—"and Jarrett did them. His wife doesn't really own half, just 49.1 percent. He owns 50.9, so he controls it all." The piranha settled back to a job well done. "Maybe she didn't know too much at the time."

"Maybe she couldn't help it."

Felson smirked. "Could be your boy had the smarter lawyer."

"Was it legal?"

"Through subsidiaries and other paper boxes, perfectly legal."

It was all a chess game of moves and countermoves, and you could do almost anything if you followed the rules of the game. Felson was so caught up in it he even forgot about hot dogs.

"Sounds like what you do, doesn't it?"

He watched my jaw drop.

"What I mean is, in your business you have to squeeze

people and lie to them to get what you need. Isn't that right? I mean, you all try to get away with whatever you can just like—"

"Shut up and eat."

My eyes did a laser lobotomy on his skull but it didn't help any. He was right, of course. In my work I pushed people too. I pushed them because somebody pushed me. Or maybe I just pushed myself.

"No trouble after that?"

Felson shook his head. "Nothing legal, anyway. With the new money Jarrett started buying up waterfront, where a lot of old plants were located. The city has eleven miles of waterfront so he got some good buys."

"And a lot of clout."

"Soon he was into subsidy housing and other city and state projects. Then he got the Harbor Terminal deal."

But sometimes people pushed back, and then people like me got a call.

"Now his holdings are impressive," Felson said. "Still peanuts to some New York developers but not bad for this side of the river."

"With more deals to come."

"He's big enough."

I thought back to the Caven Point beach where we first met. What was it Jarrett said? Soon this'll all be mine.

When I blinked again Felson was back on the dogs, one in his hand and bags in his eyes. They were stuffing it at the counter. I pulled out a roll that would choke a chipmunk and glared my way across the table.

"I know you don't like checks, so I better pay you now." I laid out the bills and scooped up his notes. "Soon I won't have enough to buy a napkin."

"Don't use 'em," he said, licking his wrist.

At the counter I asked if they took checks.

"Only in odd years."

"This is an odd year."

"Not odd enough for me."

I promised to pay him off in pennies next time.

"You should live forever, too."

"Same to you, pal."

Another Catholic! The woods were full of them.

Walking out all I could see was Laura Jarrett, who had told me she'd been disinherited by her family for marrying Jarrett. Instead she gave her new husband two million and was now worth much more.

Rich people have all the luck. Or something.

"How'd you find out all this?" I asked Felson outside.

"Does Macy tell Gimbel?"

"He did in *Miracle on 34th Street.*"

"Natalie Wood," Felson sighed. "A lovely child."

"Lovely something."

He placed the bag tenderly on the front seat next to him. A child substitute?

That was another thing Frank Barnes told me. "Malone, you have a dirty mind."

"Comes from two years in a seminary," I pleaded.

Frank had laughed. He was a Mormon and they don't have regular seminaries.

"It's all on file," Felson said behind the wheel. "Corporations have to declare ownership. Real-estate records show figures. Business directories tell the rest."

"And the stuff about Laura Jarrett's family?"

"Newspaper morgues, some stiff in the basement pasting page after page into obscurity."

He gunned the motor. It was older than mine.

"Everything's on paper somewhere," he shouted happily. "All you have to know is where."

I watched his broken taillight, thinking in a few years he'd be driving a boat. There was a lot more money in writing the papers than looking for them.

# fourteen

THE *JERSEY JOURNAL* is housed in a stone mausoleum on Journal Square around the corner from one of the best bars in town, the kind that New York and Chicago used to have, full of crusty reporters and cranky rewriters. Only now they're called journalists and copy editors. It's a serious business, newspapers.

"Here's to Ben Hecht and *The Front Page,*" I kidded Ray Price.

"Dead meat," he growled.

"Come again."

"Those guys'd never last a week today. No heat."

"Heat?"

"Sex. They had no steam in their stories."

"Heat," I said.

"They were too cynical for sex." He sighed. "Dead meat."

"Didn't you tell me they were the greatest reporters ever lived?"

"Probably."

"Well, isn't that your opinion?"

"Sure that's my opinion, but I don't necessarily agree with it."

The thing about Ray was that his mind had a mind of its own. Ten minutes with him and you'd swear it was yours.

"Tell me about the Arab," I said before it was too late.

"Arab?" Ray squinted at his glass and I motioned the bartender for another round.

"The Arab I just asked you to tell me about."

"He's North African, a Moslem."

"I knew it! I knew he wasn't a true believer in nothing."

"Not necessarily. He could be a Moslem atheist." Ray belted down the scotch. "The Moslems have one hundred names for their god, but only ninety-nine are known."

"So?"

"Suppose the hundredth name is Atheis, the god of disbelief?"

That was the other thing about Ray. You never knew when he was kidding. It was all a rubber band of possibilities to him.

"An Arab atheist could be a big draw," he said. "Not too many of 'em around. They kill for religion like we kill for Christ."

"Never make it over here," I told him. "No snap."

"Snap?"

"Bait. Arabs have no bait in their hate."

"So what've we got?"

"We got the devil and his snap's got plenty of heat." I looked at my flick to show I had zip. "Now what've you got?"

Ali Kassam was twenty-seven, a graduate of Columbia. Two years ago he'd been questioned in the murder of a young Moslem woman whose body washed up in New York Harbor minus the head.

"How'd they know she was Moslem?"

"All her pubic hair had apparently been removed, but not by shaving. Hot wax. It hardens when it cools, allowing the hair to be pulled out." His tone suggested I should've known. "It's a common practice among conservative Moslem women."

How could you trust anyone who knew that kind of thing?

Kassam had been friendly with the victim but was not implicated in the murder, which was never solved. A year ago he moved to Jersey City and subsequently joined Christians Anonymous.

"Even though he'd never been a Christian."

Ray made a solemn face. "Are we not all God's chillun?"

"It could be a setup."

"By whom?"

I shook my head. Who'd want to infiltrate a bunch of nuts trying to overthrow God? I mean, it wasn't like they were after anything important.

"See if you can learn more about the crime," I told him. "Could be an angle."

"How?"

"How do I know? You're the crime reporter."

"Not reporter," Ray corrected, "journalist. A reporter just reports. A journalist can make up dialogue."

"Can you make up something for Dancer Fitzgerald? He's looking for the money stolen from the county machine that time."

"Dancer's a good boy. What's he want with you?"

"Thinks I may know where it is."

"Do you?"

"No," I lied, "but it doesn't hurt to have them think I do. Might get me some information."

"So I'll spread the word in return."

"In return for what?"

Ray signaled the bartender. "What else? An exclusive on the whole sordid story."

"What sordid story?"

"Whatever one you're making up."

I had another beer and headed over to the West Side. It wasn't good to drink on the job—fouled-up reactions, mine anyway. Also my instinct. A lot of what I do is fishing, throwing lines out to see what snags. And a lot of it is instinctive—a smell, a feel.

I was beginning to get a feel about the Jarrett case, and I didn't like the smell.

· Traffic was light on this Saturday afternoon. Still two hours to Marilyn and I had Benziger on my mind. He'd tailed Laura Jarrett and found nothing. But maybe he was looking for the wrong something.

The house was one of those shingle jobs with a driveway in front and a No Parking sign tacked to a tree at the curb. Except there was no curb, so I eased into the driveway behind an ancient green Ford.

His office was at the rear of the house and he had the door

open, waiting for me. It was a warm spring day in Jersey City, the day I walked into Carl Benziger's life.

"If it's about the Jarrett broad, forget it," he said. Benziger had at least ten years on me, a small wiry man with big eyes and little hair. His white shirt had ring-around-the-collar and a button missing, his pants were belted with a tie and rolled up at the bottoms. He looked like what he was, a process server and tail who never made the big one.

"Yes and no," I said. "You followed her around town and got nowhere."

"Nowhere to go," he bristled. There was a whine to the voice, an excuse for every failure. "She didn't do anything."

I smiled. "In that case, you had an easy time. Did Jarrett tell you what to look for?"

"What else?"

"Another jealous husband." I put disappointment in the words.

"Like most men," said the lifelong bachelor. "Can't really trust them, you know."

"The husbands?"

"The wives," Benziger said, his voice rising. "Women." He sounded peevish.

"You're right," I said quickly.

That smoothed his feathers a little. He didn't like to be misunderstood, this Benziger. Probably been misunderstood all his life, especially by women. He'd be watching them very closely. Which was exactly what I needed.

"On the phone you mentioned copies of your reports?"

Benziger shrugged. "You mentioned something about a job."

"That's part of it," I said.

"What part of it?"

"The tail, same as before."

"The Jarrett broad?" He didn't seem pleased.

"Only this time—"

"For her ex?"

"For me. You'll be working for me. Only this time it's New York."

"Where she lives."

A look of crafty intelligence spread over the face, eyes forming points on a map of perversity.

"You'll watch her house. I want everyone who goes in, pictures of them. It's a small building, get everybody."

"No problem."

"Also anyone she talks to on the street." What else? "I want your report every day, with the pictures."

"What about around New York?"

"Stay on her, photos and names if possible." My mind kept slipping back to Jarrett not telling his tail to watch other women with Laura, which meant he could've been lying. Or just didn't want the tail to know.

"First her ex and now you," Benziger rasped. "What's she got?"

"Money," I said to shut him up. "You don't wanna get caught in it."

He laughed. "Don't worry about me. I been after people twenty years and I'm still here. People come and go, I stay."

"Must be exciting."

"One time I played watchdog for this rich guy? He loved a broad he didn't even know, bothered her all the time. He thought she loved him too, you see? That they made love together every day. It was all in his head, what they call erotomania. A week after I went off the case, he killed the two of them. They're gone and I'm here. See what I mean? Nothing to worry about."

Soon's he said that, I began to worry.

"Why'd you quit?"

"Had to. After a while the bastard decided I was screwing the broad behind his back."

"But you knew he was crazy."

"Sure I knew he was crazy," Benziger fumed, "but he had all that money. Even at the end when he talked to himself, he'd walk around naked talking like he was two people and nobody said anything. He was bare-assed and raving, but he still had *power.*"

"Just make sure you don't screw around with Laura Jarrett."

Benziger said, "You're starting to sound like him already, but I know what you mean. You want a lock on her in New York. Okay? Anyone she sees I'll see."

"What about over here the last time you looked?"

"Nobody special, unless you call big shots special. She knows a lot of them."

"Any women?"

"Some."

I watched a cloud cross his face, hoped I hadn't made a mistake.

"Ever see her with Charisma Kelly?"

"Not so's I remember."

"You know who she is."

"The Commie broad, sure. I done a job on her a while back."

My mouth sprang open in surprise. "For who?"

Benziger hesitated and I pressed him. "I need to know."

"Hell, I guess it's all the same," he said. "It was Jarrett. That's how he knew to call me on his ex."

"What was the job?"

A hand pulled at the toothpick. "Nothing much. He wanted a building she owned up on Kennedy Boulevard. Figured if he could get something on her—"

"Blackmail."

"Leverage." A shrug. "It usually works."

"But not this time."

Benziger shook his head in disappointment. "I trailed the bitch for three weeks and came up clean. She don't sleep or eat, never even feeds her cunt. It's like she ain't human."

"She's a Commie," I tossed off. "Anyone else?"

"Just an Arab who worked with her. Turned out he was a suspect in a shooting."

"You told Jarrett?"

"It was all in my report."

I nodded, a sop to his professionalism. "Anything between the Arab and the Kelly woman?"

"Not a chance," Benziger snorted. "She's cold potatoes. Anybody sticks that broad has gotta be the devil himself."

"Why's that?"

"All them Commies are the same. They all love the devil and hate people."

I took my time getting back to the car but couldn't squeeze more out of Benziger. His reports on Laura Jarrett didn't come up with anything new and it looked like a dead end unless New York was different, unless Benziger found something.

But I had to give the little guy credit. If life had dealt him a bad hand, at least he still tried to stay in the game. He taught himself to be a shadow—nowhere near as easy as the movies make it—and he'd never been a cop, never even worked for the insurance or rating companies. Benziger had no real standing in the business but I gave the guy a lot of credit.

An hour to go and another stop to make, a quick one. I wanted to know about Jarrett's son, get a line on his thinking. He'd gone with Miss Ohio, no fool, who switched over to his father, who had the money. But how did he react to it? Did he find someone else? Money always helped, unless ego got in the way.

I found Pop Wagner on a baseball diamond with the kids as usual. He was the driving force behind the local Little Leagues, a bachelor who'd served as second father to hundreds of kids over the years. A retired cop, Wagner knew a lot of people and a lot about them.

"His name's Mark Jarrett," I told Wagner. "Father's a local developer."

"Cooper Jarrett," Pop said. "I know him." Shook his head. "A rough man. You going up against him?"

"He's a client."

Pop nodded. "You wanna be careful around Jarrett, he likes to run over people. Won't stop at anything to get what he wants either."

"You know him long?"

"Ever since he was a juvenile delinquent." Pop laughed, cut it short. "A tough, street-wise punk who never changed. A real rattler."

"What about the son?"

"Don't know him, but I'll check around if you want." He looked over at his charges, anxious to get back. "If he's Jarrett's kid, he's probably worse." Was that a gleam of satisfaction in Wagner's eyes? "Ain't only the world that turns, eh, Malone?"

"Guess not, Pop."

"Sometimes it's the worm's turn."

# fifteen

"CAN I BUY YOU six drinks? I don't have much time."

It was a Jersey City evening and I was shooting for the moon. Across the table sat the moon goddess glowing, while beyond the Hudson the Garden lights already burned bright with anticipation.

"Only if they come on whole wheat."

We were in the Retreat, a restaurant run by the local Catholic parish. Every booth was filled, every table taken—which probably said more for hunger than religion.

"It's all stone-ground," Marilyn trilled.

"What is?"

"The whole-wheat croissants."

"What about the coconut oil and animal fat used to make them?"

"What animal fat?"

"Butter."

Marilyn didn't want to hear it. She loved good food and hated bad talk.

"You should show more reverence," she whispered.

"This is a restaurant, sweet pea, not a church."

"I meant for the food."

"Shoulda known," I mumbled.

"What was that?"

"Homegrown," I said quickly. "Most stuff here is grown in a home."

She liked that, showed I had some taste. Marilyn was very big on homes.

"Mae West once said a man's home is her castle."

"Yeah, well, she always did have trouble with her pronouns," I said.

"What she meant was in a home she could bake things and make meals for him." Marilyn looked over at the next table, the couple doing a *Tom Jones*. "The way to a man's heart is through his stomach."

"You're close."

She picked up the menu. "I'm ravished."

"Close again."

I followed her to the menu, which was about all I could ever follow with Marilyn. At the beginning I thought her a bit vague—until I began tripping over her tracks.

"I'm going to start with a Latin Round. What about you?"

"The Rosary and a Holy Spirit."

That was the menu at the Retreat, and part of its success. Good food was good business, and a touch of show biz made it even better. A Latin Round was melon and prosciutto. The Rosary was oysters on the half-shell, their loss leader, and the Holy Spirit a glass of wine.

"Cardinal or Pope?"

"Pope."

Other dishes included Loaves and Fishes for the catch of the day, and Vatican II, spaghetti and meatballs. The Stations were sandwiches, a hamburger the Gospel. Or you could splurge on Body and Blood rare roast beef or even go all the way with a thick filet called the Bible.

Being a slow reader myself, I usually settled for a Gospel Special.

"American or Swiss?"

"Swiss," I told the waiter in Greek.

Marilyn had the Roman Soldier, which looked suspiciously like a Caesar salad when he set it down.

"What's the breakfast menu?" I asked his back.

"Mostly Priests and Nuns," he answered my shoulder.

"What he say?"

"Ham and eggs."

An hour later we relaxed over Holy Water—100 percent Columbian—and love talk. Or at least food talk.

"A good service," Marilyn said.

"And the offering's not bad either," I said, eyeing the bill.

Whoever thought it up had a one-track mind, the secret of success. The place was a regular theme park, even to the electric candles and stained-glass windows. Showed you the power of religion.

Marilyn agreed. "Why didn't you think of it?"

"You have to be Catholic."

"You're Catholic."

"I used to be Catholic," I reminded her. "Now I'm Mormon."

She made a face. "All the same. They just leave out a few parts and don't like to drink."

Marilyn had an absolute genius for bridging differences between people, even those considered irreconcilable. If she wanted to, she could probably reconcile quantum mechanics with the unified field theory. It was a gift. I think Hitler and Stalin had it.

"When are we due in Dead City?"

That's what she called New York. Marilyn didn't think anyone should live there. I told her millionaires lived there but she wasn't very impressed. If they had any real money, they'd go somewhere else.

"Game time is eight-thirty," I announced.

"Murder Incorporated."

She took a hard line on hockey, too. It made no sense to Marilyn that twelve grown men would beat each other to death for a puck you couldn't see half the time. When I called it a sport she called me a leech, which was usually when I called her a cab. People should never mess with someone's religion, whatever it's called.

"At least in Rome they threw 'em to the lions."

But she was good about it most of the time, my Marilyn, agreeable and consenting. Every few months I got tickets for two and took her to the Garden, where the Rangers played their home games. She was always thrilled.

"Do we have to go?"

One of the last games of the season? With the Rangers fighting for a play-off berth?

I decided to use psychology.

"It's one of the last games of the season. With the Rangers fighting for a play-off berth. Think of the suspense, the tension. Won't that be terrific?"

"No."

I switched over to guilt.

"You know how long I've been waiting to see this game? Years, even longer. If we don't go, you'll be spoiling my whole evening. Is that what you want?"

"You're spoiling mine."

Male macho was next.

"I take you out to dinner, buy you drinks, even a newspaper. I watch over you because I care. Me Tarzan, you Jane. We go."

"You go."

Finally, cheap desperation.

"All right. If you don't go with me, I'll kill myself."

She just laughed.

I sat there watching her laugh, wondering why women drove men to violence. A defective gene in our makeup somewhere, but at least we tried to rise above it.

"I could always break your arm."

"Like they do in hockey?"

I looked at Marilyn, started laughing myself. Ahead of me again! All she wanted was the last word.

Tunnel traffic was heavy and New York worse. In the car I kept thinking of Charisma Kelly who'd never been adopted by her so-called mother. Why not? What would make a woman keep a child not hers, then neglect to make it legal?

"Who would do that?" I asked Marilyn.

"Do what?"

I told her about Mrs. Stiles, the tragedies she'd had in her life. Not able to have children, a good husband who died young, another who was a child-rapist and deserter.

"There's your answer," Marilyn said.

"Where?"

"With her luck she probably didn't expect to keep the child, to be able to keep it."

"No good, the kid was ten when the first husband died. Plenty of time for adoption."

"Maybe her husband didn't want someone else's child. Or maybe he wasn't her husband."

My eyes snapped shut—popped open. Closed—opened. Blinking, as in startled.

"Then after he died . . ." I whispered in thought.

"No money, maybe no records. The child is ten and they've moved, you told me."

"So after she remarries . . ."

"She knows he's no good, marries out of desperation." Marilyn smiled, not a pretty smile. "Women had to do a lot of that years ago."

I nodded, my mind on Charisma as a scared little girl. Was her mother the same? The daughter had called her a frightened woman all her life, said she longed for death.

"Gloria Steinem once said the girl is father to the woman."

I didn't believe it but I inched ahead anyway. Mrs. Stiles was the key, her life, what she did with it. I saw that now. It would explain why she killed herself, maybe even why she was murdered. Was she murdered? Charisma Kelly didn't take the suicide gun, and Henry Stiles was out of town. That left murder.

"Where will you park?"

"Thought I'd try one of those lots where they hold the car for ransom."

I pulled off Eighth Avenue behind Penn Station and clucked down the street trailing smoke. It was a gadget I'd had a mechanic rig for me. With the flick of a switch I could disappear in a cloud of dust.

"What's that for?" Marilyn said.

"So they don't think I'm the Rockefellers."

Near the corner I turned into a sign that said, *No Room, No Space, No Kidding*. I put on the headlights to find the attendant.

"You parking or junking?"

"Which is cheaper?"

"We got a special on burners today. You leave it here and we'll let you walk away free."

I settled for a spot at the end of the lot. "Less danger," said the car jockey.

"I'm insured."

"I meant the other cars."

He was nice about it, said he'd only charge me maximum.

"How much is that?"

He shrugged. "Two credit cards should cover it."

I looked at him closely, saw the start of a great career. "You should go into politics," I told him.

"Cars are cleaner." He coughed into the smoke.

I made a note to get his name in case he ever ran loose in Jersey City.

"You're lucky there's room," he gagged in my face.

"So what's with the sign?"

The attendant threw up on my fender. "We only want people who'll pay anything," he hacked. "Desperate people."

"You come to the right car," I told him.

# sixteen

**M**ADISON SQUARE GARDEN WAS built by giants for midgets. If your knees were normal you found them embedded in back of the seat in front, and if your legs were long you ended up looking like an ad for Exotic Sex. None of which bothered me whenever the Rangers were in town.

"These are very nice seats," Marilyn said. "Where's the field?"

"The field is down there." I gave her the binoculars. "You can't see it because of all the ice. It's called a rink."

"What should I look for?"

"Don't you remember?"

"Only what I can't forget."

Marilyn had a very good memory for someone who'd seen only a few hockey games. She already knew this was New York and it was April.

"Look for the exits," I told her.

The stands were full, a sellout crowd hoping to see their team nail down fourth place in the Patrick Division. Going in they were only a few points ahead of Jersey and Pittsburgh.

"Who are they playing with?" Marilyn wanted to know.

"These men," I announced soberly, "don't play with anybody."

"Isn't that a bit excessive?"

"Not when they're Rangers," I rasped. "Rangers only play *against* somebody."

"Then who are they playing against?"

"The other team."

She nodded sensibly. "Who's better?"

"The Rangers will win," I predicted.

"You said that last time we sat in these seats."

Marilyn and her trick memory!

"How you know it's the same seats?"

She pointed to the graffiti above her knees. "I remember the writing."

I bent forward and peered at the words carved in wood: Free Judge Crater.

Only in New York!

"They lost, too."

"A bad night." I shrugged. "Happens to everybody."

"Didn't I read they already have the most losses of any team in club history?"

"Where'd you read that?"

"I think they also gave up the most goals in club history."

"Where'd you think that?"

"So if they make the play-offs," she sighed, "it will be with the worst record in club history." A smile. "Is that how it works?"

I hate people with trick memories. Also people with any memory. They always remember the wrong things.

"The team that loses the most is champion?"

"No comment," I explained.

After the preliminaries ended, the shouting began. Cries of *"Kill him"* quickly gave way to more forceful sentiments, all of which Marilyn found strange.

"Why are they screaming like that?"

"All part of the game," I told her.

"But the game hasn't started yet."

"That part starts early."

The loudest cries were coming from my right, a group at the other end of the section. One of them seemed familiar, a heavy man with huge hands. I borrowed the binoculars and turned them on the group.

Marilyn followed my gaze. "What is it?"

It was Marko Bay! He was a Rangers fan! The man I fantasized sucking nymphettes like gumdrops sat there and screamed at grown men.

"Marko Bay."

"Who's Marko Bay?"

I should've known. Hockey was violent, and violence was sexy today. And who knew more about sex than the man—I shifted the glasses—sitting next to that stunning child with blond hair and heaving breast?

"Who the hell is Marko Bay?" Marilyn asked politely.

"Marko Bay"—I tried to pull my eye off the blond child in the baby-blue dress—"is a world-class sexist."

"A sexist."

"World class."

"Does his sexism take any particular form?"

"All forms," I answered truthfully. "Zoophilia, homosexuality, transvestism, necrophilia, coprolalia, pyromania, troilism, S&M-ism, M&M-ism, incest, sacrilege, exhibitionism, mass copulation, and piano."

"Piano?"

"Very fat ladies," I leered, "with very fat legs."

Something crashed, the sound of bodies. I pulled away from the heaving breast—

"And M&M-ism?"

—and focused on the other action.

"Marilyn by moonlight," I said, "it melts in your hand."

Below me the game was afoot, also astick. Two sticks, wielded like clubs. It was murder.

"Hope not." She squeezed my arm.

In the first four minutes there were two fights and two goals. The Rangers lost both.

Marilyn looked pleased, exuding an air of vindication. Twelve angry men with weapons was the perfect epitome of our climate of violence.

"Hockey is certainly a racy game," she trilled.

"Sex and violence," said her dinner companion. "As American as priests and nuns."

At the first break I turned back to the blue child in the heaving dress. King Kong had a paw on her puberty. A half-hour later she had a hand in his pocket. Both of them were shouting now, their eyes glazed, as the Rangers came from behind.

I decided they knew each other.

"Here." I handed the glasses to Marilyn, who was still having trouble finding the field. I didn't need to see any more. The heaving child in the blue movie was obviously a runaway from a bad home who'd sold herself to live and was now trying to upgrade her livelihood. Marko Bay knew many people and could help her. That's what people were for, to help each other.

On the other hand, maybe she was his daughter home from grammar school.

"What do I look for?" Marilyn said, cocky now that she could see.

"Try the puck."

"It's too fast," she complained.

I leaned into her, my hand on her leg. "A fast puck is the best way," I quipped.

"That's not funny, Malone."

I straightened up. "Then look for the moves," I said. "Hockey is like ballet, with pirouettes and positions. The three important elements are the backcheck, the forecheck, and the paycheck."

"What's the paycheck?"

"That's the most important," I confided, "same as ballet."

"Same as anything."

Always liked a woman with both feet on the ground. Sometimes.

I sat there watching the game and thinking of Marko Bay, men like him. They were all the same too, all the flesh peddlers. With them it was always sex at first feel, at least until they felt better—then it was back to business. Between the rapists and the rest, women didn't stand much of a chance. Some women.

Both Charisma Kelly and Laura Jarrett had been sexually abused by their fathers, one a stepfather.

"Looks like your Rangers might win," Marilyn nibbled in my ear.

I squinted at the rink. "Easy."

"You really think so?"

"Stake my whole professional reputation on it," I assured her.

Marilyn laughed. "I'll go even further than that," she said. "I'll bet a dollar they don't."

A pair of born gamblers!

At the last break I tried south Jersey again, got City Hall.

"Tomorrow okay? . . . In the morning, about eleven-thirty. . . . I'd rather not wait till Monday."

On the wall someone had scrawled: If you have a drinking problem phone this number.

"Won't take long. . . . Yes, very . . . eleven-thirty, then, thanks."

Afterward I phoned the number.

"Hello, I have a drinking problem."

It was a liquor store.

When I got back, Marko Bay was gone.

"Everything all right?" Marilyn asked.

"I think I have a phone problem."

"Hearing?"

"Reading."

So was his granddaughter.

"That's common in men over fifty."

"I'm only twenty."

"Then your problem is you can't read numbers anymore."

Marko never stayed to the end of anything; even in church he left before my blessing.

"No, it's people I can't read anymore."

He obviously couldn't tell when something was over, like a lot of men.

I sat there hoping I wasn't one of them. Or was it already too late?

"Here's your dollar," Marilyn said.

"What's this?"

"The game's over."

The Rangers had won it, 7–5. They were still alive, even with forty-two losses.

"Knew it all the time," I bragged.

"You're wonderful," she sighed.

"Just an average everyday guy," I said. "My hobby is

lying. I'm also interested in girls. I watch them all the time and even talk to one occasionally. You, for instance. Most people would say you were lucky to know me."

"Tell me more about myself."

"Like the bat, I spend my nights dangling upside down in the dark while the sun shines on China. But that doesn't mean I'm sleeping."

"Me! What about me?"

"I lie there thinking about Charles Weems—"

"Weems?"

"—who knew Henry Stiles—"

"Another one?"

"—who works for the redevelopment agency and gave the Harbor Terminal deal to Cooper Jarrett—"

"What is this?"

"—who was Charles Weems's boss."

"Weems again."

"Always Weems. He knew Stiles."

"Who's Stiles?"

"Charisma Kelly's stepfather."

Marilyn's eyes rounded in exasperation. "And what am I? A stick of wood? Romance me. Seduce me, damn it. *Charm me.*"

"Here in the Garden?"

"So treat me like a suspect."

"Suspected of what?"

"I don't know. Of insanity, maybe, for being here at all—"

"I'm glad you are," I said, touching her.

"You are?"

"You're all the women I haven't met yet."

Marilyn opened her mouth, closed it, opened it again. "That's beautiful," she finally said.

"I know."

On the way home she huddled next to me, her arm against my arm, a transfusion of energy, filling me with her song.

She said, "Don't you know I'm the devil? I can make things grow in the dark."

"Sounds sexy to me."

"I can even make things that don't exist in nature."

"Like an unnatural act?"

"No, really. Like the color brown. There's no brown in nature. I have to make it for my wolves."

"How can you make a color?"

"From other colors, mostly. Brown is red and yellow and blue. But to get the exact shade I want takes a great deal of playing with the mix."

"Sounds like finger painting," I said.

"That too. One time I was teaching children about color? We were in a meadow and I had no paints with me, so I broke off some grass and moistened it and smeared it on a canvas. Green is yellow and blue, so all I needed for brown was the red. I stuck a pin in my thumb and drew a little blood and smeared that over the yellow and blue—and brown suddenly appeared."

I said, "You made brown from blood and grass?"

Marilyn laughed. "And painted them a wolf."

"How'd you learn that?"

Her eyes were two hot coals. "The same way I learned how to make things grow in the dark. Guess it's just the devil in me."

There we were, right in the middle of the Holland Tunnel, when it hit me. Why did I love her? Because her world was full of magic, and mine just full of mystery.

# seventeen

SEA BRIGHT USED TO be a beautiful ocean town hugging the shoreline below Sandy Hook. Forty years ago they put in a seawall to protect the homes, and the currents soon began washing away the sand in front of the wall. Now the beach is gone and the town lies flat in the sun.

It was a little after eleven when I pulled off the parkway. The love of last night had returned to reality, and I resented it. A quick drive back and I could make it night again, but the thought never entered my mind. Not more than a hundred times in the past hour. I still had to fight the desire as I drove the last miles to Harker's house.

He was up and dressed, which for him apparently meant loose pants and a straw hat. The hat was fitted with a sweatband and had a wide brim. And this was only April!

"What'll you do in August?" I asked him over coffee.

"Wait for September."

Spring was his best time. He walked the town on the weekends, in the morning, and afterward sat in his yard. If he wanted to kick some sand he'd go over to Monmouth Beach or Asbury Park. Everything was quiet before the season started, and there was room to breathe.

"How long you come here?" I said to be polite. We sat on a terrace he'd built brick by brick.

"Thirty years next summer," Harker recalled, "and before that my family had a place in Long Branch."

"I was there years ago."

"In those days everyone from Jersey City came down. It was a big thing to have a place at the shore."

"Still is."

"Not the way it was." He shook his head sadly. "People like to move around now."

"Yeah," I said, "but some move too fast."

"Tell me about it."

"I figure you already know, being in City Hall like that." He smiled, a thin line that got lost somewhere in the jowls. "What happened to your nose?"

"I fell out of bed."

"More than once," he said. "Want to tell me about it?"

"Not particularly."

"Always like a good sex story in the morning."

"There was this mayor—"

"Just a rumor," he cut in. "The mayor wasn't even there."

"But Henry Stiles was," I suggested. "Is that it?"

Harker shrugged. "Let's say it wouldn't surprise some of us."

"Or disappoint you?"

"You're here, aren't you?"

Harker was part of the administration, an important cog in the machinery. I had to figure he'd got the blessing of others.

"They're greasing the skids," I said.

"Not an elegant way to put it," Harker protested.

"But essentially correct."

He refilled the cups. "Good government demands that the individual be responsible for his actions."

Translation: They'd be delighted to get rid of the bastard.

"It's always been that way."

Translation: They've been trying to dump him for a long time.

I took off my jacket, no match for a straw hat. It was a mistake. Harker was a gun nut, his eyes feasting on my draw holster.

"May I?"

"Steyr 9-mm," I said. "Nineteen rounds." I lifted it out of the holster. "It's armed."

"Never shot a Steyr," Harker said. "Austrian, isn't it?"

I handed him the pistol.

"Heavy."

"Adequate," I said.

He hefted the weapon, his fingers outside the trigger guard. You can always tell a careful shooter by the way he holds the gun. With the other kind you have only two choices: nail him or run.

"Nineteen rounds. That's more than the Beretta 92."

"It helps if you have big hands," I admitted.

"Doesn't look like you'd have trouble on that score." He examined the sighting. "Any accuracy?"

"Good enough. It's a gas-delayed blowback, so not much recoil."

"I like a good revolver myself," Harker said, holding out the pistol. "Nothing to go wrong in an emergency."

"That's true."

I wasn't going to ask him when was his last emergency in City Hall. For all I knew, vampires roamed the stairwells.

The gun and holster went into my jacket while Harker took off the hat to mop his forehead. He was a beefy man with short arms and expressive hands that described arcs as he spoke.

"Why couldn't this wait until tomorrow?"

"For one thing, I'm meeting someone this afternoon with ties to Stiles."

"Who?"

"His stepdaughter, Charisma Kelly."

He nodded in recognition. "The atheist."

"It would help"—my mind raced over how easily we all get labeled: Kelly the atheist, Harker the informant, Malone the dump—"if I knew what you know."

"Anything else?"

"You mentioned a document on the phone."

"Have it right here." He reached under a pile of newspapers, pulled out an envelope. "A photostat of a bill of sale for a home in Florida. Stiles purchased it six months ago."

I opened the envelope, took out the stat.

"Henry went down a number of times during the past year," Harker was saying. "Apparently he liked what he saw."

The house had been fully paid for, and delivered empty with a warranty of title. The price was $200,000.

"Except his salary didn't allow for that kind of savings."

I said, "His wife won a negligence case five years ago."

"With which they bought a house in town, among other things. Oh, yes, a place down here, too." He didn't sound happy about that. "Not Sea Bright, of course," he said quickly.

"So Florida couldn't have come from her."

"Not a chance. Six months ago they had very little in the bank—I already checked."

I sat there thinking it paid to know the right people, especially in Jersey City where anything else was wrong.

"Which means he bought the house with money he didn't have."

"Or shouldn't have," I said.

"So where did he get it?"

"Suppose you tell me." I replaced the photostat in the envelope. "You've gone this far."

Harker sighed, formed the words almost against his will. "A payoff, what else?"

"From where?"

His hands carved shapes in the air. "You ask me to check on someone for you. I already knew about Florida, that's part of my job to know those things. But I can't pin it to anything, money like that, there are ways to weasel it. Besides, nobody's out to wreck anyone, not from the inside. Not unless you have to, and even then you always do it through an outsider. That's politics. You understand?"

I nodded.

"Then you come along and I make some quick checks and now I sit here and tell you what you want to know. I tell you because you're an outsider." He paused. "You still understand?"

I nodded again.

"Good."

He took off the hat once more, wiped his brow, put the hat back on, and offered me the funnies.

"That's all?" I squeaked.

"Unless you want to tell me where you think the payoff came from. But frankly, I'd rather not hear."

"Not even my client's name?"

"I already know your client's name." The smile was not benign. "It's Cooper Jarrett."

"Then I assume you know that Stiles was instrumental in getting the Harbor Terminal deal for Jarrett."

"I do."

"And you know that Stiles knew Charles Weems, who worked for Jarrett before he got killed."

"I do."

"And you know Weems used to work for the county machine until some money disappeared."

"I do."

"Do you also happen to know how much money was stolen?"

"Wasn't it about two hundred thousand dollars?"

I was intrigued. "No connections?"

"Not unless you find them."

"If I do find them," I said in a daze, "Stiles may not be the only one to go down."

"Indeed?"

"Jarrett could take the fall too."

"Your own client?" His eyes showed amusement.

I ignored the barb, hurled one of my own. "A big developer like that. Don't your people care?"

Harker laughed. "Would you believe the list of developers waiting to come in?"

"But Cooper Jarrett is a local boy."

"Cooper Jarrett is a willful man."

Translation: He was out of favor.

I suddenly felt like an innocent in the face of evil. Or was it just a romantic in a realist's world?

"I hope you won't be offended if I say you're a cold bastard."

"And I hope you're not offended if I say I hope you're the same."

On the way back to the city I totaled up the score. Weems had his love slave steal the county money and give it to him, since the slave was found broke in Detroit. Weems then went into business with Jarrett, using the $200,000 to buy in. One percent would be about right in a company pushing $20 million three years ago. Neither man could afford to have the stolen money show up on the books, so it was used to bribe Stiles.

A perfect scheme. Weems got a piece of the action, ostensibly for his managerial talent in lieu of investment funds. And Jarrett got the Harbor Terminal deal. All he had to do was make sure Weems's one percent remained in his control.

So why was Weems murdered? And how did Stiles fit in?

Before I left, Harker told me the price of his help. "Remember that everything you learn, and everything that results from what you learn, came about through your own investigative abilities. Nobody downtown helped you in any way. In fact"—his smile could've melted water—"we never even heard of you."

"But if you want Stiles out—"

"Want him out! Are you mad? Henry Stiles"—his frown could've carved stone—"is one of my dearest friends, and among the most capable public servants in municipal government today."

That's politics, plain as a tiger's tooth.

"You understand?"

Suddenly I longed for the company of killers.

# eighteen

WE STOOD ON TOP of the mountain with the world at our feet while I waited for the devil to tempt me. No harm in listening.

"I did not lie to you," Charisma Kelly said, "then or now."

"Same thing. You evaded the truth about a hell of a lot."

"That's not the same."

"But the result is, and that's what counts."

"No, it's the intent that matters." She shook her head for added emphasis. "I had no intention of deceiving you."

"But in the process, I was deceived."

"Not by me."

I wasn't going to have this conversation. "I'm talking facts and you want to talk philosophy."

"Facts come from philosophy."

"They come from what people do."

"Based on what they believe." She smiled as to a student. "That's called philosophy."

"Call it whatever you want," I said evenly, "but the fact is she wasn't your mother and you knew it."

"Yes, I knew."

"She didn't even adopt you and you knew that, too."

"Yes."

"Thank you," I said with heavy sarcasm. Women were a pain in the ass, most of them. Some, anyway. Especially this one. While she debated how many angels sat on the head of a pin, I was trying to learn where the pin came from.

"Now that you know I'm an orphan," Charisma said defiantly, "does it help us any? Does it solve anything?"

"It solves the lies," I snapped. "Sorry, evasions. That's something."

"Is it?"

I looked at her. "At least there'll be no more blind alleys."

"Your facts will take their place."

"The truth will, hopefully."

"Your truth."

"You do remember the truth," I said. "It's what you've been seeking all your life."

"Hopefully, as you say."

"And the truth is your 'mother' couldn't have children and being a good Catholic fanatic, she saw no reason for sex. In fact, she probably did it only to keep a man around."

"Probably."

"For money."

"Not money."

"What then?"

"Protection."

"Protection from what?"

"From God."

I stared at her.

"From her vengeful and unmerciful God." Charisma shuddered against a gust of wind. Below us the roofs of Hoboken gleamed in the sun while across the river the New York skyline glistened like gold. Baghdad on the Hudson, someone had called it, meaning all the riches of the world. But the devil wasn't making me an offer.

"Why was she so afraid of God?" I heard myself say. But even as I said it—

"You were a Catholic. Can't you guess?"

—I heard the voice and knew I was in the presence of great evil.

"Jesus." I wet my lips.

"Even he couldn't save her."

"The sin—"

"—was too big for her to bear. She wanted to die for the death she'd caused others."

"Death?"

"Of the heart, yes."

"But not murder," I said mechanically.

"There are more ways to kill than with a gun, and hers was the worst."

"She never knew the woman?"

"My real mother?" Charisma shook her head. "She never even saw her. One minute I was in a baby carriage and then I was gone."

"The next day—"

"There was no next day. By then she was far away with me in her arms. Everything else she blocked out, all the facts."

"But not the guilt."

"No, not the guilt," Charisma said softly. "That was too strong for a woman of her faith. She felt the guilt for thirty-five years, but she couldn't kill herself because that was an even greater sin."

"Eternal damnation," I recalled.

"Now you see why I know she didn't commit suicide."

I closed my eyes and saw the face of God and heard the voice of the devil. Only I couldn't seem to separate the two. Someone offered me death if I stayed.

"You believe she was murdered now, don't you?"

We stood at the edge of the park high on the Jersey City bluff, a thin strip of green in an endless sea of gray. Nearby were a few swings where kids waited their turn amid squeals of joy, unaware of what lay ahead. I felt sorry for them.

"When did she tell you all this?"

"Five years ago, when she won the negligence suit. It was the only good thing ever happened to her and she thought maybe God was ready to forgive her."

"But he wasn't."

"I told her I never wanted to see her again. The next week I began Christians Anonymous."

So fate gave the wheel one more turn for Mrs. Stiles. And sealed her doom.

"Why is any of this important?"

"Do you know if she told her husband about you?"

"She did."

"He knew there were no legal ties?"

"Yes."

Which meant Stiles knew his stepdaughter couldn't inherit anything without a will, and there was no will. But why did he marry seven years earlier when his wife had nothing?

"What about the negligence case? When did that start?"

"Start?"

"Those cases usually take years to run through the courts."

"The accident occurred about eight years ago."

"Before they were married."

Charisma nodded. "Perhaps a year or so. But by then it was in the lawyer's hands."

"They were confident of winning."

"And quickly." She frowned in bitter memory. "I remember them talking in terms of a million dollars. My mother was terribly injured inside, never really the same afterward."

"Didn't you ever wonder why Stiles would marry an older woman? A woman physically impaired. And who hated sex. Didn't that bother you?"

The daughter shrugged. "I accepted it, men being what they are."

"Unpredictable?"

"Irrational."

"Men?"

"Look for yourself. They conquer worlds for a woman's smile, sleep next to a scorned wife, give mistresses money for quick release. These are not rational acts."

"Neither were your mother's."

"She was in constant pain."

"So are some men." I took a chance. "But I don't think Henry Stiles is one of them."

"You think he killed her."

"It's possible." More than possible. "He gets the house, worth over two hundred thousand by now, and the place down the shore. Not bad."

"But you said he was out of town on business that day."

"With the right money and people, anyone can have a long reach."

"Then he married her for the money."

I nodded. "He listened to the lawyers and a million dollars sounded good."

"But she got only a quarter-million."

"By then they were married, so he waited to see what happened next."

What happened was Cooper Jarrett's bribe and a house in Florida. Plus whatever the Jersey houses brought for his retirement fund. Only his wife stood in the way.

"On the other hand," I said to Charisma Kelly, "he could've got a divorce and taken his share of the property and just left."

"No, he couldn't."

I watched her face, a mask of raging thoughts. Whatever came out now had never even been framed into words.

"My mother was never married before." The voice was a whisper wrapped in defeat. "She drifted in and out of relationships because she needed men for protection, but marriage was for life in her religion. The few men she really wanted never wanted her for long. Sooner or later they all left, all of them."

"Your name—"

"Taken from a tombstone somewhere to get a birth certificate. She invented a father for me to go along with the name—James Kelly, who died of cancer."

"And Henry Stiles?"

"By then she was a middle-aged woman emotionally exhausted, looking only for a safe haven. She married him because he asked her. Whether she knew of his money motives doesn't matter. For her it was for life. She never would've given him a divorce." Charisma inhaled deeply, looked out toward Devil's Island. "She would've died first."

In the playground the children still ran back and forth in raucous good humor, blissfully ignorant of the sleek silver bird gliding in from the northeast on its approach to Newark Airport. All of a sudden I longed to be on a plane headed away, as far away as possible. Maybe some Polynesian island or Mandalay where the flying fishes play. Or even Union City.

On the way back to the car, I asked Charisma Kelly about Charles Weems but she'd never heard of him.

"How about Cooper Jarrett?"

"That's the man who wanted to buy the building we're in."

"Ever meet him?"

She shook her head.

"Who made the offer?"

"Someone named Benziger, a toad."

"When was this?"

"About six months ago."

"You selling?"

"How can I? It belongs to the foundation."

"Which you control."

"I resent that. We have an advisory board with strong—"

"You selling?"

She looked like she was going to sulk. "No, we are not."

"Good," I said. "What about Kassam?"

"We're not selling him either."

"How long's he been with you?"

"Almost a year. Why?"

"Any trouble with him?"

"Should there be?"

I shrugged it off. "What's he do for you?"

"Ali is very quick and very bright. He looks after our interests."

"He manages you."

"He does whatever needs to be done."

"Does that include suppression of evidence?"

That was the first time I'd ever seen her at a loss for sharp words, for *any* words.

I said, "Your bright boy may be part of a setup to nail you."

"For what?" she managed to squeak.

"Don't know yet," I lied. "Just make sure you don't mention I asked about him."

I knew she would, of course. Which was why I'd brought his name up. If Ali was in with Jarrett, it'd force them into the open sooner. Maybe make a mistake.

"I *demand* to know on what basis—"

"Won't work," I sighed. "I'm not the demanding kind."

Her wind was back. "I hired you, Malone!"

"To find what happened to your mother. That necessarily includes protecting your interests."

"Yes, but—"

"Which is what I'm trying to do." We were on the way back to the ashram.

"I only meant—"

"Now since you don't like cars or country, let me concentrate on my driving so I can get you safely to the city, which is up the next block."

That shut her up. Women always like forceful men.

"Why did you say good before?" she asked the next moment.

"Did I say good before?"

"When I said we weren't going to sell the building. I thought you hated us."

"Must be I like buildings."

Her laugh was harsh, as if seldom used. "You're not so tough as you pretend."

"Neither are you."

But she was right about one thing: There was something wrong with me. I was beginning to feel sorry for her again.

# nineteen

BERNIE DIDN'T LIKE MY idea.

"It's not I think you're wrong so much. Just that you're nuts."

"Look at it this way," I tried again. "Stiles decides to get rid of his wife so he can get the two houses. The one here is worth double what they paid five years ago. You know what's happened with real estate in the city."

"You telling me."

"Same with down the shore. Say he gets three hundred thousand for them, that's his nest egg in Florida. Maybe he wants to buy a business. Meanwhile he makes his deal with Jarrett and gets another two hundred thousand for the home he buys down there. Now he's all set."

"Why's he wanna leave?"

"Why does anyone leave?" I said, exasperated. "He's pushing fifty, wants to get some sun. And he knows they're gunning for him downtown."

"Are they?"

"Just a matter of time."

"That's straight?"

"He's a political hack, for chrissake. Part businessman, sure, but he's got no real power base of his own. He sees the handwriting and then he sees a way out."

"The Jarrett deal, and knocking off his wife."

"That's it."

Bernie rubbed his jaw. "How's he get the Harbor Terminal to Jarrett? Stiles ain't head of the redevelopment agency."

"But he does most of the preliminary work. They use his figures to designate a developer for a site, and the contract then locks the developer into a specific proposal."

"So?"

"So have you ever known a developer to come up with a losing proposal?"

"It's happened."

I shook my head. "Very rare. Once he gets the designation, he's got the deal."

"Okay. Jarrett's got the deal and Stiles has two hundred grand. What about his wife?"

"Could be she was part of the deal—the cash and getting rid of her."

"You say Weems was part of it, too."

"The bribe money came from him, and he had to be the middleman between Jarrett and Stiles. They knew each other, don't forget."

"Weems and Stiles."

"Jarrett set it up and Weems delivered."

"And you think that's why he was killed."

"It wasn't a sex job, even the Homicide boys know that. I told you I already had a session with them."

"But you didn't tell Harwood any of this."

"I didn't know it then. Besides, they always want proof."

"I wonder why." Bernie stared glumly at his desk, piles of paper scattered everywhere. He liked Alaska because they never wrote anything down, said he'd read it was too cold for the ink to flow. And he thought *I* was crazy.

"Why tell me?" Bernie said. "I'm just a local dick. The prosecutor's squad handles homicides."

"But not Mrs. Stiles. To them she's just a suicide."

"Me too."

"Except they're connected, don't you see? If I'm right about the Jarrett deal, then I'm right about Stiles. And that makes his wife's death suspicious as hell."

"You think it's the same two guys knocked off Weems?"

"Could be."

"And you figure Jarrett's behind it."

I nodded.

"Why Weems?"

"To shut him up about the deal with Stiles."

"After a whole year?"

"I think the phone calls were getting Weems rattled. The day I met him he was scared, said he didn't think something like this would happen. I believe he meant the calls. Which tells me something was preying on his mind. Then when I find out him and Stiles were buddies . . ."

Bernie wasn't buying it. "There's a big hole in your idea."

"Where?"

"The Harbor Terminal deal was made, what, a year ago? Can you see Stiles dealing to have his wife knocked off, and then telling Jarrett to wait a year?" Bernie raised an eyebrow. "C'mon, Malone."

He had me there. Nobody contracts for a hit a year away. "Maybe Stiles got the killer himself," I said. But my heart wasn't in it. Instinct told me it was Jarrett. So did logic, even with all the holes.

"Stiles works in an office. Where'd he get to meet killers?"

"How about on the way home?"

"Another thing," Bernie said. "Why'd they wanna make her a suicide?"

I was ready for that one. "Suicide cancels the insurance her daughter would get. Jarrett wants Charisma Kelly broke because she owns a building he's after."

"Then why take the gun away?"

"To throw suspicion on her. Jarrett hoped you would arrest her for removing evidence—that way she'd lose public support and be forced to sell him the building. He was trying for two deals with one kill."

"Except for the fact that nobody waits a year."

"I admit it slows me down."

"Wipes you out," Bernie grunted. "Anyway, why would Jarrett hire you if he's behind everything?"

"To cover himself."

"A bloodhound like you? Makes no sense."

"Could be he's an egomaniac."

"Sounds more like one of them *Columbo* fairy tales on TV."

"There's another possibility," I said. A thought that was

beginning to bother me. "Suppose Jarrett's really worried about the phone calls he's getting? That's what he hired me for, after all."

"What's your point?"

"I've been seeing Jarrett in everything. But sometimes everything isn't—well, *everything*. Suppose someone else is in the game? Hiding behind a mask. Someone we can't see."

"Like who?"

I shrugged, unsure. "Probably just my diseased imagination. You think I'm diseased?"

"I think you're nuts."

"Prove it."

"I knew it." Bernie slapped the desk. "I knew all this was leading straight to me."

"Brains and beauty," I chirped. "Who could resist—"

"Stuff the soap. I'm not there."

"Not even to catch a killer?"

"That's Homicide's job. Get Harwood."

"He's not my type."

"Neither am I all of a sudden."

I studied him carefully, the eyes. "Downtown doesn't care about Jarrett, same as Stiles." Saw them waver. "Your pension's safe."

The eyes went flat. "That's raw, even from you."

"There's bigger fish coming in," I pressed. "Jarrett's seen his best days here. I'm telling you he can't hurt you."

"But he can still hurt you. Give it up."

"If I'm right about him, he's finished."

"And if you ain't?" The frown got bigger. "He's got money and money's power around here, around anywhere. He'll get your ticket lifted. Then you'll be the one finished."

I shrugged. "Nobody gets to be a cowboy forever."

Bernie shoved his chair back, pushed himself up. "What is it with you? You got a death wish or something?"

"Something," I said.

"A guy hires you for a job and you're looking to stick him."

"I don't like to be used."

"You're sure that's what's going on."

"I'm sure."

He came around the desk and shoveled some papers away

from a corner. "I seen a picture of his ex-wife a while back." Sat on the edge. "Pretty woman."

"And you're a dirty old man."

"Reminds me a lot of your wife." He caught my surprise. "You showed me a snapshot one time."

I closed my eyes to shut him out but I was no different. We all watched everything, and filed it away.

"In that locket you always carry?"

My hand was already in the pocket clutching the locket, my last connection to the past.

"Only you never told me how she died."

Like a steer in a slaughterhouse, I heard myself scream.

"She was killed in a mugging," I wheezed. "Stabbed to death."

"And the guy?"

"They never found him."

"You did all you could." The voice was softer than I'd ever heard it.

"Everybody did," I said.

"But it still bothers you," Bernie said. "The one that got away was the only one that mattered."

"Something like that."

"Doesn't help it was a random killing, the hardest to clear."

"No," I admitted, "it doesn't help."

Bernie picked some lint off his pants. "Now you meet Jarrett's ex, the same type. Reminds you of the past. You feel something for her."

"Not like that."

"All right, not that. But she's in trouble, needs help. Maybe you can help her this time. Maybe you can save her, get whoever's out to harm her."

I looked away, my mind a blank. A piece of me was missing, caught in a time warp. I was trying to get back.

"You gonna help me, Bernie?"

He shuffled back to his chair, slumped down. "What you want me to do?"

I said a silent prayer to Saint Jude, patron of lost causes.

"Remember you told me about Stiles phoning Weems the night he was killed?"

"Sure."

"Harwood's already questioned him about the call. Stiles said he met Weems at a party and they went out for dinner occasionally, nothing more. Claims it was strictly social."

"What else could he say?"

"But if Weems was the bagman for the deal, they probably got to know each other a lot better than that. In fact"—I tried to look more confident than I felt—"I think Stiles was at the sex parties in Weems's house."

"What sex parties?"

I told him about Marko Bay's information. "The talk was four or five of them. I think Stiles was the fifth man."

"Stiles a fag?"

"More of a voyeur. His wife told her daughter they seldom had sex but whenever they did, he brought out a big dressing mirror near the bed so he could look at himself. It drove her crazy."

"So he likes to watch it."

"So maybe he watched it at Weems's house."

Bernie grew quiet.

"Maybe he liked it so much he even took pictures."

"Pictures?"

"Those people like to keep photos, to look at them. If Stiles didn't take any, maybe Weems's love slave did. Or maybe"—I sucked in air, let it out—"we could convince Stiles that someone did."

"We?"

"You."

Bernie groaned, turned to the window, swiveled back. "You want me to go to Stiles and tell him we got shots of him in an *orgy?*" He was ready to cry. "It'd be my badge."

I shook my head. "Just say you received a tip that there were nude photos of him in what seems to be Weems's house. That should do it."

"What kind of tip?"

"An anonymous call. You wondered if he knew anything about that."

"What if he goes screaming to Harwood?"

"Then you say it must've been a practical joker who called."

"And your whole theory goes down the tube."

I nodded. "But if he doesn't scream, I'm right. He'll run to Jarrett, scared and angry."

"What'll that do?"

"I'm trying to shake them up so they make a mistake."

"Jesus," Bernie swore, "you are unfuckingbelievable. If I didn't already know you were nuts, I'd swear you were crazy. Of all the stupid-ass schemes I ever heard."

"But you'll do it."

"Absolutely."

When I got to the office, Selma was her same sweet self.

"You're fired," she snapped.

"I'm the boss. You can't fire me."

"Not me, you dummy. Your client."

"Charisma Kelly?"

"Cooper Jarrett. He phoned twice."

"What he want the second time?"

"To confirm it." She rolled her eyes. "What will we do now?"

"I thought you said we had enough cases."

"That's when we had too many. Now we got too few."

Women used a logic that wasn't human. Or at least not male, which was the same thing.

"What else?"

"Some degenerate named Felson called." Her brows arched. "Does he always chew bubble gum?"

"He just sucks his hand a lot. What he want?"

"Said to tell you Charles Weems's one percent didn't show on most records because it was nonvoting."

"That's past tense," I said.

"What is?"

"Was."

"He was dead, isn't he?"

I could see the headline now: Charles Weems, Still Dead After a Week. "Who gets his one percent?"

"Who knows?"

"Jarrett," I swore. He'd never give up any more of the company. Probably had a reversion clause in case Weems died, and gave him the same. Only Cooper Jarrett had no intention of dying.

"Get him on the phone," I barked.

"Who?"

I looked at the headlines again: Weems Still Not Alive After Two Weeks.

"Whoever's left."

I went into my office and pulled the other dummy out of my chair. He looked enough like me to fool someone across the street with a rifle and telescopic lens. Whenever I was out, the inflatable double sat in my seat with the blinds open. Now he sat in the corner like Little Jack Horner. The blinds were closed.

"Mr. Jarrett?"

"You're fired."

"Any reason?"

"You shoulda told me about Weems making a tape of his calls. Now the cops think I lied, makes me look bad."

"So why'd you lie?"

"So I forgot. Who remembers calls?"

"What about the calls you do remember, like to your office? Aren't you worried about them anymore?"

"Fuck off."

I held the dead phone and considered the possibilities. There was only one. He'd hung up.

"If he made the threatening calls himself," I told my dummy double, "who was he trying to scare? He'd already planned on getting rid of Weems."

"Then it was someone else," said the dummy.

"Who?"

"Whoever knew the office routine and the private numbers."

"Someone inside," I hissed.

"Of course, you dummy."

I pumped six slugs into myself with my finger, listened to the gas escape. Releasing tension, like they say.

After that I played with the mail. A lost love I never knew had a tape of heavy breathing for me. Only twenty dollars, thirty for extra heavy. There was nothing for lightweights and they took only cash. You waited by the door for the mailman.

Another said, "This could kill you." When I opened the envelope, a dead fly fell out.

On the bottom of the pile was still another puzzle from

Jill the Slasher, who sent me nude photos of herself sliced to pieces. I was supposed to sort them out, which wasn't easy since she was a better slasher than model. The real puzzle was who took the pictures.

"You're just a carbon copy."

"A clown," I said.

"That's clone."

I shot him again, two in the pants and once around the room, and went back to my reading. Nobody likes to be corrected.

"You can't kill me, dummy."

"I need the practice."

"I'm taking over soon."

"You can take over now."

Or maybe it was Jarrett after all, after his ex-wife. Hoping she'd scare enough to sell out.

If the slugs in Weems matched the one in Mrs. Stiles . . .

I was out past Pluto when the phone pulled me back.

Harwood.

They had the ballistics report on Weems.

# twenty

I FOOLED AROUND THE office another half-hour, just to show them I wasn't anxious. It's never good to give Homicide the upper hand, they'd go right for the arm. Instead I made some calls I didn't need and took some I didn't want. The last was from Laura Jarrett.

"How are you?" she breathed heavily.

Anal regression kept me from telling her, or maybe it was common sense. "Where are you now?"

"At work. I wanted to thank you again for the other night, saved my life."

I made some deprecating noises. "Any more calls?"

"Not yet."

"Expecting them?"

She laughed. "Guess I'm still jumpy."

"You said there were at least two different voices. Could you be mistaken?"

"Definitely not. Two, maybe even three."

"Recognizably different."

"Totally."

She breathed some more and then vanished right before my ears. I didn't tell her Jarrett fired me. No use breaking her heart.

On the way out I told Selma not to expect me back till late. Late for her meant one minute after five. Well, I had a key, didn't I?

"Leaving a poor old woman with all this." She bobbed her head in misery.

"All what?"

"This whole office."

The office was two rooms stretching sixty feet if you counted all four walls and the ceiling. I had to lean out the window to water the plant, which was near the door.

"Just like a man," she sighed, "running out."

Men were always running out on Selma. She'd already buried two of them.

Lunch was over by the time I got to the end of Duncan Avenue. I'd skipped it. Two steps out of the car and my lungs filled with smoke from an underground fire that'd been burning for forty years. Who needed food? Inside, the stale air felt refreshing as I hurried to Harwood.

He was waiting in the office with Gershon, who would've waited in anything. Green pants and an orange turtleneck didn't help. Harwood was more conservative. His mohair jacket caught most of the ash from his cigarettes and what little fell all the way was quickly crushed by his black sneakers. The lieutenant had bad feet.

"Any better?" I said, pointing.

Harwood looked down and back to me. "You into floors?"

"Only female floors," I said over his bad humor. "This one's male."

"How can you tell?" Gershon said.

"It's cement. Wood floors are female, they bend."

"You ever try to bend an oak?"

"You ever stick it in cement?"

"Heard about Jarrett," Harwood cracked. "Why'd he can you?"

I made a face. "You birds cracking off about the Weems tape. Says I should've told him."

"Why didn't you?"

"I wanted to hear his answer."

"So now you heard."

"Got anything on him?" Gershon said. "We don't like his answer either."

"Anything comes up I'll call you."

Harwood sneered. "Call your girlfriend. We're getting screwed enough."

The prosecutor's squad worked out of the Public Safety Building at the edge of the Hackensack River, a narrow band of turgid water that wandered like the Parisian Seine. Eighteen investigators covered the county, but Harwood could've covered the state.

"We also hear you're friendly with his ex."

"You must have friends in New York."

He shrugged. "They asked about you."

"Nice to be popular," I admitted.

"They said you should stay on this side."

I held the smile. "Ever hear the one about the woman who was murdered and then made to look like suicide?"

"Sounds familiar," Gershon said. "Whatever happened to her?"

"She was murdered."

"Was that before she committed suicide or after?"

"During," I sighed. "A .357 Mag."

Harwood shook his head. "Must be someone else. We're pushing .38 Specials this week."

"The hell you say."

"The hell we don't."

"Weems?"

Harwood nodded to his partner. "Tell him the bad news."

"Two .38 slugs in the head," Gershon said. "Didn't need anything bigger."

"They were big enough." Harwood took a deep drag so that he looked like a dragon breathing fire. "You gonna cry?"

Gershon said, "He don't look so good, Al."

Harwood rubbed his jaw. "Aw, he can take it. Malone's as tough as they come."

"Only when you're not around," I said. "What else the slugs tell you?"

Gershon frowned. "One's not worth shit, banged up too much, but the other's still got good markings. If we find the gun, we'll be able to make a match. You know where it is?"

"I'm working on it."

"You hear that, Al?" He glanced over at Harwood. "He's working on it."

"Yeah, working."

"Weems was my responsibility," I said.

"Only Jarrett fired you," Harwood needled. "Now all you got is a suicide you're trying to push into the murder column."

"Where it belongs."

"What's the motive?"

"Money."

"Why not love?" Harwood jeered. "May as well cover everything."

"All right, make it love. There's a thin line between love and money anyway."

He waved a hand at Gershon. "Nuts. What I tell ya?"

"When we want to read of deeds done for love of money," I misquoted someone, "where do we turn?"

"To you." Dripping with sarcasm.

"To the murder column," I said.

"You don't say." Gershon tapped a pencil on the desk. "How about the murder gun? You bring it with you?"

"I'm working on that, too."

"The man's full of work."

"Full of something," Harwood growled. "Won't it be a lot easier to just ask your girlfriend for it?"

"My client doesn't have it."

"So she got rid of it."

"River's handy, right?"

"Only for fish."

Harwood said, "We could pick her up now for removing evidence, maybe even accessory."

"To a suicide?"

"Don't be dumb. Helping a suicide could lead to a homicide charge."

"Then you'd have your murder," Gershon said.

"And you'd have trouble."

Gershon rambled on right over me. "Constance Elizabeth Kelly. Born in Philadelphia 1950 to Elizabeth and James Kelly. Blue eyes, blond hair."

"Blond," I said.

"Yeah, that light stuff—you know, not dark?"

"So she bleaches it now, better for her image as the devil."

Harwood said, "What I say before? Nobody's as tough as Malone."

"Quick, too," said Gershon.

"What quick?" I snapped. "They all bleach it today."

"They all bleach their eyes, too?"

"Eyes?"

"Blue. Hers are brown."

"Didn't you notice?"

"Depends on the light," I shot back. "Look what happened at birth, they saw them as blue."

Gershon sighed, "You're right, Al. Malone's too tough for me."

"Me too."

"Okay," I said, "she's not the one on the birth certificate. I wouldn't try to kid you guys. Her so-called mother couldn't have children, you know that, so when she expropriated a baby she needed an identity." I spread my arms. "What's the big deal?"

"What's he mean, expropriate?"

"That's like transfer," Gershon said, "when you take something—"

"Shut up, Harry." Harwood turned his eyes on me, steel balls cast in black. "You wanna tell us about it?"

I didn't but I did. There was nothing else to do.

"Withholding evidence of a kidnapping," Harwood barked. "I could have your license for that. And book you besides." His voice rang with anger.

"It happened thirty-five years ago," I blustered.

"So what?"

"So she blocked out everything but the guilt. When she finally told Charisma, she couldn't even remember where it was she grabbed the kid."

"You say."

"Don't be an asshole, Harwood. The woman lived in hell most of her life for what she did. Now she's dead, which is all she wanted anyway. Why put the daughter through the same hell? Charisma Kelly had nothing to do with it. What would it help now?"

"It would set the record straight."

"What record?" I argued, my voice rising. "The kidnapping's long forgotten, the parents might even be dead. The criminal's dead too. Who benefits?"

"The law."

"The *law*"—I was angry myself now—"is supposed to protect as well as punish. And there's no one left to punish." I got up and walked around the chair, anything to stop shaking. "Did you get that?" I bellowed. "There is no one left but the victim!"

"You're left," Harwood shouted. "You should know better."

"Then nail me and keep her out of it."

He jumped up. "Don't tell me what to do."

"What the fuck," Gershon said. "You two kill each other and Darth Vader goes free." He stared out the window. "Who's gonna save the earth?"

Harwood scowled, reached for another cigarette. "What do you know about Darth Vader?"

"I read, don't I?"

Harwood inhaled, blew out streams of smoke. "It's a fucking movie," he said.

"So I listen to the words. Same thing."

"You're as dumb as the Galahad Kid here." He walked around the desk, faced me. "What's this girl got?"

"She's got nothing," I said, the voice fairly even. I was losing the shakes. "That's why I'd like to protect her if possible."

"Why'd she hire you? The real reason."

"She wants her mother buried in a Catholic cemetery."

Gershon said, "I can understand that."

"And he's a Jew," I pleaded.

"Yeah," said Harwood. He was a Catholic cop, meaning he went to church on Christmas and the feast of Saint Joseph, the cops' patron saint. "What about the insurance?"

I shrugged. "She was named the beneficiary. If I can prove it's murder, she'll probably collect."

"Does she care?"

"It wasn't her motive for calling me," I answered carefully.

Harwood grunted. "I won't be a party to fraud."

"I already told the insurance company she's not related, not even adopted. There'll be no fraud."

"All this is academic," Gershon said impatiently, "unless you're able to prove murder."

"Back where we started," I said, sitting down.

"The Weems murder," Harwood huffed at his desk, "and the Stiles suicide"—he emphasized the word for my benefit —"are not connected as far as we're concerned. Each was obviously killed with a different gun, one a .357 Mag and the other a .38 Special. Jarrett would be a suspect for the Weems job except he's got a good alibi, other people were with him at the time."

"Which doesn't mean he didn't get help," I pointed out.

"We're always hoping for proof," Harwood said sarcastically, "or even a lead. Meanwhile, we're also looking into the sex angle just in case."

"And the phone calls to his office," Gershon echoed. "Anything new there?"

"Not yet," I said. Same as Laura Jarrett. A presentiment?

"As for the Stiles suicide," Harwood smirked, rubbing it in, "that's not a concern of this office."

"At the moment," I sniffed, wanting the last word. What the hell, he wasn't Marilyn.

"You're free to go," he said.

"Am I free to stay?"

"Keep it up and you won't even be free to piss."

I gave him the last word. What the hell, he was a lot like Marilyn after all. They both had a nose and two ears.

The rest of the day was shot on errands and paperwork, closing with the car in the inspection station.

"You're borderline," the technician told me.

"Story of my life."

"Better get some work done on her."

"Soon's I can."

"Whenever," he said, "long as it's today."

I failed inspection again.

Back in the office I watched the sun go down with a bottle of Jack Daniel's. Wine for dinner and relaxing, beer on the job, and the hard stuff for all the lonely times in between. What a life. Terrific! Now if only I didn't have any problems.

"If you didn't have problems, you wouldn't be alive," Frank Barnes used to say. "Even worse, if you were alive you wouldn't know it."

Funny how Frank kept coming back over the years, the things he said. Like a good song or the moon dance in *Picnic*.

"All life is trouble, only death is no trouble. Look for trouble—and live."

There were always two glasses with the bottle since drinking alone was the kiss of death. I raised mine.

"Here's to you, Frank."

I swiveled round to the window, sat there in the dark with the blinds open. Now all I had to worry about was the infrared sight on the rifle pointed my way from across the street. I was reaching for my $2,000 night binoculars to find the bastard when the phone rang. If it was him, I'd press the magic button that sent a death ray through the wires.

"Malone?"

"Yeah."

It was Bernie. ". . . just got the call from New York. Was he working for you?"

Not anymore. He'd been shot in the back of the head.

Carl Benziger was dead.

# twenty-one

IN MEDIEVAL EUROPE WITCHES were said to have no souls, so they were presumed to weigh less than normal people of the same size. Weighing stations separated the humans from the demons, and a lot of thin people were murdered because they were a little light, their bodies burned at the stake.

Today the same could be said of the dead.

The medical examiner's office was on First Avenue across from Bellevue. I followed measured feet down empty corridors to view the body. Nobody hurried here and time had no meaning. I half expected to see clocks without hands. Inside the room my guide pulled back the sheet.

I stared at Benziger, smaller in death. The eyelids were protuberant and purple with the blood collected behind them.

"How many shots?"

"One in the head was all it took."

"Meaning the guy was a pro."

"Or just lucky," said the voice at my elbow.

I nodded in relief; at least I wasn't talking to an idiot. New York bulls could be divided in two: those who've seen it all and those who think they have. The good kind remained skeptical of everything.

"Jersey City said he was working for you."

"A tail job."

"Laura Jarrett. Is that her name?"

"Could be just an accident," I said. "Some kid at a window trying out his Christmas present."

"Tell me about it."

I told him all I knew. Which was nothing.

"That's it? Your man was watching the Jarrett woman to see who she met?" He sounded skeptical.

"I'd be lying if I told you more."

"Go ahead. I like stories."

His name was Vergil, a black man who'd taken all the ribbing he could handle over the name. I was too tired to try for new heights.

"Laura Jarrett was getting death threats over the phone. Her ex-husband, too, and another man, who's already been killed. I'm working for her ex."

"In Jersey City."

"He's got an office there. That's where the calls came in. I thought whoever it was might try to get to her over here."

"Where's your client live?"

"Fort Lee, by the Washington Bridge."

"You got someone watching him, too?"

"No," I admitted.

"But his ex works for him."

"She owns half the company."

The eyes went blank. "A family affair?"

"I don't think so," I answered truthfully. "At least not in the usual sense."

"What other sense?"

"I won't know until I find out who's making the calls."

"Ever think it could be your client?"

"You telling me my job?"

He shrugged. "Just seeing if you know it."

I decided against war. He was probably overworked and undermanned. Meaning I might need a favor sometime.

"When's the autopsy?"

"In the morning. Expecting a surprise?"

"Not unless he turns out to be his sister."

Vergil smiled at the thought. "A transsexual P.I."

"Just castrated," I said. "That's what happened to the one I mentioned before."

"Castrated?"

"Probably a fad."

"Not this one." He yanked the sheet off. "See for yourself."

Walking away, Vergil started on a case he'd had a few years back. "This fifteen-year-old punk raped a little girl and the judge told him if he ever did it again he'd be in real trouble." The detective squinted at me. These kinds of things were never repeated to the public. Who'd believe it?

He grunted, satisfied. "Few months later he raped another little girl. Naturally, since he saw the law wouldn't touch him. This time he was sent to a country club for kids—he was sixteen by then—and six months later he was back on the street. Only now the girl's people had bought some justice of their own."

I saw what was coming. "Castrated?"

"They shoved 'em in his mouth before dumping him outside Bellevue emergency room." His smile was a triumph.

"What happened to the buyers?"

"What buyers? We figured it was some maniac."

"New York's full of them," I said helpfully.

He made a face. "Would you believe it? We never caught the guy."

"It's a big town."

"Never will, neither," Vergil said softly. "He's long gone."

I read the official report at the precinct. Benziger had been found slumped over the wheel of his car at 8:20 P.M. by police responding to a passerby who'd noted his condition. The driver's side was away from the curb, with the window down. Death was approximately an hour earlier; the entry wound indicated a .22-caliber slug, point-blank. In the glove compartment police found a .45 pistol, presumably the victim's, not recently fired and—

"You're a slow reader."

"I'm counting the typos."

"Any conclusions?" Vergil asked.

"Seventeen so far."

He gave me a long look. "You thinking of moving here?"

"You making an offer?"

"Only to get out of town. We got enough troubles now."

"Why should I move?" I told him. "They're gonna make

me police commissioner and mayor. Plus Jersey has one-fifth the state tax over here, no city tax, and less crime."

He wasn't convinced. "Maybe you'd like Brooklyn."

"The people are so happy they sing all night."

"Ever hear of Coney Island?"

"You'd love it. They even dance in the streets."

"I can't dance."

Black people have no rhythm. I don't know why that is. Someone stuck a head in the door. "You Malone?"

"I try to be."

"You got a call."

It was Bernie. Cooper Jarrett had attended a political dinner for the upcoming elections.

"Been there since seven."

"Kassam?"

"At a meeting with the atheist and her advisory board. You can scratch him, too."

"Nobody's perfect," I said, and hung up.

"Trouble?" Vergil looked hopeful.

"Nothing I couldn't handle if I were you." I rubbed the bridge of my nose, an excuse for a silent scream. "You mentioned a surprise on the way down here."

He gave a tired smile. "I was thinking of holding you as a material witness. Now I'm not so sure. You'd probably contaminate the others."

"Suppose you tell me what's on your mind."

"You first."

Vergil was even bigger than me, so I told him. "Benziger was taking pictures of everyone going in or out of Laura Jarrett's building. He had twenty years' experience, so the killer must've come up from behind, stuck his gun through the open window, and fired. A .22 doesn't make much noise and it was already dark out."

"Barely."

"The report says about seven-thirty."

"It's not an exact science. Bodies differ."

"We're still on eastern standard. Dark enough."

"Why not a silencer?"

"If it was an automatic, maybe. You find a casing?"

Vergil shook his head. "How was the guy in Jersey killed?"

"Two shots from a revolver."

"You say they were pros."

"All the way."

"Think the killings are connected?"

"Probably not," I lied.

He nodded. "Why was your man taking pictures?"

"I intended to sort them out later, see if anyone familiar pops up."

"This Laura Jarrett a suspect in the other killing?"

"Not at the moment, but I like to know what everybody's doing."

"She could also be in danger."

"Never thought of that," I said with a straight face.

Vergil frowned, sat quietly.

"You just gonna sit there?" I said.

"I'm wearing you down."

"With what? ESP?"

"It's a new technique."

I measured him for a straitjacket. "You thinking of moving to Jersey?"

"Only after I die."

I went back to finishing the report. They'd found a .45 in the glove compartment—locked so it wouldn't be a felony —and $200 in his wallet. On the floor of the passenger seat was an empty camera case.

Empty!

"So that's your surprise," I said in a strangled voice.

"You're not surprised?"

"It's robbery."

"Is it?"

"What else?"

"They didn't take his wallet," Vergil said.

"No time."

He let out a sigh. "Maybe."

"They wanted the camera," I said carefully.

"Or the film."

It was after midnight when I headed home. I made one stop on the way, a call to Laura Jarrett. Her hello sounded drowsy, as if she'd been in a deep sleep. I hung up without saying anything. A silent bed check.

The next thought was my professional liability coverage.

I'd call the agent in the morning to make sure everything was in order, just in case.

Canal was an east-west artery bisecting the isle of Manhattan, deserted now but during the day filled with hawkers and gawkers of every stripe, a commercial street that ran right to the river. If you stood on the wharf looking downtown, you could see a new city growing out of the water. Cancer Rising!

I drove mechanically, my mind brooding on Benziger.

Eventually Canal fed into the tunnel, which emptied in south Hudson County: Jersey City, Bayonne, Hoboken. The county also had a north and a west, but no east, unless the lost land of Atlantis lay under the Hudson somewhere between Jersey City and New York. Those who saw New York as Atlantis called it East Hudson and demanded annexation to New Jersey. Another separatist movement sought statehood for the river itself.

I saw Benziger in the windshield, his features granitic, the kiss of death already on his lips. The little guy was too good to be caught short like that. Whoever did him knew him, at least by sight. Walked up to him smiling, but the smile had teeth. One shot and the film was gone.

Or else an impulse killer who wanted the camera and didn't take the time to search for a wallet. Plenty of those in New York, wounded animals with nothing to lose.

I watched Benziger's face turn into the Easter Bunny. Sometimes I believed anything.

# twenty-two

LINCOLN PARK STRETCHES FROM West Side Avenue to the Hackensack River, 273 acres of condemned land that rises in the east to at least an inch of grass and falls in the west to impenetrable jungle. It's the largest park in the county, which has the fewest parks in the state, but it's home to a lot of wild birds and some very strange animals.

I found two of them seated at a small table whose surface resembled a chessboard.

"Why do you always sit in the same place?" I asked Manny.

"Because it's here."

"But if you go west," I reasoned, "you'd see a whole world of wildlife out there."

Manny looked around us. "It's a zoo up here, too," he snorted. "A regular Ring-a-ling."

"He means circus," said Luther.

Manny and Luther spent the nice days near the park's east end where they could almost see their houses, about a block apart. Both their wives were dead.

"We never go past Lake View Drive," Luther said. "Never even saw the lake."

"There isn't any," I told him.

"I knew it," Manny cackled. "Didn't I tell you the mayor was smart?" He pronounced it "mare."

Legend had it that the Hague political machine set aside a

half-million dollars of county money to build a lake across the highway that cuts through the park. When the state naturally said no, they simply renamed one of the winding roads Lake View Drive instead. Signs pointed to the lake on the other side of the highway but since there were no roads on the other side, no one ever found the lake which was never built.

"Whatever happened to the signs?" I said to Manny.

"I think the city set aside some money to take them down."

"Typical," Luther huffed.

"They're down, ain't they?" Manny argued with unassailable logic. "Nobody was trying to steal anything."

I wasn't going to bring up the half-million for the lake.

"There's that damn squirrel again." Manny pointed, and when Luther turned around he slyly moved one of his chessmen. It did no good. A few moves later Luther beat him.

"I lose on purpose," Manny boasted. "What's a friend for?"

"Did he ever win?" I once asked Luther.

"Never."

"Why do you let him cheat?"

"Can't help it. He has to cheat even to lose."

"I read about Weems," Manny said while Luther set up the next game. "Funny thing, eh? You ask about the guy and right away he's dead."

"Not funny to him."

"You get hurt?" Luther wondered.

"Only my pride."

"Not for nothing," Manny said, "but who you wanna know about now?"

I put on a face. "Can't I ever come to see you just for the joy of it?"

"Sure, sure. The joy."

"You got a suspicious mind," I pouted.

"Comes from all this living."

Nobody spoke for a moment.

"So who you wanna know about now?"

"Henry Stiles," I groaned in defeat.

Manny shook his head wisely. "He'll be dead in a week."

"All I need"—I took a deep breath while Luther tied his shoelace and Manny cheated—"is a line on how he thinks."

"He thinks like all of them think—stay on the pad."

"Suppose he wanted to get off?"

"Then he'd get a bankroll first."

"Could he get it where he works?"

The voice was a sneer. "Ain't that what government's all about? Opportunity?"

"The redevelopment agency?"

"All the same—city, state, or feudal."

"Federal," said Luther.

"That too."

"You know anything about the agency?"

"I know Hague never had none," Manny said contemptuously. "Didn't need it. He ruled this town for thirty years and built everything himself."

"Mostly his bank account," Luther sniffed. "Lived like a king on an eight-thousand-dollar salary."

"Things were cheaper in them days."

"When he retired, the city sued him for fifteen million."

"What'd he do?" I asked.

"He left town."

"That what Stiles gonna do?" Manny said.

I tried to dodge it. "Haven't talked to him yet."

"But you got a good guess."

"It's possible."

"That means for sure," Manny told Luther.

"What's his reputation?" I said.

"A political hack. He was a double dip for a while, worked two city jobs before he got this."

"Looks like he picked the right one," I suggested. "Plenty of redevelopment going on."

Manny's eyes turned sad. "The whole town's changing."

"For the better," said Luther, whose eyes were turned forward.

The next minute Manny cheated twice—getting even!—as Luther picked up a fallen bishop.

I said, "That Caven Point beach area? I think he's working on a project there."

"Caven Point beach?" Luther studied the rearranged board. "That wouldn't be redevelopment, would it?"

"Why not?"

"Nothing's there now," said the retired teacher, "so what could they redevelop?"

"He's right," Manny admitted grudgingly. "That's waterfront. They'd need permits from all the regulatory agencies. And preliminary approval for any new plans."

"Where would a developer go for that?"

Manny nudged me as Luther made his move. "He cheats, but I don't know how."

"Hypnosis," Luther laughed.

I watched as he trounced his chess partner again. "That makes eight million zlots you owe me."

"Forty cents," Manny confided.

"What about new development?" I said. "Who handles plans for that?"

"The city planning board. Who else?"

Manny knocked half the pieces off the table, probably practice for the next game. "You bring me bad luck," he complained.

"To tell you the truth," I lied, "your strategy's way over my head. Where'd you learn to play like that?"

"That's no-show biz!" he bragged.

"He means a no-show job," Luther explained. "Since they didn't have to show up for work, they passed the time in the park playing games."

"That's politics," I said, getting up.

Bufano's Gym was near Pershing Field and on the way I mulled over Manny's information. If Jarrett was working on a deal for the Caven Point beach area, maybe Stiles wasn't involved this time. They'd already done one deal. So why did he call Weems?

When I got there Dancer Fitzgerald was waiting inside. "I like to watch 'em work out," he said as we found a couple of chairs in the corner. "Makes me feel good, you know?"

"Like when you were up there," I said.

"Hey, that's right," he wheezed and slapped my shoulder. "Not so long ago neither."

"Bet you could still go a few rounds with these young punks," I told him.

Dancer laughed. "Until they catch me." But the voice was wistful.

"You used to train here," I recalled.

"Still work out a little," he said, and punched a fist into his palm. "Pow!"

"Sounds good."

"It could still tag a few." He squinted at the boys in the ring. "Word's out you got a line on the two hundred thousand."

"Who told you that?"

"Word gets around," he said mysteriously.

Ray Price's word, a favor to me.

"I think it's connected to the killing."

"Weems?"

"Your people checked him out at the time and found no money. And the one who took it was found dead broke." I glanced at Dancer. "But maybe Weems knew where it was all this time."

"And maybe you're guessing to get help with looking for whoever killed him."

I keep forgetting that people are often dumb but seldom stupid.

"I could use help, sure, but so could you," I said angrily to throw him off-balance. "It's what, three years now and your keepers don't know a damn thing yet. At least I know why Weems was murdered." The men around the ring were looking at us now.

"You don't have to shout," Dancer growled. "I got ears."

"Then help or stop wasting my time." I stood up.

"Hey, don't get sore."

"I don't get sore, just busy."

It was Dancer's turn to sweat. "But why'd they cut his nuts off? Ain't that revenge?"

"That's why," I said. "To make it look like revenge."

"You mean if you get them, we'll get the money?"

"Probably not, but at least we'll know where it went."

He nodded. "Hey, sit down. No kidding. I got something for you." Dancer reached into his jacket as I sat, my eyes on his arm. If it came out with anything but fingers I was gonna break it off his shoulder.

"That's why I called you." He took out an envelope,

handed it to me. "When the dude hung himself in Detroit, the cops sent back what he came in with. Didn't amount to nothing except maybe for these two pictures."

I pulled them out. The first was a photo of two men posing for the camera. Both were almost naked and one of them was Charles Weems.

"That's the one who croaked," Dancer said, pointing to the other man. "He was Weems's asshole."

"He stole the money and left town."

"I don't know the others, just some more fruitcakes he must have known."

I looked at the other snapshot of two men wearing only some sex devices. I'd seen them once before. No, twice. At least the thin one, a silhouette in the dark. I hadn't recognized him but there was something about his walk, a young walk. The older man was taller by a head, and broader.

I was staring at the two nudists on Caven Point beach that first day with Cooper Jarrett!

". . . we couldn't use the picture of Weems to make him open up about the money," Dancer was saying, "'cause we didn't want everyone to know a fruitcake'd been a big shot in the Party. But we kept them anyway, in case something turned up."

I swore at myself, a prize sap. It was there all the time, right in front of me. Jarrett's shooters, who'd killed Weems because he was ready to talk about the deal with Henry Stiles.

So why wasn't Stiles in the pictures? Because he'd taken them. I felt it, knew it. He was the fifth man.

"Think you can use 'em?" Dancer whispered at my side.

"Maybe," I said, and slipped the photos into my pocket. "Let's see what happens."

He gripped my arm. "We're real anxious."

"So am I."

"You'll call me."

"If I have anything to say."

At the door I looked back and saw Dancer shadowboxing his way to the ring, throwing cream puffs right and left. Some dreams die hard.

In the car I took a few big breaths to clear my head. If I had Harwood pick them up, I had nothing. No gun, no positive ID, no case. They'd never talk, and neither would Jarrett. He'd laugh me out of Jersey. Plus there was still Charisma Kelly's mother. If I was right, they did her too.

And there was Carl Benziger, a funny little guy who called women broads and chewed toothpicks and dressed like Halloween. But he was a P.I. just like me, a loner, and I'd sent him out to die.

My hands shook so hard I couldn't even light a cigarette, which was a good thing since I didn't smoke.

The sonofabitch, I kept telling myself. He played me for a sucker from the start.

I patted the pictures in my jacket. Okay, there were many roads to Jerusalem, and some were meant to fall by the wayside. Some would even die.

I gunned the motor and shot down the street in a swirl of smoke.

The Lone Ranger rides again!

# twenty-three

MARILYN HATES IT WHEN I've got the shakes.

"You care too much," she said.

"It was my fault."

"And you always blame yourself."

"Who else is there?"

Marilyn was a metaphiliac who suffered from a consuming search for meaning. More meaning, unfortunately, than existed.

"It was God's will."

"At least."

We sat in her studio drinking coffee made with champagne rather than water, a favorite trick of hers to get me relaxed. Mostly it just got me drunk.

"Did I ever tell you New Jersey has the highest suicide rate in America?"

"No."

"New Jersey has the highest suicide rate in America."

"It could just be accidental."

I studied her over my cup. "How could suicide be accidental?"

"New Jersey's near New York."

Sometimes Marilyn got a little drunk too.

"I'm gonna quit it all," I announced eventually. "The whole game."

"What game is that?"

"A good question," I said, and quickly forgot it.

Marilyn liked to hear about my cases so I told her things, only to help her out.

"He had everything planned for Florida," I said, "a house and all the money he'd ever need."

"Who?"

"Remember I told you about Henry Stiles at the redevelopment agency?"

A foolish question, with Marilyn's memory.

"Only his wife stood in the way."

"Good for her."

I knew my Marilyn didn't mean that.

"So he had her killed."

"I think I'll marry Peter."

"No, really. I just can't figure out how he did it. Jarrett's trying to get something from the city planning board, so he doesn't need Stiles anymore."

"Doesn't this Stiles do the same thing at the redevelopment agency, the same kind of thing?"

"What kind of thing?"

"As the planning board."

"Roughly," I granted.

"So maybe he knows someone there."

They were God's gift to men, women. Marilyn had made the connection I'd missed. Weems was dead and Jarrett needed a new bagman for his new deal.

"That was the payoff," I raved. "He didn't need more money."

"Who?"

"He needed her dead."

"Stiles."

I sat in the corner like Little Jack Horner, a dummy.

"I've lost the touch," I told Marilyn at my side.

"Not with me." She took off the painter's smock and her panties.

Much later I opened my eyes and saw an angel brandishing a sword, a green sword that slithered into a snake. By the time I focused, the snake had become a phone. Marilyn held it, wearing a smile of love.

"Your office," she said.

It was Selma sounding the end of the world. Not tomorrow, right now.

"It's two minutes after five," she warned, "and you're not here."

"I'm here."

"Refreshed, I suppose, parts of you."

"Fit as a fizz."

"You never called in."

"Mellow as a martini."

"You ever coming back?"

"In the morning."

"That soon, huh?"

Holding the phone I felt a surge of power and dialed Ray Price at his paper.

"Kassam."

"Kazoo."

I dialed again.

"Is this the famous Pulitzer Prize journalist I been waiting an hour to get?"

"Lucky to get me at all. Some nut just called."

"What'd he want?"

"An obscene sneezer."

"How about an obscene Arab?"

"Nothing much," Ray said. "The woman was stabbed a dozen times—"

"Stabbed? I heard she was shot."

"Hold on."

I smiled at Marilyn, back to the wolves.

"Got it right here—punctures of the heart, the lungs, the liver . . . then it gets nasty."

"That lets him out."

"Out of what?"

"He must've learned about guns in North Africa."

"Plenty there."

Which meant Jarrett's hold was money. "What else?"

"Nothing, unless being pregnant is something."

"So what's the mob doing these days?" I asked Ray.

"All they can."

Damn, even the Arabs were for sale.

"They take over anything new?"

I decided never to see *Lawrence of Arabia* again.

"Don't have to. They already own fifty percent of you."

Afterward I sat at Marilyn's feet and watched her work, which was only fair since she listened to mine. I really liked what she did, too, especially the werewolves. She had them in boardrooms, as cops, on TV. Werewolves as people in positions of power. They all seemed so . . . *real.*

"But there are no werewolves," I told her.

"Are you sure?"

What a question. Was I sure the moon wasn't made of cheese or little green men didn't live inside the earth? Was I sure there wasn't a hell where sinners would burn forever?

"Of course I'm sure."

"Look again."

I had to admit one of the werewolf cops bore a strong resemblance to Al Harwood. Not the face so much as the body contortions and the *intensity.* And the more I stared at some of the others, the more they began to look like people I'd known.

*"Lycanthropus erectus,"* Marilyn said.

"But there are no werewolves."

Her eyes were patient. "If a person believes he's a werewolf, and gives the appearance of a werewolf, and acts like a werewolf, what have you got?"

"A nut."

"You're a nut," she laughed.

That's when I first learned to like Marilyn. She accepted me for what I was, at least in her eyes. A nut, maybe even a werewolf. Loners on the fringe of society.

But there was no malice or scorn or condemnation.

"If I were a werewolf," I'd said to her, "what would you do?"

"Paint you."

"How?"

Two months later she painted me as the werewolf who stalked the sleeping city, looking for killers who lurked in the dark. A one-wolf crusade against crime. She called it *The Howling* and gave it to me for Christmas.

"It's not only got the higher brain functions working for it," Marilyn said. "It's got pituitary too. There's a lot of passion in that beast."

Naturally I hung it over the fireplace. Since there was no fireplace I had one built, and then had to do the same for the upper two floors.

When Bernie saw it, he asked how much it cost.

"Thousands," I told him truthfully. "It was a Christmas present."

# twenty-four

**A** HOMOSEXUAL HIT TEAM? Don't make me laugh."

Bernie didn't believe me.

"Where you been the last few years? They're like the rest of us now."

"What's that supposed to mean?"

"That means they're like the rest of us now. They bleed when they're cut and piss when they drink."

"And fuck whenever they can."

"Same as you and me, just that we use women and they use each other."

"But a hit team?" His voice rose sharply.

"They kill, too," I said. "Probably caught it from us."

"You know what I mean."

I nodded into his stare. Homosexuals didn't often turn pro, and those who did usually stayed in their own yard. The mob was not an equal-opportunity employer.

"Could be they have special talents," I ad-libbed.

"What talents?"

"They blend in better, put up a good business front. Look at Weems, he had sex parties with them. Jarrett hired them. Maybe they specialize in business deals."

"And maybe you're into fairy tales."

"These guys may be fags," I told Bernie, "but they're no fairies."

"Same thing," he grumped. "You can't find 'em."

I'd spent a couple days watching Caven Point beach and tracking the city's few homo haunts. No sign of them. Since I had no informants there, I decided to open up to Bernie.

"My guess is they're from out of town. Probably Bergen County."

"Why there?"

"Jarrett lives in Fort Lee. Lots of homosexuals up that way."

Bernie leaned back in his chair. "How come you never call them gays, a liberal like you?"

"Liberal? Me?"

"You like women, don't you?"

My eyes shrank to pinholes. "Exactly how do you mean that?"

"I mean you really *like* them."

"They're nice people."

"That's what I mean."

Bernie adored his wife of twenty years, doted on her. He also had three adopted daughters. Yet here he was giving the impression he merely tolerated them. Men were hopeless, I decided. But so were women.

"I don't call them gay," I explained, "because I never saw one who was. Now can we go back to Mutt and Jeff?"

"Why not go to Harwood?"

"He'd find them and lose me Charisma Kelly."

"Still pushing that one," Bernie droned.

"She's my only client."

He made a paper airplane and sailed it across the room. It was a way to whittle down the piles on his desk.

"They're pros, right? And you expect them to use different guns in the killings."

"Happens all the time."

"The gun itself, sure, but—"

"The real pros always get rid of the murder gun afterward."

*"But they don't change calibers."*

I started to say something and thought better of it.

"That's your fatal flaw," Bernie said with a grin. "One .357 Mag and one .38 Special makes two separate hits."

"In the new math, one and one sometimes equals one."

"Tell it to Einstein."

"He's dead."

"So's your idea."

I let it pass. "Stiles didn't scream to Harwood about your tip of his nude photo. Doesn't that surprise you?"

"You don't know he went to Jarrett either."

"He will when he sees that." I pointed to the picture of Weems on the desk.

Bernie shrugged. "There's nothing to tie him to this."

"It'll scare him anyway."

"You hope."

The redevelopment agency was on Kennedy Boulevard. When I got there Stiles ushered me into his office, his face one big frown.

"The only reason I'm seeing you is because my step-daughter is your client. Why I don't know."

"I appreciate that."

He sat at his desk, pencil in hand. "Make it short."

I showed him the snapshot of Weems. "Recognize it?"

"Should I?"

"You took it."

He tapped his pencil on the desk. "The police apparently received a tip about a photo of me. This isn't me."

"You're next."

His smile said he didn't think so while his voice wondered if I was the tipster myself.

I'd lost that round. There were no nudes of Henry Stiles, he was too careful. And nothing to prove he'd taken any. But that wasn't the whole game.

"Here's another photo you took. Let's call them Mutt and Jeff."

One glance wiped the smile off his face for a second. Too late. That round was mine.

"Who are they?" he managed to squeak.

"They killed Charles Weems. Didn't you know?"

He tapped the desk again, much weaker. "Charles Weems was a friend of mine."

"Of course he was." It was my turn to smile. "You even called him the night he was murdered."

"I merely wanted to—"

"You wanted to get together, talk about the new deal you've got with Cooper Jarrett. Maybe get some advice."

"What deal?"

"Caven Point beach. You're the bagman for that, right? Just like Weems was the bagman for—"

"Get out!" The pencil snapped in two.

"It's the city planning board this time, isn't it?" I stood up, leaned over the desk. "How you gonna work it?"

*"Get out!"*

I turned at the door. "You'll want to be careful, Mr. Stiles. Look what happened to your friend."

Outside I was so mad I could eat meat. Jarrett didn't like me poking around so he cut his losses, thinking that was the end of it. There'd been no more calls so who needed me? Two dead and him in the clear, as always.

All the way back to the office I kept thinking about the calls stopping like that. Did it have to do with them being taped? If Jarrett was trying to scare Laura into selling, he wouldn't stop them. This was the right time to get her out, now, before the new deal with Stiles went through.

If it was Jarrett.

"Who do you think it was?"

I always asked Selma the important questions. She had a woman's intuition plus she was older, which made her wiser. Selma liked to think of herself solving murders by proxy—with me doing just the legwork—and she was always thrilled to give me the benefit of her vast knowledge.

"How the hell do I know? Not enough I have to manage this arena and handle the phones and the mail and the weird people coming in all hours of the day, now I'm expected to do the thinking, too, and know what all those crazy people are planning and I suppose the next thing you . . ."

I staggered into my office and shut the door, softly so I wouldn't disturb her answer.

Sometimes you have to put principle aside and do what's right.

Behind the door was the dartboard and I quickly threw three straight bull's-eyes for exercise. Which wasn't hard since the whole board was one big bull's-eye. But it was still a lot smaller than the wall.

By the time Pop Wagner called, I'd thrown twenty-seven consecutive darts. I felt in control again.

"Yeah, Pop."

"You asked me to look into Mark Jarrett for you."

"The son, right. What you find?"

"Pretty much what I'd expected, seeing who he's got for a father."

"Trouble?"

"He's no cowpuncher."

Pop loved the old West, saw himself as a cowboy riding the range. Except the closest he ever got to a horse was Monmouth Raceway.

"Got a sheet on him?"

"A stabbing when he was sixteen, later some assaults and D and D's. Charged with wife beating at eighteen. Jarrett paid her off to get rid of her. The kid liked cars so Jarrett made him a mechanic, same as he was before he took up real estate. When that didn't work he got impatient and had the kid's arm broken to teach him a lesson."

"His own son?"

"What the hell, it worked. Mark saw the light and went to college, then last year he started full-time for Jarrett. The talk is he still shits whenever his old man's around."

"So why doesn't he leave?"

"Too much money, I suppose. And Jarrett keeps him out of trouble, probably paid off plenty over the years for the young punk. There's all kinds of rumors."

"What about now?"

"They say the kid's settled down this past year on the job. Even Jarrett's impressed. They say he's showing paternal feelings." Pop laughed. "Sooner trust a snake."

"How about the kid?"

"Like snake, like son."

The rest of the day was downhill and the night was no better. While Marilyn worked the exhibition circuit, the TV played laugh tracks. I sat in my living room and watched the static, me and Jack Daniel's. In the morning I threw out the empty and took a shower and toasted a bagel, topping it with cheese that looked green and smelled blue. My coffee was the usual black hole from which no light escaped.

Afterward I found clothes I hadn't worn since yesterday and went to the service. It was billed as a funeral but was really a burning and I stood in the parlor and waited for Benziger's body to go up in smoke. They liked to do a cremation early so it didn't mingle with all the other things burning in the city.

I couldn't help thinking of the witches. Benziger's soul had left his body when he died, so he looked smaller in death. Now he was being burned at the stake.

"He wanted it this way," said his sister, who sounded unconvinced. She was a cripple from Kansas, had taken two days to get here. "Carl never liked earth, couldn't stand the thought of lying in it."

We were the only two at the service, unless you counted the paid mourners who handled the transubstantiation. I recognized one, a night bartender up the street.

The all-denominational minister read the eulogy for the all-dead. It held no surprises, a good man gone before his time because God called him.

In all of religious history, no one had ever been called by the devil, and death was the ultimate reward for living.

"Dust to dust—" intoned the minister.

Before the ceremony I took a last look at the body, but I'd seen too many of them. The man had changed from flesh and blood to a stuffed animal. Was that the loss of the soul? I couldn't seem to leave the myths of my youth. Or were they the reality and death the dream?

"—and ashes to ashes."

During the Inquisition they pulled people apart in search of the soul. Now I sought those who did the pulling. Yet I wouldn't exist without them.

"He feels no more pain," I comforted his sister. A priest tending his flock.

"Amen," said the minister.

The service was over.

"We'll wait in the office for the ash."

Almost over.

"Your body's worth nearly two hundred thousand dollars," Dorsey once told me.

"Only to a pathologist," I'd laughed.

"No kidding. The blood in your veins goes for twelve hundred at a hundred-fifty a pint charged by blood banks. Then there's five thousand dollars' worth of albumin, a protein, and four thousand of hemoglobin, a blood substance."

"That's only ten thousand."

"Did I mention a hundred grand for the myoglobin, which circulates oxygen in muscle? And forty thousand worth of blood-clotting substances?"

"So kill me," I said.

"No need for that. We could just drain you to death."

"Drain me?"

"It's the fluids that count," he raved in a Romanian accent.

Children of the night!

"If you should want a more ornate urn," said the consoling voice to Benziger's sister, "we have them, of course."

"This will do," she replied wisely. "My brother is already in heaven."

"Of course."

I left a vengeful man, and probably doomed to hell. But there was still the devil to pay.

# twenty-five

**I** HEADED FOR HOME again, my mood too fragile for the office. I was sore, and a little scared. From the beginning I'd played the sap for them, made to play the fool. That hurt. I didn't know what I might do.

What I needed now were a few kind words, maybe even a pat on the head. I let it ring six times, which meant she was working. Whenever Marilyn painted in the studio she pulled the plug on the phone, a nasty habit. I thought of going over and breaking the door down. Instead I stretched out on the couch with some Chablis and dreamed I was saying mass, using grape juice for wine because I was an alcoholic priest. When I placed the host on Laura's tongue, she bit my fingers.

The phone saved the rest of my hand. Gershon, to let me know that Ali Kassam had accused Charisma Kelly of taking the suicide gun from beside her mother's body so she'd get the insurance money. How did he know? She'd told him the next day but he was too scared to say anything. Now she could be charged with falsifying evidence.

That did it. I shaved again to draw blood, which always calmed me. Then I laid out my Captain America costume. It was the same suit I'd worn on the way in. Then I reached into the drawer for my nineteen-shot semi and strapped that on and climbed into the Dodgemobile and went gunning for Mutt and Jeff.

Traffic was light on the way to Kassam's hotel, a downtown dive called the Half Moon. Soon the moon would fade away, slated for the wrecking ball as Exchange Place turned into Wall Street. Not that Kassam cared where he was going.

The police knew Jarrett owned the property around Charisma's ashram. They'd been told he wanted to build a big condo development there and needed her lot, but they couldn't make the connection to the Arab's story. Didn't want to make it, afraid of the pressure.

I double-parked next to a truck to hide the car and hurried into the lobby. In the dark I felt my way to the desk.

"A little Arab lives here," I told the dismal clerk.

He wasn't impressed. "Arabs everywhere. They're like *cucarachas.*"

"That's the Spanish-speakers," I said. "This one's called Kassam, which is Arab for Smith."

"Plenty of those, too."

"Know where he is?"

"Is it worth a buck?"

I ripped one in half like you do for the hookers.

"What's this?"

"Fifty cents."

"Try the diner down the block."

I threw him the rest.

"Hey, I got no tape."

"Spend half at a time."

The diner was a blue-plate special that served six meals, all of them the same. I spotted Kassam in a faded red booth that had two holes punched in the wall. The other man looked like he'd done the punching. He had a wide neck between big ears, and his big nose between Ali and me.

I walked past the counter and whispered to a hefty trucker dribbling strings of meat, "Your mother sucks elephants." Then I floated back to North Africa.

"Done just like you told me," I said in a loud falsetto, and squeezed Kassam into the booth and faced the wide neck with the big nose. His eyes were small.

"What's the idea, Bo?"

"I'm taking the Arab with me. You're paid to watch him, but now you've lost him. Maybe you should go into some other business."

"Maybe you should go back to milk."

I saw the trucker rolling down on us and screwed up my voice: "I told you he'd be mad," I swished, and opened my eyes wide at his approach. "Don't blame me," I yelped when he hit the table. "He made me do it." I pointed to Big Nose. "He likes to get fat people mad and then beat them up."

The trucker was set to smash someone but a homosexual was something else. He'd never live it down on the road. With a roar they could've heard in Harlem he swatted Big Nose like a bug, then piled into the booth on top of him as I dragged the Arab out. He was still screaming when I carried him under my arm to the car.

Inside I tossed him on the seat, kicking and clawing. I bent down to push the legs further in and his nails raked my face and I belted him more from reflex than anger but it did the job. The next second I was around the corner and racing for the moon. Half Moon.

His room was on the third floor, a dump. It took me five minutes to pack his clothes in a suitcase and another five to search the place. I didn't know what I was looking for—a big knife, maybe—but it didn't matter. Nothing turned up, not even a roll of bills.

I left the key in the lock on the way out. Kassam wasn't coming back.

In the car again I pulled him onto the seat and removed the gag. He was conscious, but his hands were still tied.

I said, "You're going away."

"So are you," he blustered. "This is kidnapping."

"Not kidnapping," I told him. "Just helping a friend out of a jam."

"You're not a friend," he screeched, "and I'm in no trouble."

"You're in over your head and you don't even know it."

"Let me out." He tried to work the door handle with his knee and I made him sit on his legs. Then I eased into traffic.

"You threw in with Jarrett to ruin your boss so she'd have to sell the ashram." I kept glancing at him. "He wants it and you want money. How much he give you?"

"Nothing!"

"Five thousand at least so you got about two up front. You wouldn't put it in a bank, which means you're holding it."

"You're crazy."

"If I have to search you, I'll keep it all."

That shut him up.

"Now you're gonna run out on Jarrett."

"Why would I do that?" he sneered.

"Because I got something worth more to you than his money."

"What's that?"

"Your life."

He thought that over while I headed north.

"You picked the wrong side," I told him. "Jarrett's taking the fall, soon he won't look so good to you. That's the first thing." I checked to make sure he was paying attention. "The second thing is I don't want the woman hassled. She's been through enough."

"But she's an atheist."

"So are you."

"It was just a job to me," he said.

"That's why I'm giving you a chance to get out while you can."

"What if I don't?"

I took out the pistol and put it against the side of his head and pulled the trigger.

Kassam screamed and almost passed out again.

"That's the only free ride you get," I whispered. "The magazine's full."

Behind us Jersey City was thinning into air as a few trees popped up now and then. I shoved the Steyr back into the shoulder rig.

"I'm offering you freedom along with your life. There's a homicide dick in New York who'd want to talk to you about the murder of another Moslem, a young woman around eighteen. Remember?"

"I already talked to them," he whined.

"Not this one you didn't. He's better than the rest. And there's a lot I could tell him."

"Like what?"

"Like the name Kassam is common in your country,

187

same as Smith and Jones over here. It's often used as a name of convenience. Also there's a fair amount of intermarriage in Moslem villages, where people end up with different names but are still related."

"And so?"

"So if the police checked further, they might find there's more to your name, maybe more to hers, too"—good research always paid off—"or they might even find the two of you were related."

Kassam shrugged. His nerve was coming back now that the pistol was gone. "What if we were? It's no crime."

"But it would change their view of you," I said, "make them check even more. You know about guns, maybe you've killed before—plenty of wars in that part of the world. Plenty of women get killed over there, too. They're just like slaves, right?"

We were nearing Fort Lee; ahead loomed the Washington Bridge. "And the knife, a dagger perhaps. That's your national weapon, it goes with the clothes your people wear."

Thank God for *Lawrence of Arabia.* I made a mental note to see it every six months. Blessings upon Allah.

"Even if she was a relative from the same village," Kassam said heatedly, "that's not a motive."

"And then there's Moslem custom," I sighed. "How could the police know that a Moslem girl who wears lipstick or has a date disgraces her family? Or that it's part of age-old Moslem tradition for male members to kill the offending daughter? To bring honor back to the family, of course."

"That's all changing."

"How could they be expected to know," I continued, "that some Moslem women remove all their pubic hair as a religious ritual? Or that in certain other classes, let's say, it's a sign of debauchery."

"She disgraced her family," shrieked Kassam.

"But I don't think that's why you killed her."

"I didn't kill her."

"I think you killed her because she was pregnant."

We were approaching the ramp to the bridge now. I pulled off at the last exit and cut his hands loose. The bridge was less trouble than the tunnels for when I dumped him in New York, and gave me time to let Kassam see what he faced.

"I don't care myself, but my friend in New York, he cares. He'll break you down till you confess. Even if you didn't do it, he'll nail you for it. It's good for him, another homicide solved." I let that sink in. "I could also turn you loose over there. You've got money in your pocket, go see the world. Disappear. If you set foot in Jersey again, I'll feed you to the shark. His name's Vergil."

"All this," he said, "so I don't testify against Miss Kelly."

I shook my head. "You wouldn't be believed anyway. You can't produce the gun and you have no witnesses. And she didn't put in for the money, so there's no fraud."

"What about falsifying evidence?"

"It's her word against yours. With your background that would come out, who'd they believe?"

"Then why—"

"You still don't get it." The knock in the motor was louder now, a ring job for sure. "I'm giving you a trade. Your freedom for where they are."

"Who?"

I reached into my jacket and Kassam cringed, started babbling. Probably prayers to the Ayatollah Khomeini.

"You already had your last ride," I reminded him.

"Allah be my judge, I know not what you mean."

The words sounded stilted, English in his own idiom as he'd learned it. He was scared.

"Jarrett used you to get something he wants," I explained patiently. "That's what he does with people. But he doesn't like to take chances, especially with money. Before he gave you any, he sent his boys to throw a scare into you. Not the stumblebum in the diner." I flashed back to the beach. "One of them's tall, about forty and balding. The other's in his mid-twenties, thin, clean-cut. What's his name?"

"I don't remember."

"You remember everything. What's his name?"

"Alec," Kassam whispered.

"I can't hear you."

"Alec!"

"And the other?"

"He called himself Dack."

"Good. See how easy it is? Now where would I find them?"

"How would I know?" he pouted.

I exhaled, still patient. "They gave you a number to call in case of trouble. Okay, I'm trouble, so we'll call."

"I can't!"

"You, being a meticulous man, would've checked the number for an address. It'd be a drop, of course, but still something to trade if everything went wrong." I held out my hand. "Everything just did."

"They'll kill me," he squealed.

"They're going over, same as Jarrett," I assured him. "Besides, how would they know it's you?"

"They're crazy."

"So am I."

"No, I mean really crazy."

"This time tomorrow you'll be far away. Why should you care?"

"They'll find me."

"Or you can be in jail and I'll tell Jarrett you told me everything. That way they'll find you for sure, even behind bars." I put out my hand again. "The number."

Kassam closed his eyes to jog his memory. "Six-nine-nine-five-two-eight-five," he groaned.

"Jersey City?"

"Bayonne."

"You got a good memory," I said. "But let's check it just to be sure."

I drove to a corner phone, got the operator on the third ring. When I gave her the number, she gave me the address. Bayonne!

"You're a smart boy," I told Kassam going over the bridge. "Now get yourself lost for good. Stay smart."

I left him at the bus station on the other side, suitcase in hand and two grand in his kick. He'd made another killing.

"May your death be a turning point in your life," he shouted after me.

Any Arab curse was better than wishing I'd live forever.

"Shalom," I snarled into the rearview mirror. To the Arabs that was the biggest curse of all.

# twenty-six

**B**AYONNE WAS NEXT TO Jersey City, with Hoboken on the other side. Years ago they were called the three sisters because they hated each other so much. Hoboken had all the gin mills and Jersey City all the rest. Bayonne was part of Poland. Now everything was different, with Hoboken becoming the Venice on the Hudson and Jersey City the Boomtown of the East. Bayonne was part of Puerto Rico.

The address was a rooming house run by an old man with gold glasses and bad teeth. Next to him I looked like Hulk Hogan. He looked American so I figured he spoke money.

"I think this fifty dropped out of your wallet."

"Must be magic," he wheezed. "My wallet's got a rubber band around it."

"Maybe the rubber band broke."

He grunted at me over the glasses. "You need a room?"

"Just a number," I said.

"What number?"

"Can I come in out of the rain?"

"It ain't raining."

"If the bill gets wet," I mumbled, "it washes down to a fiver."

He opened the door to let me by, his eyes on the magic bill. I could've been a Mongolian for all he saw.

"Just got into town." I smiled. "There's a couple guys I'm supposed to see, but I lost their number."

"What's their names?"

"Dack, he's a big guy about my size. The other one's Alec."

"Never heard of 'em," he said, and took a step toward the door.

"This fifty," I said quickly, "has a twin sister."

That stopped him. "You must want them bad."

"Been a long time." I shrugged. "We're old friends."

I looked at him while he looked at the bill. "You said two?"

"Two friends, two bills."

I opened my other hand to show him the second fifty. More magic.

"I just got a number to call when there's a message," he rasped.

"That's all I want."

He licked his lips. "For a hundred?"

I put both bills in his hand.

"Wait here a minute."

He opened a door off the dark hallway while I counted to ten slowly. When I got to eighteen he reappeared with a slip of paper. The bills were gone.

"Don't never say where you got it," he warned me. "I don't want no trouble."

"No trouble." In my business, grease almost always worked better than muscle. Sometimes.

I put the paper in my pocket and took out the pistol, all in one smooth motion. Pure poetry, from all that Kung Fuing around I did to stay in shape.

The old man stared at the gun.

"Don't be scared," I told him. Which scared him more. "Just I can't have you calling them."

I marched him into the room and tied him in knots that would fall apart in an hour, enough time. The gag went on next.

"Relax," I said, and got the operator. The next moment I had the address. Then I dialed the number.

"Yeah?"

"Sunny's Pizza?"

"Fuck off."

I waited a few minutes and dialed again.

"Yeah?"

"Is this Sunny's Pizza on Broadway and—"

"I told you to fuck off, joker. Now fuck off."

I hung up instead. Fuck him.

Only one of them was home. Unless the other was too lazy or in the can or another room or sitting on the ceiling.

Some people are happy only when they're creating problems. We're called cataclonics.

When I left I told the old man the money was his, and I swore his eyes smiled. Gave me a good feeling. Always leave 'em laughing, even when they're gagged.

Twenty minutes later I found the house, a stucco two-story with the driveway on the side and a garage in back. The rest of the block looked the same. I parked near the corner and walked up the next driveway to the rear of the house. The first thing that struck me was everything seemed so goddam normal. Here they were, the two of them living as man and wife in a working-class neighborhood. Whatever happened to killers lurking in sleazy hotel rooms until dark, playing cards in overcoats and hats? Another Hollywood myth!

The only thing that looked out of place was me, prowling someone's backyard. That was my second thought and I moved fast to the windows. They were old, wooden casements with pulley ropes. I pushed one up and crawled into a pantry. Gun out, I slipped on silent feet through the kitchen and front room. The noise came from upstairs, a radio. Or a trick; I'd used it myself a few times.

In retaliation I employed a defensive maneuver from the FBI rule book. The book we'd used. The book not written. I banged on the front door, from the inside, and skirted behind the landing. The next minute Dack trooped down the stairs. He wore a sweat shirt and beige pants and his hands were free. He hit the bottom step in hiking boots and swerved to the door as I stepped out of the shadows. We met with a gun between us.

I said, "Sunny's Pizza?"

He froze. "The joker."

"Beats a pair of queens," I said pleasantly.

His eyes saw everything but a way out.

He was big as me but not wide enough. His shoulders

sloped off the neck and gave his head an elongated appearance, something like a swan. I fixed my sight just above the collarbone and brought the gun crashing down, a five-pound lead weight. It dropped him like a sack of shit.

"That's for cold-cocking me in Weems's house," I said, and kicked him in the gut. "And that's so you remember who did it." I bent down and doubled his right hand on the floor and then I stepped on it. "And that's so you don't do it again."

He was no sissy. It had to be plenty of pain, but Dack said nothing. There was nothing to say. I had the cannon.

"Now you're thinking, I had my oats so why don't I go. Only I can't go." I sat him up with one hand, jabbed his head against the banister. "I don't wanna have to kill you, least not now." I banged his head again. "But I can't go until I know."

He was dazed, out on his feet. Except he lay semisprawled on the floor and I held him by the sweat shirt, bunched in my hand.

I said, "You're working for Jarrett."

Dack raised his eyes in question and I brought the gun up again, over his head.

"Jarrett," he wheezed, and spit on the floor.

"He hired you and Alec for the heavy stuff."

Dack nodded.

"Only Jarrett? He's the only one you saw?"

He nodded again.

"Never talked about somebody else being his partner?"

"Nobody."

"You did the Weems job."

He gave me a look of pure hate.

"Nobody's here," I said, "no witnesses, no recorders. Just you and me." I tightened my grip. "The Weems job."

"Yeah." He coughed it out and let his head sag.

"For Jarrett."

The shoulders hunched.

"And the Stiles woman," I pressed, "last month over on Fairview. Mrs. Henry Stiles. That was for Jarrett too."

He didn't say anything.

"The Stiles job was for Jarrett, wasn't it?"

Still nothing.

"Wasn't it?" I snarled, my gun in his neck.

He raised his head, slowly, and locked his gaze onto mine, and when I looked into his eyes I saw only death.

"Go on," Dack whispered hoarsely, "kill me."

And then I knew I'd never get it out of him. I'd have to kill him and still get nothing, not Mrs. Stiles or Benziger or anything else. I understood him. He'd admitted to the Weems kill because I was there, that made it personal. We'd shared the confrontation, a bond between us. Even if we fought to the death, the bond was there on Weems. For the others, we were perfect strangers. A shooter and a snoop, two professionals. Kill or be killed, it was all part of the game.

I stepped back and belted him twice to put him to sleep and then I walked out his front door and down the street and got into my car and drove away. It was no use looking for any murder guns in the house; they would've been broken up or dropped in the river, or if a favorite was kept it'd be in a safe hideaway. Inaccessible. Ready for the next time.

That was my one hope.

At the Jersey City-Bayonne border, I pulled over and flagged down the blue Ford behind me. I crossed to the passenger side and opened the door and climbed in and turned to the driver.

"What's the idea, Harry? Why the tail?"

Gershon snorted in good humor. "When'd you spot me?"

"First time I saw you. What's the idea?"

"Harwood's idea." He pulled in behind my car and cut the motor. For the whole length of the block there wasn't a soul in sight, nothing moved. "The guy alive?"

"He's breathing," I said.

It looked like the set for a doomsday movie.

"He do Weems?"

I nodded. "Him and a young punk named Alec."

"He tell you that?"

"They work for Jarrett."

"What else he tell you?"

"Nothing else."

"I thought you were hot on them for the Stiles thing."

"I am."

"But you didn't wanna bother him with too many questions," Gershon said sarcastically.

I shrugged. "He's a pro."

"Dangerous?"

"Very."

"Where's the other fit in?"

"They're lovers."

Gershon took that like a duck takes water.

"You already knew about them," I moaned.

"Sometimes we get lucky too, right? We got a tip about them so we went for a look."

"What you learn?"

"The house is rented, two guys. The older one done time for murder and armed robbery. We think the young one's clean."

"You think?"

"We just got the tip." He sounded hurt.

"Always some reason to talk, eh? Like maybe the mob doesn't want independent contractors around?" I shook my head. "Where would you guys be without informants?"

"Out of business, same as you. When were you gonna tell us about them?"

"Come Christmas, when you tell me something."

Gershon grunted. "I *am* telling you something. Harwood don't like you holding out on us. Me, I'm easy. But now Al, he gets cranky when he feels the short end. You know what I mean? You don't wanna get him too cranky."

"What's to tell? I can't make a positive ID and you can't make the gun. We'd look silly bringing them in. Plus there's no link to Jarrett yet."

"You said he admitted it."

"To me, not you. He wouldn't admit anything to you."

"So we change his mind."

"Not this one."

"How about the other?"

"He's probably worse."

Gershon turned the key and the car roared to life. "Harwood thinks you're being cute 'cause you wanna nail them for Mrs. Stiles so your client can get the insurance money. He says to tell you that don't cut no ice with us.

They're suspects in the Weems kill and if we get anything concrete, we'll take them in."

"Why tell me?"

"Al says you want them free so you can watch 'em dance till they trip up something on the Stiles dame. He says you don't care how long it takes."

"What do you say?"

Gershon shrugged. "I say whatever Al tells me to say. That's the way the job works and the pay is good."

"And the livin' is easy," I snapped.

"So don't make it hard for us."

"What about Benziger? Wouldn't you like to get them for that one?"

Gershon put on a frown. "There you go again, getting cute. You know the autopsy found a .22 slug in him. That's not their style." He gunned the motor.

"Harwood doesn't care he did a couple jobs for Jarrett?"

"We don't care, period. Benziger was made in New York, that's their worry."

"So it's just Weems."

"All the way."

"And Jarrett?"

"If we can."

I worked the door handle, suddenly pissed. "Now who's being cute? It's Jarrett the prosecutor really wants and that's why you birds are giving me all this room. Jarrett's dead downtown and the big boys are worried he's involved in more than they can cover. Murder's not on their menu, so he should pay for what he's done because justice demands punishment, especially if you're caught, but if he turns up dead then that's okay too. That way everyone can go home nice and neat with nothing to worry about. Weems is perfect to bring Jarrett down, only it's not so easy all of a sudden. That's where I come in. I can do things you eggsuckers can't, just so long's I don't do them too loud. All right, I understand that now. Now I'll waltz around until I can tie these bums to Jarrett's tail and give your boss what he wants, but in the meantime tell him to stay out of my way. I've got some loose ends of my own to tie and I don't need you clowns sucking up my sleeve." I kicked open the door, turned back to Gershon. "And by the way, tell your girlfriend he can forget about the Arab's charge against Charisma Kelly. It was all a joke."

"He'll be glad to hear that," Gershon jeered. "Al likes a good laugh same as me."

I grunted, feet in the air. "Thanks for the lift."

"Anytime." He waited until I'd cleared the car. "Just give us what you got when you get it."

"Got it."

"Just don't take too long."

# twenty-seven

**W**E CALL IT THE electronic mask."

I was in the high-tech lab, where spectrum analyzers and infinity transmitters were yesterday's news. The research vice-president wore an encryption module that scrambled his speech. The only reason I understood him was the conversion chip in my ear.

"Electronic mask, you say."

"That's the baby."

To the rest of the world we were talking Mickey Mouse.

"Hides the caller?"

The VP nodded. "Disguises the voice so your own id wouldn't know you."

His laugh was in English.

"And doesn't need a decoding device?"

"Nope."

"How's it work?"

"Micronics."

I said, "Oh."

He shrugged. "It's kinda complicated, but what it does is simple. It gives you a whole new identity every time you pick up the phone."

I'd come forty miles to learn about the phone calls to Jarrett's office. Electronic spying was the flip side of the security game. For two decades it'd been big business, until the government clamped down on civilian monitoring. Now the same companies specialized in protection against such spying and it was even bigger business. All the hardware was the same, too, only the name had been changed to protect the profits.

"You heard the tape," I said, "so you know the voice was clear."

"Clear as a bell."

"But low."

"Because the electronic mask slows down the speaker's voice," the VP crooned. "That's what makes it lower. The words are recognizable but not the speaker's identity."

"You mean the man spoke normally, in his natural voice?"

"Who says it's a man?"

I stopped, stunned.

"Could be a woman," he said. "The mask turns them into men." His voice leered electronically. "Handy little gadget, eh?"

The gadgeteer had a sense of humor.

"We're working on one now that'll turn men into women. That'd be even better."

"A woman," I mumbled. The thought opened new possibilities. Laura had heard at least two different voices, so she said. Both male. Jarrett—and Virginia?

"Why not?" the electronic genius trilled. "God made woman out of man. We're just reworking the original circuits."

I had to check my chip to make sure I'd heard right. A biblical scholar, too?

"Might even make them interchangeable."

If he turned out to be a brain surgeon in his spare time, I was gonna turn off. The human ear can take only so much chocolate.

"Anyway, to answer your question, yes, you speak in your normal telephone voice. At the other end they hear someone entirely different."

"But can you make it sound like different people?"

"Different enough," the VP said. "You just turn the knob to make the voice lower and lower. Theoretically, there's any number of voices you can achieve."

"So if someone said they heard different people talk, that's very possible."

"Oh, sure." He pivoted left past some silver shapes out of *Star Wars*. "Unless they run it through a voice analyzer," he said as an afterthought.

We entered a glass booth filled with phone equipment. The electronic mask was a Touch-tone receiver in a flowered tissue box. My guide pointed to a regular phone on the next table.

"We don't need the encryption modules in here. The booth's got a force field around it." He smiled. "Bugproof."

I took the chip out of my ear and put it on my shoulder. "Maybe we were all better off when we wanted people to hear us."

His head bobbed. "You mean when man came out of the caves."

"I mean a few years ago."

He picked up the receiver and I did the same. What I heard had nothing to do with the alien standing next to me. The voice was clearly not his. As he worked the control knob, the voice wasn't even itself any longer but a continuity of disembodied spirits.

I frowned out of some atavistic fear. What this gadget needed was another called the Electronic Exorcist, preferably worked by a priest who still believed in God.

Back in his office I asked the alien about the voice analyzers. "Could they really pick out the speaker?"

"A good one probably could, at least give a pattern." He rubbed his hands in dismissal. "Of course, you have only the one tape."

"At the moment," I hissed.

April in Jersey is not Paris, but it beats hell out of December. I drove down the Garden State listening to Jersey music and sucking on a Jersey tomato. In my wallet was a Jersey license and on my face a Jersey tan, white and yellow as Jersey-baiters used to say.

Too bad my head was in New York.

Laura Jarrett had staged the break-in at her apartment for my benefit—sat downstairs in the lobby and waited for me so I'd be there to find it—and Jarrett had probably helped her. To make her look like a victim and thus above suspicion. Which meant they could've made the calls, her to him supposedly, him to her, and two of them to Weems. That would explain how the caller knew the private numbers.

The thought held me all the way into the city.

"Life doesn't always imitate art," I said to Selma.

"She's in your office."

"I'm glad you asked. Laura in the movie, for example, was suspected of murder and brought to headquarters for questioning. But she was innocent."

"So's this one."

"Who?"

"Laura in the flesh."

"Here?"

"She's in your office."

"Why didn't you tell me?"

"I'm glad you asked."

Women are oddly perverse, some of them. Selma liked to test me, find my weakness.

"I don't have any," I confessed on the way in.

Laura Jarrett jumped, her hand on my thigh.

"You certainly don't," she laughed.

"That's my double." I lowered the blinds and tossed the dummy out of my chair. "He keeps me modest."

I circled the room to get my bearings. Everything was in place except Laura. I remembered the first time I saw her more than twenty years ago during a revival run of classics. I'd walked in on a close-up of her face and sat through the movie three times, then I walked out and went home. We met again that night in my bed.

Now here we were, old friends, and it was too late for either of us to just be passing through.

She said, "Cooper's fired you."

I said, "That's not news."

She said, "The news is I want to hire you."

She was no less beautiful today, a female Dorian Gray. But what of her portrait? Her eyes smoked of pure passion while her mouth promised rich rewards under the secret smile. She was wearing a white blouse and black skirt. She had no color.

I said, "Why do you want to hire me?"

"I think Cooper's trying to kill me," she said. "Planning to, anyway, and I want you to stop him."

The rest of the afternoon was spent on the phone, talking to Jack Conners in New Haven among others. Conners was one of the best private eyes in the East, a relentless tracker who knew Connecticut well.

"We'll see," I'd told Laura Jarrett. I didn't want to make any commitments, not just yet. Not while I had evil thoughts of her, suspicions of her. She and Jarrett—so why would he want to kill her? Or was it just jealousy on my part? "I'll help you all I can," I'd said confidently.

When she stood I gazed up at her, Bogart looking up at Laura. Loving her and lost in his love because she was lost. Thinking she was dead. Was she dead? A lost soul, beyond redemption? Or was the evil portrait just in my suspicious mind? I cursed my suspicions, and then, remembering my first love, I began to suspect my cursings. And my motives.

I took out the locket and snapped it open to Karen's picture. She looked so much like Laura, their faces entwined in my memory. Of course I'd married her and loved her madly. But she was dead and it was I who would be lost if I didn't exorcise my ghosts. Corruption comes slowly at first, with the patience of a devil.

"When a person lies," Frank Barnes had said, "they always tell a little bit of the truth."

I had to find that little bit of truth in Laura—and in myself.

"Anything else?"

Selma's way of telling me it was five o'clock. One of our daily rituals, the things that bind people together.

"You go on," I said.

Another thread of our corporate life, meaningless yet important. If I ever tried to stop her, she'd black-belt me down to street level.

The last call came an hour later, Charisma Kelly to let me know Kassam had disappeared.

"Gone, just like that." She sounded mystified.

"Maybe he got a better offer."

She didn't find it funny. "Ali felt at home here, that he was doing something important."

"How much you pay him?" I said.

"He believed in our work."

"How much?"

"Since we're barely breaking even," she sighed, "naturally—"

"You see?"

"No, I don't." Her voice turned suspicious. "Did you have anything to do with this?"

"What would I know of life at the top?" I said quickly.

"Don't you dare get bizarre with me!" she snapped. "I asked if you know anything about his disappearance."

I put a smile in my voice. "Absolutely not."

More lies, bigger and better lies. Soon a litany of lies that you use for survival. And sometimes even to save people from themselves.

I locked up and went home. When I didn't see anyone I liked there, I went to Marilyn's home.

"Tell me about your day," she said in my arms.

"A simple story of greed and passion," I told her. "I got up this morning and now I'm here."

"Sounds like something's missing."

"Nothing important."

She kissed me for that and I held on to her, feeling better already. "Amazing what some people can do for you," I said.

"Or *to* you," she whispered, pressing against me.

"Only natural," I bragged.

Marilyn giggled. "I've felt worse."

"No war stories," I warned her. "Men are not that sophisticated."

"Neither are women."

I let her go to make the drinks while I made the music. "Rodgers and Hammerstein coming up."

"But they're so corny and sentimental," Marilyn squealed.

"So is life."

I sat in my favorite chair, a brown Barclay lounger I'd given her for Halloween so I could relax. I was just too hard on the easy chairs and too small for a couch.

"A lounger," she'd laughed, "at your age?"

"My weak back," I started to say.

"Your weak back," Marilyn groaned, "is strong as steel."

"Then my poor front."

"Hard as a rock."

"Only for you," I leered.

"Now?"

"Here."

Afterward I'd told her that a chair was like any other weapon. "Only as good or bad as the man who uses it."

"What about a woman?"

"That too," I said. "Just another weapon."

But Marilyn had a good sense of humor. She'd laughed all the way to the bed and left me in the lounger.

Now we sat in front of the *Mona Lisa* sipping wine. I liked it the best of all her paintings. A she-wolf smiling out of those cool gray eyes, her cubs huddled around her. When I first saw it, I told Marilyn the Mona Lisa had no kids.

"Sure she did," Marilyn said, "only they were still inside of her."

"Inside?"

"That's why the Mona Lisa's smiling," said the painter. "She's pregnant. My portrait's after the birth."

"Then why's she still smiling?"

"Wouldn't you?"

I sipped some more, my eyes on the portrait. "To you," I said.

"And you."

We kept sipping and refilling, me in the Barclay and Marilyn on the bearskin by my side. Mona Lisa and his brood.

"Did I ever tell you about Kranko?" I said after a while.

"Who's Kranko?"

"He resembles a Jap about two feet high, not counting the tail."

"What about him?"

"He always brings the flies with him. Wherever he goes there's always flies around him." I shook my head. "There's something wrong with that boy."

After a long time Marilyn said, "You were going to tell me about someone."

"Who?"

"I forget."

Later I got up to fetch still another bottle but lost my way. They had put the kitchen in the bathroom.

"What are you looking for?" Marilyn asked.

"A girl who likes to suck her thumb."

I finally found the bottle and popped the cork.

"I like to suck corks," Marilyn said. "Will that do?"

I almost missed the chair, which was almost impossible. "They moved that, too," I mumbled. Trying to rattle me. I turned all around, there was nobody but Marilyn. She wouldn't do that to me, I burped. Do what? I shook my head, wondered if I was getting drunk.

"Only humans and the two-toed sloth mate face-to-face," I announced eventually.

"Back to back is better," Marilyn giggled, and slipped off my lap.

"So now I chase only women who are going downhill," I said.

The last thing I remembered was trying to remove some wine stains from the cat, except she had no cat. I was lying on the rug, on something softer than any rug had a right to be, and all the lights were out and a voice kept calling for the werewolf to come and I waited there in the dark for the werewolf and all I could think of was the Rangers. They'd made the play-offs with the worst record in Rangers history. Now if I could only make the morning . . .

# twenty-eight

GREENWICH WAS A DREAM dressed in dollars. The main street sold sable coats and cornish hens, the side streets Mercedes and mink. Only money talked and everybody listened.

I pulled off the Merritt Parkway at the North Street exit and wound my way down to the town. The back country was a picture postcard, the kind bankers send to clients of million-dollar trust funds. At the Post Road I turned left into Cos Cob and looked for the restaurant on my right. Another five minutes got me to the Clam Box, more restless than hungry.

My hangover headache was gone but the stomach lingered on, a mailed fist. It'd taken me a half-hour to clank out of bed and forever to find my face in the mirror. By then Marilyn was already chirping away in her studio, which didn't help my manhood any. Men were supposed to be big boozers, it said somewhere.

Breakfast was a finger down my throat. For lunch I'd probably just have the thumb.

Inside, the hostess took a chance and smiled. When I didn't rip her clothes off she led me to a back table, her eye over the shoulder all the way. I think I was too big for her. She watched me squat and clasp my paws together before she skitted away, her body breathing relief.

"One or two?" said the waitress, who didn't seem afraid of anything.

"One and a half," I told her. "I'm the half."

"I can hardly wait."

"I can't. Could I get coffee now?"

"Cream?"

"Jam."

She reined, a trained pony.

"For the coffee," I explained.

"You put jam in your coffee?"

"All the time." I smiled. "Got a sweet tooth."

"What kind of jam?" she asked suspiciously.

I shook my head. "They're all the same."

"Is this a home remedy?"

"At home, yes," I said. "Here it's a restaurant remedy."

"For what? Living?"

She brought the tools and hung around while I whipped up a batch of magic elixir. "Puts a lining on your stomach," I told the waitress.

"Do you dip an apple in that?" she said.

"Only when I find Snow White."

I took a few drags and she took a powder, prancing off to call the Galloping Gourmet.

Nursing my paranoia, I sat there sipping until Jack Conners saved me. He hadn't changed, a polite man who shocked easily and never let on. An efficient man, even prodigious.

"Two parts to your problem," he began efficiently, "the parents and the money."

"Possibly related," I said.

Conners grimaced. "That's what you need to find out, isn't it?"

"That's why I called."

He glanced at his notes. "Laura Cross from Greenwich, married March 1980. Her parents died in California that July. A few months later she inherited half their estate."

"How much?"

"Almost nine million before taxes."

"After?"

Conners shrugged. "Maybe three each. My contact at the bank will fill you in on the money."

The waitress returned for our order. Conners had a fish and I needed more coffee.

"Jam too, please."

She didn't bat an eye, probably afraid of crowds. The two of us covered the table.

"But Laura was disinherited," I griped when she'd gone.

"He'll fill you in," Conners said patiently.

I waved him on.

"There were two daughters and a son. The boy drowned about ten years ago, the other daughter lives in Carmel. She's two years younger than Laura. Married and a mother herself."

"In 1980?"

"She moved there in '79 with her new husband."

"Any connection between Carmel and the parents being in California?"

"According to the insurance report, they took a month's vacation to tour the state and see their daughter. The father bought a Mercedes there, intending to drive back."

"To Connecticut?"

Conners grinned. "I guess he liked to drive."

"Another nut," I said.

"Being cooped up in an office all day could do it."

"Yeah, must be tough in those executive towers with the gold faucets and private dining rooms. Go on."

"They drove up from southern California to spend the third week in Carmel, before heading home." He referred to his notes again. "Got there July sixteenth. The accident occurred four days later."

"What kind of accident?"

"With the car. It went over a cliff." He saw my face. "You didn't know that?"

A bell rang in my head and I heard Pop Wagner telling me how Jarrett said his son should be an auto mechanic, like *he*'d been before he went into real estate and got lucky.

Cooper Jarrett was a mechanic! He knew all about cars, how to fix them and how to . . .

"Jesus H. Christ."

And Laura was married to him, four months married and hating her father for raping her and probably hating her mother for letting him get away with it. Plus she was lost without money; she'd grown up with it, needed it. They had it, millions, and now they'd disinherited her. It wasn't fair, not fair.

"So say something."

"Christ!"

"Something else."

I shook my head, bent a finger into the palm and pressed until I felt the pain, the adrenaline rushing to my brain. A cheap charge.

"California."

"A seemingly nice place," Conners said. "Lots of cliffs, especially around Big Sur and Carmel."

He was ahead of me, as usual.

"When can you go?"

"Not tomorrow."

"The next day."

"In the morning."

I nodded. "Start with the police who made out the report, and the scrap-metal yard that got the wreck. Jarrett would need a car, so check the rental agencies too."

"What're we looking for?"

"Anything," I growled. I was as dumb as the other dummy in my office, probably dumber. "Then try the daughter, see what she's got to say."

"What's my cover?" Conners asked.

"Play it straight. Someone thinks maybe it wasn't an accident. Get her reaction. But no names."

"She might call her sister."

"Good. That might rattle them."

The bank was a white mausoleum smack in the center of main street, which naturally was called Greenwich Avenue. A cop stood on a box in the middle of the street directing traffic, oblivious to the ebb and flow of cars at his back. It would probably be considered vulgar to hit him.

The bank official took me into his office and closed the door. What he had to say was highly confidential and done only as a favor to Jack Conners. Did I understand that? I understood he wanted me to know it was a favor. I told him I appreciated his taking time out to talk about Laura Cross.

"Yes indeed, John Cross was a fine man. We all felt it keenly when he died. And Mrs. Cross, too, of course."

That's the way they talked in Greenwich.

"His daughter?" I prompted. "Laura Cross?"

"Laura was a fine girl, too."

I decided to give it one more try, thinking maybe Conners was toying with me. His idea of a joke.

"There's some talk that she might've been disinherited. I mention it only because we all know John Cross was a fine man before he died. And that goes for his wife as well," I added. "And Laura, of course."

The bank official shook his head sadly. "Fine people, all of them. Of course, John always hoped that Laura, who was the elder, would marry in the community, so to speak." He peered at me over his glasses. "John had no son, you know. His only boy died at fifteen, a tragedy."

"I heard he was a fine boy."

"Very fine. John had him enrolled in Yale at birth." He raised the glasses on the bridge of his nose. "Did you attend Yale, Mr. Malone?"

"No, I'm afraid I missed Yale. All those years abroad, you know."

"Great Britain, wasn't it?"

"And all the other great countries."

"Umm. Well!" He clasped his hands on the desk. "Naturally John had to cancel the Yale enrollment. Broke his heart."

"And Laura?"

"Hers, too, I'm sure. They were very close, you know. The whole family."

I decided to tell him I was raised a Catholic, which would cancel everything. To hell with me.

"So when Laura married a person from New Jersey"— the emphasis was on Jersey—"John naturally was upset. So was his wife, of course."

"Of course."

"In retaliation," he sighed, "I'm afraid they took the ultimate step and divested themselves of future fiduciary responsibility for poor Laura."

"They disinherited her."

"In a word, yes." Another sigh. "As coexecutor, naturally I tried to talk John out of such a drastic step."

"Was that the only reason, her husband came from Jersey?"

"Well, there was talk at the time, I recall, that he dabbled in rooming houses, of all things." He sounded personally offended.

I was beginning to catch on to the Greenwich mentality, in a word. They needed reassurance that you were human, though naturally not of their order. Which was fine with me, yes indeed. I decided not to tell him that I thought Henry VIII a sheepsucking swine with all the morals of an English lord.

"So who would get the money?" I said instead.

"The younger daughter, Elvira. An equally fine girl."

"All of it?"

The official peered at the only scrap of paper on his desk. "Eight million, six hundred ninety-two thousand." He looked up. "In round figures, of course."

"Then how did Laura end up with half?"

A whole series of sighs seemed to erupt from the chair. "In a sense that is truly the tragic part of all this, though naturally not for Laura." He removed his glasses and gently rubbed his eyes. "There was talk in town, unfounded talk, I must emphasize that, unfounded talk!" His stern look made me nod. "Nevertheless there was some unfounded talk"—the voice dropped to a whisper—"that John Cross had made his younger daughter, Elvira, his mistress."

I sat there enthralled, not daring to speak.

"Such a revelation, even such an *accusation,* would have created an unprecedented scandal for the town. John Cross was a deacon of our most prestigious church. Not only that, he was"—the man searched for the properly persuasive illustration to show the severity of the threat—"he was head of the southern Connecticut branch of the National Rifle Association." The thought seemed to stagger him. "The town would have been ripe for ridicule. Can you imagine the sensational headlines in *The New York Times* and other scandal sheets?"

"I can imagine," I assured him.

"Naturally some of us were concerned when Laura threatened to take her sister to court over the inheritance. She claimed to have proof of these vile accusations, numerous witnesses to whom Elvira allegedly confessed and John boasted. Her threat implied that such a finding would show undue influence on John Cross in the preparation of the will."

"So some of you talked to Elvira," I said.

The bank official nodded. "We merely pointed out the danger to her, not for a moment doubting her complete innocence, of course."

"She'd also been recently married, what, the previous year?"

"And living in California." He looked relieved. "I see you grasp the situation. Elvira decided for the good of the town she loved, and for her own peace of mind, to be generous to her elder sister who, after all, had done nothing more sinful than marry a person from New Jersey."

I couldn't let that pass. "I heard somewhere he too was a member of the NRA, the New Jersey branch."

The banker literally shuddered. "Such a thing could never occur in Greenwich," he confided.

I saw I was out of my class, and nearly out of my mind. "Elvira consented to give her sister half."

He consulted the paper again. "Four million, three hundred forty-six thousand, in round figures. Naturally the inheritance taxes were taken out first."

"And the executor fees and banking costs."

"Of course."

"Naturally."

"Since that day," he sighed, "I'm afraid the two sisters have hated each other."

So Laura had got her money without a fight. Meaning John Cross had attacked both his daughters, and made one of them his mistress. A fine fellow, yes indeed.

I drove home wondering if Laura had hated her father because he attacked her or because he rejected her for her sister. Sibling rivalry was a strong force, sometimes even as strong as the father-son bond. Or the father-daughter?

If my suspicions were right, Laura Jarrett was certainly her father's son.

It was almost six by the time I got back to Jersey City, so I headed for home. Everything seemed to be going my way for a change. I just had to keep pushing Stiles, to goad

Jarrett until he made the wrong move. I had a feeling the case was about to break.

Meanwhile, it'd been a nice drive on a nice day and the evening would be even better. I was meeting a friend for dinner, a priest who'd been at the seminary with me. Now he was married to a former nun and they had three children. There was a lot to talk about.

The double garage was on the side of the house, toward the back with a gravel area in front. The doors were white with brown trim and worked electronically. I reached into the glove compartment for the remote control and sat there for a moment lost in a fantasy of my wife greeting me with a smile and a kiss. That had always refreshed me, no matter how tired I was.

Now I was tired and alone and all that greeted me were bills and I pressed the remote control to kill the waves of self-pity and the world blew up in my face.

# twenty-nine

FRANK HAGUE BUILT THE Jersey City Medical Center as a monument to himself. Hospitalized, I lay in bed and promised to praise him the next time I saw Manny.

"Saved your life," Bernie said.

Harwood grunted in the corner.

"Just luck," I said.

"Good or bad?"

"That depends," I told Harwood, "on who's asking."

They both sat up straight, in deference to the sick, while I sprawled on my back swathed in gauze.

"Remote control," Bernie gushed. "What'll they think of next?"

Police humor.

"Obviously they didn't think of it at all or I wouldn't be here."

"You're here," said Harwood, "because you were fifteen feet away when she blew."

"Bad?"

"Bad enough."

"Blew out the doors, destroyed the garage, and wrecked your car," Bernie cataloged in awe, "and you walk away with a faceful of Band-Aids and some burns and bruises."

Nobody liked their injuries slighted. "In the first place I didn't walk away. I was scraped off the ground, they tell me.

215

And in any other place this white suit I'm wearing is no Band-Aid."

"Tough monkey," said Harwood.

"King Kong at least," Bernie growled.

"There were more than a hundred glass shards in me."

"Musta been the windshield."

"Burns all over."

"Front end gone as well."

"Bruises, too."

"Even the tires."

I saw I'd get no sympathy from these sadists. Anyone who'd pick on a man near death who couldn't defend himself—

"So when do you get out?"

"Tomorrow."

"That long?" Bernie said. "Must be serious."

"Maybe even longer," I crowed.

Harwood lit another cigarette. "Got any ideas?"

"You wanna buy a used car?"

"About the bombing."

"What was it, by the way?"

"It was no prank."

"No kidding."

"Jersey tomatoes," Bernie rasped. "It was Jersey tomatoes."

"No prank," Harwood echoed.

I nodded agreement. Jersey tomatoes was mob talk for dynamite, especially Hercules dynamite, reddish sticks that sweat in the dark and need to be turned over frequently.

"That's it, then," I said.

"What is?"

"Jarrett tried to take me out."

"Why Jarrett?"

"His two goons."

"No," Harwood wheezed.

"Why not?"

"We had a man watching them."

"In Bayonne?"

He shrugged. "So a Bayonne man."

"So they slipped out the back."

"And got a bus at the corner."

"It could happen."

"With the dynamite in a knapsack."

"That too."

Harwood pulled his chair closer to the bed. "Think about it. These guys are shooters. What do they know about dynamite?"

"They could've learned," I said stubbornly.

"Whoever did it," Harwood persisted, "used too much. Half would've done the job."

"So they didn't learn too good."

"He also didn't see the electric eyes on the garage doors."

"He?"

"Two guys would've seen them. But only one came at night with a flashlight." The lieutenant took a deep drag. "What we got here is an amateur, someone who's never done this kind of thing before. Someone who wants you out of the way." Ground the butt under his heel. "What you working on now?"

"Just Jarrett," I said.

"He fired you," Bernie yelped.

"So what?"

He turned to Harwood. "One of them eccentric millionaires."

"If we're poor we're just crazy, right?"

"Now you got it."

"What about the atheist?" Harwood asked. "You still on her?"

"She's part of him."

They exchanged looks while I studied the ceiling. What they said made sense, a guy so scared he wired the stuff to the door and never even noticed the electric eyes in his rush to get out. An amateur.

"Any idea who it is?"

"Whoever it is don't belong to Jarrett," Bernie said. "He'd get more pros if he needed 'em."

"Malone?"

"Not yet."

If they were right so was I, my feeling that Jarrett didn't know about the phone calls. Someone else was out there, someone besides Laura.

"How about this Ali Kassam who disappeared?"

I smiled into Harwood's stare. It was just a needle, to let me know he knew what happened. Not that he wasn't glad; the last thing he needed was a newspaper battle with an atheist.

Bernie said, "Maybe someone you put away."

"They're all away."

"Maybe one of 'em walked."

"They don't go after professionals," I reminded him. "If they're into revenge it's usually family or friends, citizens."

"Hey, what about a woman?"

"You got one?"

We all agreed to do nothing. I didn't want them watching Jarrett's shooters, and Harwood couldn't move against them without evidence or at least probable cause. Searching the house might turn up personal drugs, but they'd be out the next day, and wary.

"Better this way," I told them.

"Better for you."

"I'm the one on the firing line."

"Then get off," Harwood sneered.

"How?"

"Tell us what you got."

"When I get it."

"You're holding out on us," he snarled, "like always."

"That's an accusation!" I shouted. "Don't I have any rights under *Miranda?*"

"You're sick!" he screeched on the way out.

"Nice of you to notice!" I screamed.

Bernie posted a guard at the door just in case. I didn't argue because I tried to get along with everybody.

At noon Dancer showed up on my call and I told him where the $200,000 went. Charles Weems gave it to Henry Stiles of the redevelopment agency to get a deal for his company. Stiles used the money to buy a home in Florida. There was no direct proof because Weems was dead, but I was working on it.

Telling Dancer about Stiles would increase the pressure. Not telling him about Jarrett was a risk but I didn't care. He was mine.

So was Marilyn. She came in the afternoon and painted animals on my bandages. They all had tension in them, untold stories. That's what I loved about her work, the sense of drama. Like in Balthus, something was unresolved. The viewer had to finish the story.

"The lion's laughing," I said.

"Maybe he's happy," she said.

I said, "It's good to be alive."

She nestled in my arms.

"I'm a tiger."

"Two tigers."

"One."

Women like the warm sensation of being held. So do men.

"I wouldn't want anything to happen to you," Marilyn said after a while.

I laughed it off, to shield her. That's what men did.

"I wish you were the wax cowboy," she sighed, "who stands motionless on street corners."

"Why wax?"

"Then you'd just melt in my hands."

"Hot hands," I said, "are a sign of health."

Marilyn said, "Let's stay healthy." I put a damaged paw around her waist and we nuzzled.

At 4:50 Selma called for the tenth time to ask how I felt. With all her troubles handling that huge office and the constant chaos, she still found time to think of me. I loved the woman.

"What is it now?" I barked so she wouldn't think I cared. Women were so perverse.

"Mark Jarrett finally called back."

"What he want?"

"He wanted to know what *we* want." She sounded annoyed. "We called him, if you remember."

"What'd we want?"

"I don't know," she said sweetly, a danger sign. "You didn't tell me."

"How long you talk?"

"As long as I could was what you said."

"Good girl."

"I am not a good girl," she huffed. "I'm a good woman of forty-five—"

"Fifty-five."

She started again, out of spite. "I am not a good girl—"

"It's just an expression," I said.

"So's fuck off."

*Click!*

I hate it when they talk dirty, especially good women.

For supper I had a dish of glop laced with goo. When I threw up, they told me it was a plea for attention. I asked them what it would be when I pissed in bed.

The last call I made was to an informant who knew the price of Jersey tomatoes.

# thirty

FUNNY HOW THINGS NEVER work out the way you planned. Or even dreamed.

I walked out of the hospital two days after they wheeled me in. The sun was shining and people smiled at each other. When I told the cabdriver where I wanted to go, he didn't argue. Even Selma was courteous and kind.

"You look terrific."

"Same to you, pal."

What else could I snarl in the face of such provocation?

"Your tapes should be ready this afternoon," she purred.

And efficient, too!

All phone calls to the office were taped, and a log kept of the caller and time. What I wanted were the voices of Jarrett and his son and Laura and Virginia matched against the one to Jarrett's office. According to the electronics expert, there was some hope for voice identification.

"Jack Conners'll call you tonight at home," Selma sang. "He said about six, that would make it nine P.M. our time."

I tried to smile through the Band-Aids, which wasn't easy. Most of the flying glass had found my face. Apparently I'd been on the cutting table for hours, the doctors poring over me with tweezers. Fun for them but not me. Even my sore ribs squeaked.

"Nothing from Dancer?"

Selma shook her head. "Only someone who wouldn't leave his name. Said to tell you no tomatoes were sold privately this week." She looked up. "Are we into white slavery now?"

"Worse," I said and went into my office. That meant the mob wasn't involved, which left just the rest of the world. Basically Jarrett and his son and Henry Stiles. Except Jarrett was too smart to bungle a stunt like that and Stiles too dumb. But Jarrett Jr. was a field engineer who worked around construction sites where they used dynamite. He'd at least know what to do with it, an amateur.

But why?

Because, said the dummy in me. Meaning I knew I was right though I didn't know the reason.

At 4:30 I did.

"Looks like you have a winner," said the director of the security agency.

I'd taken a quick hop over the Pulaski Skyway to Newark for the voice analysis. His agency specialized in voice identification and trained law-enforcement officials in its procedures.

"We compared the control tape with each of the four samples given us. Indications are that's the person on the office tape."

The one I held in my hand wasn't Jarrett or his Virginia or even Laura. It was a twenty-four-year-old punk named Mark Jarrett who was supposedly afraid of his father, who'd taken Virginia away from him. And who had he taken in return? Only his father's wife.

"The patterns seem to match," said the director.

"You're positive?" I pressed.

"Nothing's positive," the director beamed.

"That's where you're wrong," I growled, clutching the tape. "It's guaranteed I'm gonna beat the living shit out of him."

"With that obvious exception," the director sighed, unruffled, "we say nothing is positive. And the electronic mask makes the chances of uncertainty even greater." His fat face was anything but a mask, jovial and unlined. "Still, we think we know our job pretty well."

I'm suspicious of people who always use *we* instead of *I*. If a group's involved, no single individual can be held responsible. The malaise of our age.

"But within parameters, you're sure," I huffed.

"In a word, yes."

I felt like I was back in Greenwich.

On the Skyway again I toyed with the idea of stomping the little rat right now, which would get me nothing but satisfaction. What I needed was proof. To get that I needed help.

"He's in it with Laura Jarrett," I told Bernie on the phone. "They're lovers, probably since her divorce. Jarrett took Virginia, so he took Laura to even the score. Or maybe it was all her idea and she went after him. With her looks she could get anybody."

"Maybe she got you," Bernie said. "You sound bitter."

"She almost did," I admitted. "It's a long story."

"Why'd he make the calls?"

"They intended to kill Jarrett, take over the company. This way they set up a phantom killer who's after the owners for some reason. When Jarrett got hit, they wouldn't be suspected even though everything went to them."

"Then why stop the calls before the hit?"

"They got scared when Jarrett pulled me in, especially the taping, but after Weems died they couldn't resist one more. It was perfect: Take credit for Weems and Jarrett'd be next." I frowned. "That was their big mistake, the last call."

"So far you got Junior on threats and nothing on Laura."

I ran a hand over my face. It was still sore and so was I. "There's more," I spit into the phone. "They didn't want Jarrett knowing about them, so they'd meet in New York. It was safer there since Jarrett had no more interest in Laura. Then a few months ago he decided it was time to buy her out, get rid of her. Only she wouldn't sell, so he got a local P.I. to tail her."

"Benziger!" It was an explosion of breath.

"You see my drift. Benziger tailed her only in Jersey because Jarrett wanted something on her here so he could blackmail her out."

"How?"

"By catching her in bed with a local woman."

Bernie made noises and I told him it looked like Laura

might be AC-DC. "Whether she is or not doesn't matter. The point is Benziger didn't get anything on her but somewhere along the line he saw her with Junior. He didn't think anything of it, of course, the boss's son and his former stepmother, both of whom worked for the company. But now he knew what Junior looked like."

"So when you sent Benziger to watch New York—"

"He must've seen them together, maybe acting real friendly. He shot a picture, that was his job. Somehow Junior spotted him with the camera, thought he was working for Jarrett—"

"—who would've ruined their plan if he found out."

"Probably have them killed," I said. "Junior had to get the camera and Benziger too."

"He wreck the apartment that time you were there?"

"To show Laura was in danger from the caller who'd already killed Weems."

"But Jarrett had Weems killed."

"Good for them. Now it was Jarrett's turn and they'd own it all."

"So Jarrett thought the calls legit."

"Sure he did. But when they stopped, he figured them for a crank and bounced me. Suddenly I was the danger."

Bernie snorted into the phone. "Now you got Junior for murder but still nothing on the woman."

I didn't like what I was thinking. There was no evidence against her for any of the kills—not for Weems, even though she probably told Jarrett I'd be seeing him that night; not for Benziger, though she must've known what Junior intended; nor for Mrs. Stiles, though Jarrett might've told her. And there'd be nothing to mark her for the murder of her parents, either.

"Malone?"

"Here," I rasped.

Who'd believe a multiple killer against a woman of obvious quality? Or a weakling like Junior against a woman like that?

"She's out of it then," Bernie said. "Unless the Jarretts turn on her and get somebody to listen."

"What're the chances?" I asked him.

"Without proof, zero."

I stared at the wall and watched my soul burn. Evil was everywhere and mostly in my thoughts and suddenly I envied the atheists, who didn't believe in good and evil beyond the grave and so were saved.

"What'll you do?"

"Do?"

"About the Jarrett boy? Where's the gun?"

"He's an amateur," I forced myself to say, "so he probably still has it."

"Does Harwood know all this?"

"Says he's not interested in the Benziger kill, that's New York."

"He still has to know," Bernie said.

"I'll tell him. But meanwhile we search Junior's house."

"We need a warrant, something."

"Use the tapes. That's enough to pick him up on suspicion and do the search. When we find the gun, Harwood can take over and send it to New York."

We left it for the morning, early, a time that wouldn't look unduly zealous to a judge in case we found nothing. Bernie would do the paperwork.

"Looks like you got two killers," he said, "instead of the one you were after."

"How's that?"

"Jarrett and his shooters and now Laura and Junior."

I didn't tell him about Jarrett and Laura killing her parents five years ago. I had no proof and he wouldn't have believed it anyway.

On the way in to dinner I fondled the locket from Karen, trying to recall something of our time together, feeling the dream turning to ash, losing another thread of my life.

Father John was already seated. Even in the seminary he'd loved food, a celebration of life. Some years later he discovered celebratory sex.

Now he showed me pictures of his wife and children, all of them beautiful.

"The oldest is four," he said proudly, "and then three and two."

"What happened last year?" I quipped.

He shrugged. "Guess I didn't eat well enough."

Talk soon turned to the priesthood. Father John was not

sanguine about the American Catholic church. "Almost half of our priests doubt the existence of God." He seemed appalled at the thought. "The Center for Human Development in Washington did a survey last year. And they also found out that sixty-six percent feel tension over the church's celibacy rule." He drew nearer. "I was one of them when I practiced the priesthood."

"And now?"

"Now"—he relaxed—"I have no doubts and no tension. God is good."

"Maybe the church will change some of its rules," I suggested.

He didn't think so. "You have fifty thousand priests in this country. The way things are going, fifteen years from now there won't even be half that."

"Then they'll have to change."

"By then it'll be too late."

Over the next two hours we discussed everything from organized religion to murder, using good Jesuitical tactics of equivocation and guile. It was helpful to hear of old intrigues and new insights. Father John thought the pope a madman for traveling to third-world countries, whose children were starving, to tell parents they shouldn't use birth control. On the other hand, he was scandalized by my belief that people hopelessly ill should be allowed to die.

"Life is sacred," he cautioned me. What he meant was sentient life outside the womb—that was his definition of life. Mine was much more restrictive. I believed only the good should be allowed to live.

Going home I marveled at how our paths had widened over the years. Father John was a staunch Catholic who believed in the perfectibility of man, while I knew for a fact that evil devils roamed the earth.

At 9:10 Conners called from California. The police reported three witnesses to the accident, one of whom lived nearby and was interviewed. He remembered the car gaining speed on a downhill, as though unable to stop. It failed to make a curve and swept over the cliff. The junkyard found nothing unusual in the wreckage but noted that any mechanic could booby-trap a car.

"What about the local rental agencies?"

"We're in luck there. A Cooper Jarrett rented a Ford in nearby Monterey on July fifteenth, five days before the accident."

"In his own name," I clucked. The ego of some killers!

"Never thought anyone'd come looking," said Conners.

"And the other daughter?"

"She hates her sister, says she's not surprised."

"Think she'll call her?"

"Only to gloat."

I sat in the darkened room soaking my sores with Jack Daniel's but it didn't help. Jarrett got away with murder, just like Laura. At least Weems and Mrs. Stiles would nail him. Stiles was the weak link, and cracking. He'd already called Harwood about me harassing him, the next time would be for immunity.

The phone rang again at ten, Dancer watching the Stiles house at my suggestion. More harassment, anything to shake him up. But someone else had a better idea. Two men came for Stiles.

"Cops?"

"Not these," Dancer sputtered. "They were the guys in the picture."

"What picture?"

"That I gave you from the fruitcake in Detroit. Hey, I recognized them."

"The tall one carries himself like walking death and the other looks like the devil?"

"That's them."

Jarrett's shooters!

# thirty-one

**D**ANCER TAILED THEM SOUTHEAST toward the river and the Bayonne line, then lost them on Garfield Avenue and called me. I told him to get Bernie at police headquarters, have him cover the Bayonne house.

Their direction gave me only two possibilities: where they lived or where they played.

"Caven Point beach," I said to Dancer. "Tell him maybe there."

By 10:15 I was over the wooden trestle beneath the turnpike and racing down the deserted road to the beach. My mind clicked off the landmarks, fierce silhouettes on a frozen moon. I was taking a stab, working a hunch, what Marilyn would've called guessing. A shot in the dark, maybe, but more than a guess. Stiles was marked for murder and a body needed dumping. For fifty years Jersey City had been a dumping ground for the mob, and Caven Point a local favorite. So popular that the mob moved on as the citizenry took over. You didn't have to know its history to see its potential.

I came to the first fork and swung left, continued a half-mile and stopped. From here it'd have to be on foot. Harwood's men would find the car because Bernie'd call them, that was part of his job. And this was part of mine.

There was another reason for my banking on the beach. I was up against a pair of homosexual sadists. The pictures showed gladiator gear, leather stuff that meant sadomasochistic sex, and in Stiles they had a ready victim. He'd been with them before, at least to take photos, but this time there'd be no camera.

It was still a few hundred yards to the beach. I moved up the dirt road past scrubby shoots sticking out of earth strewn with debris. On either side of me, tangled undergrowth struggled to survive. In the distance the river was black, a solid ribbon. No sign of life. The path veered southward and I followed, silent with caution. I'd learned night infiltration at the FBI school in Virginia, where we stalked straw men. But that was straw and this flesh and blood. After fifty yards I began seeing the skeletal spires of oil derricks.

Closer still put the abandoned piers into view, misshapen demons importuning a departed god. I crouched for a moment, trying to separate sounds. They would be up ahead now, somewhere along the beach in front of me. Maybe.

The beach at night was a lunar landscape, but at its watery edge life throbbed and the surrounding shallow wetlands were a nesting site for dozens of waterfowl species. The two men, in their own nesting, probably never noticed the canvasback ducks, who in turn paid no mind to the nearby metal scrapyards and tank farms and derelict buildings. Urban blight that at night became softer in shadow. Under a quarter-moon I picked out the spot where I'd stood with Cooper Jarrett that first day, now whiter than I remembered it. Reflected light threw the shells and refuse into relief and brought out the white, grainy sand. I changed the angle of my gaze to include the fishing pier just south of me, with its wooden steps. There was no sign of people on the beach and nothing moved. I worked my way closer to the pier, the gun heavy in my hand.

There were sounds now, soft scrapings and later low murmurings, a kind of drone that charged the air. I crept forward, a snake slithering, blending into darkness, *implacable.*

The pier lay ahead, a beached whale. I had to climb its tail, one step at a time. It would have helped if I'd known both of them were up there. Stiles, certainly. There'd be no sense coming this far without him. They had taken him from his home to here, a captive slave for their sporting pleasure.

I thought about rushing them. Trying to catch them by surprise, a sudden mad dash. But the chances were slim. I might get one on the run before the other brought me down. The pier was too long, too open. There was no cover anywhere. And they'd kill Stiles first thing.

I didn't want that. Stiles could tie Jarrett to the killing of his wife, maybe even to Weems. Which was why Jarrett wanted him dead. He'd become too shaky, a threat. The Caven Point deal was dead too, at least with Stiles. Jarrett probably had found another way, someone else to corrupt or destroy or kill. Had they already killed Stiles? Were they devils dressed as men? There was only one thing to do with them, I told myself.

In the name of justice, which had many other names.

Amen.

I oozed up the steps, caressing each board, and held my breath at the top. If they saw me, they had me. I took the chance, peered over the edge.

I was back in Denver, my first kill. At the window.

I'd said, "Let them go."

He said, "We all want to die."

I said, "Only saints and psychotics want to die."

He said, "You want to die too," and started to raise the rifle.

I said, "If it's revenge you're after, you'd better dig two graves."

And he smiled at me and I saw death in his eyes and I pressed the automatic fire and said, "I'll pray for you, soldier."

Now I looked down the length of the pier, longer even on the flat. There'd be no chance to get them both running, none at all. They would kill Stiles and turn to me. It was too light to miss, a silver moon on silvery water, and we were all pros.

They were at the end of the pier, a huddled mass. Only the drone of voices filled my ear, nothing distinct. That and occasional giggles and snorts of laughter. I lowered my head and looked for an answer. When they returned this way, it would be without Stiles, who would be dead. I had to go to them.

Shifting my position I glanced at the pier's underpinnings, a row of piles driven into the seabed. A latticework of beams connected the piles and supported the deck. The beams formed a horizontal ladder, or so it seemed to me, that stretched to the end of the pier. I could walk the ladder's edge all the way out, if I could walk the ladder's edge. One slip would bring them running.

I took off my shoes since the brine made the boards too slippery for leather soles. To reach the first beam, I'd have to hang from the deck and wriggle hand over hand around its corner and about ten feet forward. I removed my jacket and rolled up my sleeves, made sure the shoulder rig was securely fastened to the belt. With a mental sign of the cross I eased myself off the stairs to the deck planking, hanging now in midair, moving slowly, one hand and then the other. At the corner I followed the curve, teeth gnashed, my ribs screaming, and an eternity later my stocking feet touched the first beam.

Carefully I inched ahead, sometimes astride the beam and sometimes on all fours. Where there was a crossbeam I would stand and hold on, moving faster. The wood had the smell of ocean. The crossbeams came every ten feet and were bolted to the base. The bolts were rabbeted into the wood. There was sea scum everywhere.

I had come almost halfway. Resting a moment I checked the rig again, then my hands. They were claws, raw and without feeling. I flexed them a few times and went on. My mind was a blank, attuned to nothing but noise. I could hear the sweat running down my back. The moon dropped behind a cloud now and I hurried, using touch as much as sight. I kept blinking the sweat away from my eyes. Above me all was quiet. I took a deep breath and held it and squeezed it out in silent gasps.

The river itself was silver but the water below me was a slick black, all definition gone. I quickly looked away. Absolute darkness was alien to man's nature. Another crossbeam soon came up and I grasped it. There were only four more to go and I used that as my incentive and then there were three.

If Stiles was still alive I would save him, use him to get Jarrett. I had come too far to fail and I felt the excitement welling inside of me. A danger signal. I stopped at the second section to get my breath. Voices sounded, disjointed mumblings. I shut them out, concentrated on the skiff ladder at the end of the pier. I'd be able to rise up behind them, so to speak, from the sea side. My heart was pumping, pushing me forward. There was phlegm in my throat and I swallowed it silently. When I reached the last crossbeam, I carefully rounded the corner and clung to the ladder. It rose from the depths, a lifesaver for men who went down to the sea. Or came out of the land.

I could've kissed it, my catwalker's cross. Wrapping an arm around a rung, I wiped my hands on my pants. First one and then the other. I wondered if I'd ever learn to swim.

"I think he's dead," someone said.

"Shit." It had a disapproving ring to it.

My hands flew to the railings, gripping them. There were six rungs to the top and I took them one at a time, forcing myself to rise slowly. It was too late for mistakes. When I brought my head level with the dock, the gun was in my hand.

Stiles was stretched out about fifteen feet from the edge, his body pointing inland. Dack and Alec were crouched around him. They looked like two monkeys on the floor of the cage, which was where they were going.

Dack shook his head. "I told you to be careful."

"You shoulda told me how," Alec snickered. "Anyway, who cares? He was supposed to be dead."

Nearby, a man's voice said, "I care." It was an angry voice but still under control, still rational. I held the gun steady. It was my voice.

The voice said, "You'll get up now, both of you. And take out the guns, one at a time, and lay them on the pier. You first, boy."

"Suppose we don't wanna?"

The sneer was there but so was something else. There was madness, too.

In the moonlight we looked like the dancers on the pier in *Picnic*. Except everyone here was male and the dance was death. I motioned to Dack and he rose slowly, his hands showing with the palms out. A pro all the way. But I kept my eyes on Lucifer rising for the second time, only this time there was no one behind me.

His hair and skin had a sickly reddish cast and his face was the ugliest I'd ever come across. Not so much distorted as vacuous, as if he'd lost all human attributes. Or never had any.

"Now the gun," I said. My hand was steady and so was my voice, but I knew true evil could not be taken alive.

Lucifer didn't move.

"The gun," I repeated. "Out and on the floor."

"Come and get it," he giggled, and my eyes turned into cross hairs and I pulled the trigger on the empty chamber, a favorite trick. It's the loudest sound in the world, and always means the same thing.

Almost always.

Dack hissed, "He's empty," and began to move his hand toward his jacket but my eye stayed on Alec, who already had his gun coming up shooting when I shot him dead in the forehead. It was the fastest draw I'd ever seen in my life, so fast that the bullet slammed into the deck only inches away.

The blink of an eye had passed as I shifted my gun hand slightly and caught Dack clearing his holster and I put one in his groin to let him know I was angry. He tried to hold on to the pistol, but it flew out of his grasp as he doubled over. On the way down I shot him in the head.

# thirty-two

HARWOOD SAID, "TOO BAD you had to kill both of them."

"Too bad they got fresh," I said. "You saw the bullet hole in the deck."

"What the other one do, try to kiss you?"

"He was getting ready."

"So you shot him in the balls."

"My hand was sweaty. I must've slipped."

"Dead center?"

The two bodies were gone, more meat for the bugs who'd inherit the earth. Nobody cared.

Harwood looked out over the water. "They could've given us Jarrett," he complained.

"No," I told him. "Our only chance was Stiles."

"You screwed up."

"They were dangerous," I said. "Especially the young one."

"How come you didn't shoot him twice?"

"Didn't have the time."

"But you beat them both," Harwood said.

I shrugged. "Just lucky."

"Ain't we all?"

"I mean it. If I'd watched Dack instead of the kid, I would be dead now."

"That'd be too bad." His sigh said it'd be about right.

The ambulance was backing the length of the pier,

coming for Stiles. He'd been left for last, a murder as opposed to justifiable homicide.

"Strangled," Dorsey said as we hovered over the corpse. He pointed to the tissue bruising that was consistent with strangulation. "Never had a chance."

The body was naked except for a hooded leather mask over the face and a leather device tied to his penis. Sado-masochistic sex.

"Fucking animals," a cop said, looking down.

"What's the body worth now?" I asked Dorsey.

The pathologist shook his head. "Losing thousands every minute," he sighed. "All that money going up in air."

I'd tried to save Stiles so I wouldn't lose Jarrett. Now all I had was Manny telling me whoever I asked him about soon got killed. The Prince of Darkness, he'd called me the last time. Catholics were very superstitious.

"Why didn't they kill him at home?" Dorsey wanted to know. "Like Weems."

"They didn't want to disturb the neighbors," I said solemnly. "It's a nice block where everyone goes to bed early. . . ."

My story drove him away with the body. It couldn't tell us any more, and neither could he.

Ray Price drew nearer. "Why'd they kill him at all?"

"He was gonna sing soon and Jarrett didn't like the tune."

"You got proof?"

I told him I'd call when I did.

Bernie'd arrived later than Harwood's crew. First he'd gone to Bayonne with the local cops to stake out the house. While he was there I was here, waltzing the bodies. I kicked Dack's automatic out of the way, just in case this turned out to be the night of the living dead, and stepped over Stiles and picked up Alec's revolver and opened the cylinder and examined the bullets and sat down to think. It was a cheap gun, a Saturday Night Special.

I told myself it didn't make sense, a talent like that deserved a Stradivarius or at least a Colt. Unless, of course, there was a reason for his choice. The gun wasn't new.

When the Homicide van came, I told them to bag the gun carefully. It was the evidence I'd been looking for or my name wasn't—

"Malone?"

Bernie.

"C'mon with me."

There was nothing left here, just a beach in the middle of industry. Soon it would all be residential and somebody'd make millions.

"Billions," Bernie said.

I said, "Long's it's not Jarrett."

"Don't make it personal."

Nothing personal, I told him. "Make it a sense of justice."

"Or maybe revenge?"

"Good and evil really exist," I snapped, "and somebody's gonna have to pay."

Bernie nodded. "Just remember he didn't kill your wife."

We were walking off the pier now. The vans were gone, and most of the locals. Soon the sun would soak up the blood and no one'd ever know the difference. A moment in time, a blip. Like all of us.

"Harwood don't want you on the bust," Bernie said.

"He told me."

"Says you might fall on Junior."

I admitted it was possible since he'd tried to kill me.

"Harwood says you got no sense of humor."

"What else does Harwood say?"

Bernie shrugged. "You know Al. He don't talk much."

They were going to pick up Mark Jarrett now, instead of morning. Stiles changed everything and Harwood wasn't taking any chances. With all the bodies, he needed someone alive.

"Call me at the office," I told Bernie.

"It's midnight."

"That's where I turn into a pumpkin."

The river road was deserted. I drove slowly past the park behind the Statue of Liberty, thinking of murder all the way. With Stiles dead, Jarrett was home free, and so was Laura who looked like Karen who looked like *Laura*. Both had wanted me killed, Laura with Junior and now Jarrett with his shooters. One hired me and the other tried, in order to cover her own tracks. And they had one more thing in common: Both had committed murder five years ago, a dual murder. The same murder.

I passed unnoticed through the empty city streets, a reminder that the darkness was there before the light and man merely a temporary aberration. At the moment it seemed like a good idea.

Upstairs I sat by the window with the bottle on the desk, my mood somewhere between yellow and gray. Yellow meant I was idealistic and imaginative to the point of paranoia, and gray meant I wanted to conceal myself from the world. After a few drinks the yellow and gray turned to black. That meant I was getting drunk.

When Bernie called I put the bottle away. Never drink on the job.

"It was where?"

"In the refrigerator, under a carrot casserole." He sounded insulted professionally. "Must've seen a bad movie."

"A .22?"

"Like you said. They're matching the bullets now."

"It's the Benziger gun," I told Bernie. "What's Junior say?"

"Everything."

"About Laura?"

"That too."

A punk to the end, just like his father.

"When's Harwood picking her up?"

"In the morning at work. He figures she ain't gonna run. Besides, she don't know about Junior."

"And Jarrett?"

"What's he got to do with it?" Bernie squawked. "You aced his two goons, remember?"

"We'll still do the ballistics on that revolver," I said.

Bernie grunted. "Don't mean nothing to Jarrett. So it's the gun that killed Weems, but now the goons can't tell who paid them."

"Not Weems, Stiles—"

"Stiles is dead too."

"So's his wife."

There was a long pause. Then: "Jesus, Malone, that was a .357 Mag." The voice carried concern that maybe I was cracking.

"I know."

"And the revolver's a .38 Special."

"I know."

"Even if . . ." Bernie sounded mystified. "Anyway, it wouldn't change Jarrett. There'd still be no tie to him."

"I know that too."

"For chrissake," Bernie barked, "you can't fire a .357 round from a .38 Special."

I flashed back to Charisma Kelly in Pershing Field, telling me her mother couldn't have committed suicide.

Somebody was wrong.

"Anything's possible," I said finally. "The test's at ten."

"I hope you know what you're doing."

"We'll see."

I took another drink for luck and switched off the recorder and went back to work. It was only a phone call away.

"Do you know what time it is?" the voice growled.

"I'm a detective. It's after twelve."

"It's almost after one."

"Soon it'll be after two."

The silence was threatening, even the sigh. "What's on your mind, Malone?"

"I'm afraid I have some bad news, Mr. Jarrett."

"So tell me."

I told him. Everything. It hit him right between the eyes.

"Laura and my son?"

"Lovers."

"Planning to kill me?"

"All set."

*"Me!"*

A scream of rage, exactly what I needed. I fed it more.

"Your son would have half the company, and she has the other half. Plus they'd get your money."

"If this is a joke, I swear I'll kill ya."

"No joke. But who'd you get to do your killing? Your two shooters are dead."

I told him the rest. "The cops'll call you in the morning."

"They got nothing on me." A pause. "And Laura?"

"There's no proof," I said, "only your son's word. Nobody believes him."

"She's clean?"

"Clean as you. Isn't that good? Looks like she's your partner for life," I sneered. "Unless she decides to blackmail you for your half."

"With what?"

His anger was fearful and I kept feeding the flames.

"Remember when you killed her parents in California?"

The muttering stopped, the curses, even the breathing.

"You rented a car in Monterey," I said. "Witnesses could identify you around her sister's home in Carmel. You were a mechanic. Years later you told Laura what you'd done. Now she's not married to you, so she could testify against you. Now she could blackmail you." I heard nothing on the other end. "Still there, Mr. Jarrett?"

"It's all hearsay."

"Sure it is when *I* say it, means nothing. But her words would matter if she says you told her personally. Then it's not hearsay anymore."

"How come you know so much?"

"Who you think told me?"

The line went dead.

I was sweating bullets. There wasn't much time now, wouldn't take him long to get down there. Or maybe I was just scared. And mad, too. They'd been ahead of me all along, both of them. Right from the start, playing me for a sap.

Only one more call to make.

I wiped my hands on the bottle, emptied it. The whiskey hit my gut as the voice answered. She was in bed.

"Sorry to bother you, lover, but they just took your boyfriend. I thought you oughta know."

"Who is this?"

I gave a short laugh. "After all we've been to each other? Don't break my heart."

"Malone?"

"The cops've nailed Junior for junking Benziger and trying it on me. He says you were in on it."

"How—"

"There's no time for that now." I kept my voice low, rushed. "They plan to pick you up in the morning at work,

*239*

that way they don't have to bother with New York extradiction. With Junior's confession, they figure to have enough on you."

"But I know nothing about this," Laura said.

"You'll tell them that, and maybe they'll believe you. Meanwhile, Stiles is dead too. He was in business with your ex, but you can tell them you knew nothing about that either. Jarrett had him strangled and now they've got him as well."

"Cooper?"

"At least you don't have to worry about him coming after you for planning to kill him."

"It's not true."

"I told you, Junior's confessed everything—how the two of you planned the murder and even faking the calls to the office."

Now she believed me. "What can I do? Help me."

"Not a chance."

"Please!"

"I told you I could help you and then I told you I would help you. Now I'm going to tell you. I can't help you."

"I'll give you anything. Money—"

"Stop it."

"Anything," she sobbed.

"You should've played straight with me from the start."

"I was a fool."

"But I won't be. Not anymore."

"Come over." Her voice was a silent scream. "We can talk, make plans."

"What plans?"

"You and me. Mark has turned against me, telling lies—"

"What about you and me?"

"Any way you want it." The voice began to purr. "I know you like me, I've seen how you look at me. . . ."

I let her talk me into it. I would come over to her apartment, now. There was no time to lose. I would help her beat these malicious lies, stand by her. Afterward we'd be together the rest of our lives. Just the two of us, together, me and Laura.

Those lies, how familiar they seemed. But she was only a dream.

"A half-hour," I said. "Buzz me up right away. I don't like to stand in lobbies. Same with upstairs."

"I'll be waiting at the door."

Yes you will!

"Malone?"

"Yeah?"

"It'll be great, I promise."

"So do I."

# thirty-three

**I** MADE IT THROUGH the tunnel to West Tenth in fifteen minutes and parked across from her apartment house. Almost where Benziger was found but on the other side of the street.

It was 1:20, just about a half-hour since I'd called Jarrett. He would've taken the Washington Bridge and come down the West Side Highway to the Fourteenth Street exit and across Greenwich Avenue onto West Tenth. Which meant he'd be along any minute.

And he'd be alone. His help was dead—a few phone calls would've convinced him—and it would take time to set something up, days at least. Too late for Jarrett. He knew if the cops got her, she'd talk. Women were like that. Even if he beat the rap his business'd be ruined, the contacts scared away.

The other thing was more emotional, an egomaniac who suddenly felt himself threatened. He would strike out of blind fury.

I sat in the car and fantasized our life together, me and Marilyn. Maybe I'd begun to come out of my shell. Was that love? I only knew that being with her was like looking into a Rembrandt portrait. There's no bottom.

Someone rounded the corner and I watched him hurry to the building and disappear inside. Jarrett, probably parked up the block. I followed a minute later, using my picks on the outside lock. The stairs took me to the top and I came out in the carpeted hallway with mirrors and a package table between the two apartments. Hers was the front and the door was closed.

Jarrett was taking no chances.

I studied myself in the mirror, gave it a passing grade. I was no Robert Redford, but could he cook up a perfect oyster stew? Or run a six-minute mile? Or remember everything he didn't forget?

After that I examined the designer wallpaper, a kind of Art Deco down on the farm. It looked like eight maids a-milking while being sodomized by nine pipers playing. I was on my second maid when I heard the first shot, a muffled pop. It was a gun. Nothing else makes that sound, not the pop of popcorn or even a balloon. You know it when you hear it if you hear it enough.

Then a second shot. Just to make sure.

I steadied the Steyr with both hands. The next moment the door swung open and Cooper Jarrett stormed out, empty-handed. When he saw me he stopped dead in his tracks.

"You!"

"And you."

He looked in my eyes and when he looked in my eyes he saw, and then he knew.

I waited patiently while he fumbled in his pocket before I shot him through the heart, just to make sure.

Then I called the cops.

Vergil's people came about twenty minutes after the patrol cars confirmed a homicide. Ten minutes later Vergil came.

"You again!"

Laura Jarrett was dead and so was her ex-husband. He shot her and I shot him.

I told Vergil what I could, which wasn't much. Her boyfriend, who was Jarrett's son, had killed Benziger on the street. They were planning to kill Jarrett, who was involved in some killings himself. When he heard about them, he rushed here and shot her. I came too late.

Vergil didn't believe a word of it.

"How'd he hear about them?"

"I don't know."

"How'd you know he was coming here?"

"Just a feeling."

He was ready to feel me into fifty years.

"Look at it this way," I told him, "now you don't have the Benziger case on your mind."

He told me to shut up.

"And you got the murder gun on the woman, so that's no problem."

He told me to go away.

"And you can see I shot the man in self-defense."

He told me to shut up and go away.

"I can clear all your cases just like that."

"Take a walk," Vergil said.

"Where?"

"Around the bathroom," he growled.

Black people have no sense of humor.

An hour later Bernie came, with Harwood right behind. They didn't seem too happy with me, but everyone agreed there wasn't enough evidence to convict me of the Kennedy assassination or the bombings in Beirut. Harwood wasn't sure about the Lindbergh kidnapping.

"Are you just a normal homicidal maniac?" he wanted to know. "Or is there something wrong with you?"

"He's got a sense of justice," Bernie jeered.

"A sense of shit is what he's got." Harwood shook his head in disgust. "Shit sense."

I took it like a man. You get used to this kind of abuse in my business or you get out.

"Yeah, but he makes more'n we do," Bernie reminded him, "and he don't worry about who's mayor tomorrow."

Harwood puffed on his cigarette. "Probably a Russian spy, too."

"I resent that."

Vergil told me to shut up.

"But he tried to save the woman," Bernie pressed. "Rushed here so fast he couldn't even call us." He gave me a dirty look as Harwood snorted. "How'd he know she was in danger?"

"Says he had a feeling," Vergil fumed.

"What can I tell you?" I cried out. "Sometimes I get these hot flashes—"

"Shut up!"

"I dunno," Bernie said to Harwood. "Sometimes his feelings are pretty good. Remember the Hardy rape-murders last year?"

"Even shit's got some good points," Harwood agreed.

While they debated my points I went into the bedroom and called Marilyn. It was late and she liked her sleep, but I had something on my mind. I fingered Karen's locket while I talked, told her I'd been involved in a shooting but I was all right.

"Are you sure?"

"I'm fine."

"And the other man?"

"Jarrett. He's dead."

"You killed him."

"I had to."

That's what I wanted, needed, to hear myself say it. To see if it really sounded all right. If I was all right.

"You'll tell me about it someday," Marilyn said.

"Someday."

I told her I'd be over when the case was finished.

"Is it finished?"

"Almost," I hinted.

Vergil wanted to hold me on a concealed-weapons charge —"just so he don't skip the state," which I thought was pretty funny under the circumstances—but Harwood reminded him that New York and Jersey had an understanding when it came to cops carrying their guns next door.

"But he ain't a real cop."

"What're you bitching about?" Harwood groaned. "You had two murders over here, Benziger and now the Jarrett woman, and he cleared both for you."

It was nice to hear Harwood sticking up for me, it happened so seldom. But I was one of his for the moment. Sometimes shit was even thicker than blood.

Vergil probably saw himself getting a commendation for solving two murders, and released me in Bernie's custody pursuant to my appearance before the Manhattan DA. I knew that'd be the end of it. Everyone was relieved although none could say so officially.

On the way out Harwood said he expected to see me in the ballistics lab at ten. "On time. You got that?" He poked a finger in my chest to show me we weren't brothers anymore; he was head of the Homicide squad and I was still shit. "And it better be goddam good or I'm gonna have your ass for lunch."

He slammed the door in my face and the car pulled away from the curb and I watched it blow up behind my eyes. Another fantasy.

Riding home Bernie was quiet, not like him. When we got to my door, he turned off the motor and cleared his throat. "I know what you done, Malone. Not how—I don't know exactly how you done it—but I know what you done. And I don't like it. I want you to know that, too."

"What're you telling me, Bernie?"

He made a face. "That's your thing, communicating. Right? But it ain't mine. I'm into talk. So that's what I'm doing. I'm just talking." He looked the other way, out the window. "You set 'em up, both of them. You figured we couldn't get Jarrett for Weems or his ex for Benziger, so you set 'em up. He'd nail her and you'd get him." He took a deep breath. "Maybe you're right. Maybe we couldn't get them for anything. But what you done was still wrong."

I told him about her parents murdered in California by Jarrett and Laura. "Should they get away with that, too?"

He shook his head. "Don't make no difference. You took the law into your own hands. You executed them."

"I did what the state couldn't do."

"You did what you wanted to do."

I respected Bernie. He was one of the best cops I'd ever known. But I didn't understand him. "What's your beef?"

"I work for the law, that's my life. Not justice as you see it or I see it, the law. If what you done is right, then my life's a joke. You make a mockery out of my life." He started the car. "We won't talk about this no more. I just wanted you to know how I felt. Now go to bed."

I got out and watched him pull away, the taillights fading into darkness. The two of us came up the same way, but somewhere along the line we started serving different gods. Or maybe it was just different roads to the same God.

I went upstairs and took out the locket and opened it to the photo and kissed Karen goodbye and put the locket in the strongbox and closed the safe.

Then I went to sleep and got up and went to work.

# thirty-four

THEY WERE ALL IN the lab to watch me make a fool of myself. Gershon and some of the other squad members traded gibes while Harwood wore an air of impatience. Bernie sat quietly; he didn't think I was a fool, just the devil's disciple. I didn't blame him. It was a hard road to realize your friend worked for a darker power. How could he know I saw everybody in shades of black?

The ballistics lab used a water trap, a recovery tank ten feet long and three feet wide and four feet high. It was set horizontally and test firings were shot into the tank of water.

The technician nodded to me that he was ready and signaled Harwood.

"Pipe down," he yelled. "I wanna hear his last words."

Somebody snickered.

"We're here," I began, "to look at this .38 Special"—held up Alec's nickel-plated revolver—"and these two .357 Magnum cartridges." I showed them in the other hand.

"Are they live?"

"Lemme out of here."

"Quiet!"

"Now everyone knows you can fire a .38 caliber bullet from a .357 Magnum," I said, "but not the reverse. You can't fire a .357 bullet from a .38 Special."

"Everyone's right."

"Everyone's wrong."

Someone said, "He's crazy."

"So let him hang himself."

"Everyone thinks that," I emphasized, "because the .357 bullet's too big. It's a tenth of an inch longer than the .38, but you have to ask yourself why. They're the same bullet in land diameter: .357 inches. But the Magnum bullet develops thirty thousand psi, which shoots it out of the barrel at around fifteen hundred feet per second. Almost double the regular .38 police load. So while the diameter is the same and the length is the same, the load is simply too hot for the .38 Special."

"But the length isn't the same," Harwood objected. "It's a tenth of an inch longer."

"Only in the case. Originally the length was the same, along with the diameter and weight. But the gun couldn't take the hot load, the higher ballistics. That was the problem. So they lengthened the case just enough to prevent it from being chambered in a normal .38 cylinder."

"They made it so you can't use it in a .38 Special."

"That's right."

"But you say you can."

I nodded. "Ask yourself what stops the .357 bullet from fitting in the .38 cylinder. If it fit snugly, the cylinder would turn and feed as you pulled the trigger."

"What stops it," Gershon said, "is obviously the chamber shoulders."

"Exactly," I noted. "That tenth of an inch is just about a tenth of an inch too long for the shoulders." I put both bullets on the table. "And that's why they made it longer."

I saw Bernie's face tighten with interest. Some of the others, too.

"Now suppose, just suppose you had a cylinder without any chamber shoulders."

"In a .38 Special?"

"In a .38 Special."

"There ain't none," said one of the squad.

"Yes." It was the lab technician. "Some of the cheap revolvers have cylinders without chamber shoulders. I've seen 'em."

"What kind?"

"What they call Saturday Night Specials."

"Like this," I said, and held the gun up again. "Not all Saturday Night Specials are piss-poor. The RG, for example, is a good one for the money, and there are others."

"What about the one you're holding?"

"No chamber shoulders." I broke open the cylinder, showed them.

"Even if it fits," Gershon said, "wouldn't the hot loads blow up in your face?"

"Depends on the gun." I retrieved the two .357 cartridges and inserted them in the cylinder. "What you need is a revolver that's cheap enough not to have shoulders"— clicked the cylinder shut—"but made well enough to take the shock."

"And you think this one can do it."

"Don't stand too close to him."

"I think it's already done it more than once."

I took the .38 Special with the .357 bullets over to the trap and put on goggles and ear mats. With everyone crowding around the tank, I shot through the firing tube at a thirty-degree angle into the water.

Once.

Twice.

"Sonofabitch," Harwood said.

The bullets had lost their velocity after five or six feet and sunk to the bottom of the tank. Now the technician was fishing them out with a scoop.

Gershon said, "Where in hell'd you learn that one?"

"A Tibetan lamasery," I kidded.

"I heard they were nonviolent."

"Only with their own kind."

Harwood came over smiling like we were brothers again. "The gun had .38 ammo when he shot at you on the pier."

"A regular load, right."

"So you're saying he sometimes took out the .38 ammo and used .357 instead."

"Probably on most of his hits."

"Why?"

"To fool us in case he was picked up with the revolver. Who'd test a .38 Special in a .357 killing?"

"But Weems had two .38 slugs in him."

I shrugged. "Maybe he used some kind of alternating system."

"You mean Mrs. Stiles." Harwood gave me a shrewd look as the lab technician brought over the two spent slugs.

"Get these to talk," I told Harwood, "and you'll find they match the one in Mrs. Stiles. Fired from the same gun."

"Which you already knew."

"For a while," I admitted. "A hunch, anyway."

Harwood didn't like it but he was a good cop, and honest. "So I was wrong on that one," he acknowledged. "We'll change the disposition to murder and your client can collect the insurance."

"It wasn't the money," I said.

"'Course not. How much is it?"

"A hundred grand."

He winked at me, comrades in arms. "Minus your cut."

"Only five hundred a day."

*"What?"* He wheeled around, yelled for Gershon. "Get this shit civilian out of my sight. Now!"

Harwood walked away muttering to himself. Just for spite I didn't tell him I was only kidding.

"Why you always upset him?" Bernie said on the way out.

"Guess I like to see people sweat."

"Should've seen me in there."

"You mean the test?"

"Craziest thing you ever did. The danger—"

"No danger," I scoffed.

Bernie snorted. "Listen to Superman."

"I knew it would work."

"How could you be sure?" he said.

"Because I'd already tried it."

He stared at me, mouth open.

"On the pier," I said, "while I waited for the rest of you to show. I'd brought along a .357 cartridge and put it in the empty chamber and shot it out to sea."

"You're saying that," Bernie insisted, "because you like to see people sweat."

"That's true," I lied.

# thirty-five

HOLY CROSS WAS IN North Arlington, strictly Catholic and very consecrated. To me it was just another dumping ground.

Charisma Kelly wanted her mother buried in a Catholic cemetery to relieve her own guilt feelings, and it made me wonder about her commitment to atheism. But I kept my doubts to myself. She'd have to find her own road, like the rest of us. In the limousine she told Marilyn to love those who loved her, and Marilyn said she tried and looked at me. I suddenly felt red and yellow and blushed all over and looked out the window at the hearse with Charisma's mother, or whoever she was.

The three of us stood over the grave and Charisma squeezed my hand and there were tears in her eyes. She was dressed in black and Marilyn in white, a commentary on life. Hope and despair, reward and punishment, the living and the dead. I said a prayer and Charisma bowed her head. I wondered who she was praying to; at times this atheist business could be tricky.

It'd been two weeks since the shootings, and events were fading from the newspapers. Charisma had attended the annual Atheists Convention in Dallas on Easter weekend, then took the long way home. It was just as well. Paperwork took time, and so did the insurance check.

Now, back in the city, Charisma hugged me and told me she would never forget what I'd done for her. She held me and for a moment there I saw in her face the future of mankind, and then the lids quickly closed over the secrets of her eyes.

When I told Marilyn I thought I'd had a religious experience, she reminded me that sex between consenting adults was often the same thing.

"Strangely enough," she said, "we're adults."

"But is it an experience?"

"Only if we consent."

She was Madge and I was Hal and we danced in moonglow.

Later I learned the Rangers had been beaten in the playoffs for the Stanley Cup, and right at the start. What could possibly be worse than that? I was in the county seat calling the office and I turned around in despair and there was the same uniform standing behind me. It smiled.

"Funny seeing you here," he said.

"Not funny to me."

"We've been looking for you."

"Tell 'em you couldn't find me."

"But we found something that belongs to you."

Now he had me. I always like to get what's coming to me.

"This was ripped in a dozen pieces," he said, reaching into his jacket, "but we managed to put it back together."

He handed me my parking ticket, the same one he'd given me last time.

"A conscientious citizen," he explained, "witnessed a criminal dispose of a legitimate summons from a fleeing automobile. Of course he collected the pieces and brought them to us."

I looked into his eyes and saw parking meters sucking in coins like slot machines. Then a bell rang and three lemons came up. I'd won.

"Take me to your pit boss," I told him.

"This might go all the way to the director." He made it sound like the Big Casino in the Sky.

I pleaded insanity and was given 500 years or a fifty-dollar fine. I chose the 500 years and the judge said that proved my plea and found me innocent. After I paid the fifty dollars court cost, I walked out a free man.

I love America.